London Blue

London Blue

Lord & Lady Hetheridge Mysteries
Book 8

Emma Jameson

Copyright © 2025 by Emma Jameson

All rights reserved.

No part of this book may be reproduced in any form or by any electronic or mechanical means, including information storage and retrieval systems, without written permission from the author, except for the use of brief quotations in a book review.

❧ Created with Vellum

For the loyal readers of my Lord & Lady Hetheridge mysteries. I am eternally grateful to each and every one of you.

And with special thanks to the ladies who helped me make this book as good as it could be: Kris Basset, Tina Miles, Kathy Stohrer, Kathy Froelich, Merrily Taylor, Uma Sarma, and Barbara Franklin, as well as two of my fellow authors: mystery and crime writer Cyn Mackley and romantasy author Tara West.

Chapter One

Anthony Hetheridge, ninth Baron Wellegrave, private detective, and occasional consultant to Scotland Yard, was awakened by a brush of lips against his earlobe.

"Sixty-two years old," purred his wife.

"Not yet, I'm not." He declined to open his eyes. If she wanted to get a rise out of him, she'd have to work harder.

"Fine. Sixty-two years old in two weeks."

"More like three."

A soft bite on his earlobe, and his eyes flew open. Kate Hetheridge was propped up beside him on one elbow, an impish smile on her face. Behind her, streaks of pink glowed between silhouetted trees.

"I'll never forget what you said the first night we worked together," Kate continued, her tone calculated not to wake their son, five-month-old Nicholas, in his nearby cot. "There you were, looking insanely shaggable in evening dress, doing your impenetrable aristocrat routine. I asked how old you were, not because I thought it mattered, but because you seemed to have such a hangup about it. And you said"—she did her best imitation of his most cutting tone—"'I'll be sixty in three weeks.'"

"It was true."

"It was meant to warn me off."

"I was your superior officer."

"We were off duty. And we both knew you wanted me."

"Which is precisely why I tried to warn you off."

"Lucky for you, I don't scare easy." Her fingers played across his bare chest. "How's the knee?"

"Aches."

"Been there. Fight it. Gimme a bed slide."

Tony smiled wryly, but his groan wasn't entirely in jest. He was twenty-seven days post a total knee replacement, and the required rehab was still torture. Not medieval torture now, true, but Industrial Revolution torture without a doubt.

Slowly and somewhat painfully, he performed the rehab exercise called a bed slide, drawing his left foot toward him. When he achieved ninety degrees of flexion and held it, Kate threw back the duvet to verify his achievement.

"Top marks!" She glanced toward the cot. "And you know what? Nicky's still dead asleep."

"He was up half the night. Now it's daylight. Of course he is."

"We could make good use of the time. Unless you'd rather do more bed slides as I cheer you on." Raising her arms, she shook invisible pompoms like a Crystal Palace Premier League cheerleader. Given that she wore nothing but a smile, Tony did find the sight distinctly cheering.

"Tempting. But I'm in no shape, I fear, to get a leg over."

"No need. I've got you right where I want you."

* * *

"Tony! Grab that, will you?" Kate called from the bathroom. The words sounded garbled, coming as they were around a mouthful of toothpaste. She was due at New Scotland Yard soon, and because of their dawn tryst, she was running half an hour behind.

Kate's secure MPS mobile trilled again from her bedside table. Leaning heavily on the crutch under his right arm, Tony stumped around the bed to intercept the device before it woke Nicky. It was unusual for Kate to leave it behind; like most coppers, she took it everywhere, including the loo.

That's down to me, he thought, secretly smug because she'd left their bed in a blissful haze, her work lifeline forgotten. *Bollixed up knee or not, I do some of my best work before breakfast.*

"DI Hetheridge's phone."

"Chief! How's dad life treating you?" It was DC Kincaid, sounding upbeat as usual.

"I don't sleep. I don't leave the house. I've never been happier. What about you? How are you these days, Sean?"

"Oh, you know. Job's never been busier. Working on the Toff Squad has always been my dream. Hoping for a regular place if the stars line up. Otherwise..." He tailed off. "Nothing to report, really."

Tony *mm-hmmm*ed, which was all he could do without putting the younger man on the spot. Grief was tricky to discuss, especially copper to copper. DC Kincaid's rub-along-with-everyone, we're-all-mates-here attitude was his armor, and he rarely removed it, even for a moment.

A few months prior, Kincaid and a fellow detective constable, Amelia Gulls, were entwined in a secret love affair. The relationship had been serious, probably building toward an engagement, when her sudden demise had rocked Scotland Yard. And no one had been rocked harder than Kincaid, who was briefly the prime suspect. Amelia's murder had touched off an investigation into police corruption that was still sending shockwaves to this day. False evidence, some Joe Public defendants stitched up while elite Met-connected defendants went free, a DI executed and dumped dead in the street. The culmination would have been Tony's worst day on the job in a very long career—except his son Nicky had been born that same day, infusing hope into an otherwise hopelessly tragic situation.

Oh, Amelia. You didn't die for nothing, Tony thought. *But what I wouldn't have given to save you.*

"What's it all about?" Kate demanded between swishes. "Did Seannie boy ring just to hobnob?"

"I heard that. Tell her no, this is official business, and she's to meet me in Shepherd's Bush," Kincaid said, sounding grateful that he'd escaped direct questions about his emotional life. "Number 9, Bulwer Street. Near the old village hall. The blue and white tape isn't up yet, but DI Bhar is already on-scene. One of us will flag her down. Ask her to be discreet, no lights or sirens."

"Why? Is it a hot scene?" Tony asked, unable to stop himself. He didn't like the idea of sending Kate to a location where the murderer was believed to be still on the premises.

"No, sir. Only—" Kincaid broke off in search of the right word.

"Getting in the shower!" Kate called from the bathroom.

"Only this murder seems to be politically tricky," Kincaid finished. "Not that I've been let in on anything. But reading between the lines, I'd say it's already turned a bit fiddly."

"Right. Well. Carry on. Kate will be along ASAP."

After ringing off, Tony thumped his way to the deep walk-in closet to select the day's shirt, tie, and trousers. Most new fathers lived in T-shirts and trackies, or so his friend, Paul Bhar, had assured him, but old habits die hard. Besides, now that he'd mastered the crutch, it felt good to meet his own standards again.

It had not been his intention to undergo a total knee replacement while Nicky was still a newborn. In fact, he'd never intended to undergo it at all, if he were being honest. But when Kate returned to work at New Scotland Yard, he'd taken over much of Nicky's care, including late night/early morning distress calls.

Pressing pause on his detective career to parent his youngest had been a no-brainer. Moreover, it was a privilege—one he'd long believed out of his reach. One night, when he was pacing the nursery with Nicky in his arms, coaxing the fussy infant back to sleep, his left knee suddenly gave way. Tony had fallen hard, and Nicky had fallen with him.

Instinctively clutching Nicky to his chest, Tony had narrowly averted a disaster. The *thud* awakened Kate, a very light sleeper, and even roused their son, Henry, who was sleeping on the floor below.

Kate, whose PTSD still flared in moments of stress, had burst onto the scene, scared of a home invasion. Henry, who'd also come running, had said, "If you're waiting for a sign to get the surgery, I reckon this is it."

As for Nicky, he'd stared at Tony in mute disbelief for a moment, then started burbling in delight. Babies were resilient, as their pediatrician liked to say. Nicky had taken his old dad's pratfall as part of the evening's entertainment. The only person angry about the accident had been Tony. He was worse than angry with himself for leaving it so long. He was incandescent.

By calling in old favors, he'd managed to get himself in front of a private orthopedic surgeon right away. A week later, he'd gone under the knife.

The procedure had gone off without a hitch and was declared a success. Tony received everything the doctor promised—on paper, anyway. But the intensity of his postoperative pain, and his excruciatingly slow progress during physical therapy, was like cold water to the face.

After three days of sheer hell, his friend, Lady Margaret Knolls, a veteran of two TKRs, arrived to check on his progress. Her *amour*, Lady Vivian Callot, also the recipient of a double total knee replacement, came along.

"The surgeon muffed it," he'd told them angrily. "The wrong implant, the wrong technique, something. It's outrageous. Kate had emergency knee surgery with a TKR, and she didn't go through anything like this."

"Is that so?" Lady Margaret's gimlet eyes had narrowed. "And how, pray tell, do you know that?"

"I was beside her every step of the way, thank you very much."

"I see. Viv, dear, enlighten me," she barked as if Lady Vivian were in another room rather than three feet away. "Who is this 'Kate' of whom he speaks? He can't possibly refer to his wife. *That* woman is famous, nay, infamous, for her pain tolerance. To wit: she mistook advanced labor pains for indigestion and nearly gave birth at home as a result."

Lady Vivian, a gentle soul, had mercifully ignored Lady Margaret's invitation to pile on. "Yes, Peg, that's true.

London Blue

Kate's tough as nails. But they say every patient is different."

"Fine. If you won't tell him, I will." Turning back to him, Lady Margaret had said, "Tony, it is a fact universally acknowledged that when it comes to bearing pain, women are tougher than men. Far tougher. Don't compare your progress to Kate's. And don't whinge. I find it completely disorienting to hear you whinge. Remember your ancestry. Summon up the blood."

"Bugger the blood," he'd muttered.

"Swearing helps," Lady Vivian said cheerily.

"Indeed, it does." Lady Margaret had softened slightly. "Listen to me, Tony. Rant. Rave. Put your fist through a wall. But whatever you do, don't skive off on your rehab exercises. If you do, you'll end up leaning on a stick like me." She thumped it against the floor for emphasis. "Probably for the rest of your life."

"Peg doesn't actually need the stick. It's an affectation," Lady Vivian said. "She likes to threaten people with it. Like Lady Danbury."

Tony knew what *Bridgerton* was but refused to admit it. Between Paul, Henry, and Ritchie, he suffered through enough pop-culture nonsense as it was. But he took the threat of a permanent walking stick seriously. After Lady Margaret's dressing-down, he'd applied himself religiously to his rehabilitation routine, swearing all the while. Once past the wheelchair, he'd tried to leapfrog straight to crutches and suffered another excruciating fall. After his surgeon checked him out, declared him bruised but otherwise unharmed, and sent him home with more exercises, Tony had resigned himself to the one thing he'd hoped to avoid: the Zimmer frame.

He knew it was pure egotism. That didn't change the

fact that he'd loathed, hated, *despised* the necessity of using an aluminum walker to get through the day. Were he still a bachelor, he could have borne it philosophically, confident that his manservant, Harvey, would delete the image from his memory banks once it was over. But in front of Kate, it was insupportable.

The Zimmer frame was the universal sign of a pensioner, at least to his way of thinking, and using it in her presence was agony. He wasn't deluded enough to believe she'd never reckoned on him reaching the Zimmer frame stage of life long before she did. That didn't mean he wanted her to see him like that. Not so soon.

Old age comes to all of us. All the lucky ones, he reminded himself. *No whinging, or Margaret will cane me.*

"Well?" Kate emerged from the shower, her voice echoing off the lavatory's tiled walls. "What's the story?"

Rather than shout in response and risk touching off one of their son's crying jags, Tony crutch-thumped his way to the bathroom and stuck his head in. Kate was attacking her wet hair with a fluffy white towel. Their eyes met in the mirror.

"Murder?" she asked, almost hopefully.

"In Bulwer Street in Shepherd's Bush. A touchy situation for someone up the food chain. Off you go."

Chapter Two

DI Kate Hetheridge arrived on the scene in twenty-eight minutes flat, a feat she attributed to something she'd never dreamed of in her pre-Tony days: support. Loads of support. Specifically, her husband, her husband's personal assistant, the family manservant, and Josie, the full-time companion of her brother, Ritchie.

Josie made sure he ate regular meals, as opposed to nothing but crisps and candy. She kept on top of his doctor visits, accompanying him when Kate could not. Sometimes she even got down on the floor beside Ritchie, doing a thousand-piece jigsaw puzzle while he worked with LEGO bricks. Her presence took the pressure off the rest of the family, especially Henry. He loved his uncle, but since Kate and Tony's wedding, he'd too often fallen into the role of junior caregiver. Little boys needed private time to read, think, or do nothing at all.

Mrs. Snell was Tony's longtime administrative assistant turned personal majordomo. In addition to answering Tony's professional phone line and weeding out inappropriate queries—he refused to take cases about infidelity, disputed child custody, or industrial espionage—she handled all the tedious household details Kate despised. Had Kate really once called Mrs. Snell, that invaluable creature with white curls and hugely magnifying specs, "ghastly?" Talk about the foolishness of youth. She'd been on vacation for less than a week, and it felt like a decade.

As for Wellegrave House's indispensable manservant, Harvey Sixsmith, his role had evolved. During Tony's bachelor years, he'd been valet, cleaner, chauffeur, and cook. Now, he supervised kitchen staff and day cleaners, cooked once or twice a month, and played chauffeur only on special occasions. These days he spent more and more time in the walled garden, nurturing David Austin roses. As Nicky grew older, Kate knew that Harvey's deep reverence for the house, the Hetheridge name, and the barony of Wellegrave would come in handy. He loved sharing such knowledge; Tony hardly gave a tinker's damn.

Finally, there was the man himself. Her husband: detective, self-proclaimed dinosaur, and the world's best new dad. Tony's embrace of fatherhood was complete. He did feedings, changed nappies, and answered Nicky's nighttime wails when Kate could barely crack an eye open. And later, if she awakened in a frisky mood and bit his earlobe, he was up for it. Being the man he was, Tony allowed Kate to be the copper she was, which meant turning up at a murder scene in record time. She was itching to get stuck in.

Number 9 Bulwer Street turned out to be one of those lovely, if cookie-cutter, Victorian-style new builds. Playing spot-the-difference, she picked out only a few signs of individuality from house to house. One had a satellite dish, another had a flowering vine trained up the wall, and one brick fence was painted white when all the rest were plain red brick. Beyond that, only the front doors, painted an array of unharmonious colors, saved Bulwer Street from looking like conjoined clones. What exorbitant fee had each owner paid for their slice of upper-middle-class *meh*?

I shouldn't turn up my nose, Kate thought. *Maybe some of these people clawed their way out of council estates, just like me. In which case, they're probably thrilled to bits, living someplace without used needles scattered in the garden and nasty words chalked on the walls.*

"Guv!" called DC Kincaid. He waved at her from no. 9's narrow porch.

"Hiya, Sean." She hurried up the steps, eager to get inside where it was undoubtedly cooler. Her skirt suit was autumn/winter weight, but she was wearing it anyway, which explained the perspiration on her lower back. After splurging so much for her Harrods dress-for-the-job-you-want professional wardrobe, she wore them in all weather, including days like today, when the temperature was expected to hit 32° C by two o'clock.

"Hiya, DI Hetheridge."

"So, what's the story? I clock no crime scene tape. No news van. Not even a SOCO glaring at me through his spacesuit helmet. I'm intrigued."

"DI Bhar's inside with three ladies. The dead woman, her daughter, and her cleaner. The cleaner discovered the body," Kincaid said.

"The daughter lives with Mum?"

"No."

"Then why is she here?"

"Because the cleaner rang her instead of 999. The daughter rushed over from her home in Brixton. She's the one who rang 999."

"From Brixton to Shepherd's Bush," Kate murmured.

"Yeah. A reporting delay of at least thirty minutes."

"Besides that, it's odd, don't you think? Daughter lives in Brixton, while mum lives here. I suppose the daughter might be an artsy type."

Kincaid looked dubious. "There's an odd air about her. I think they were estranged. And they both have connections. She wouldn't admit it, but I'd lay odds that before she rang 999, she phoned someone in government. High up in government."

And that someone has the power to order Scotland Yard to have a discreet look-see before local coppers, SOCOs, or the media find out something's up, Kate thought. A murder house had been unilaterally declared off limits until Kate, Paul, and Kincaid evaluated the evidence. *That's old-school Toff Squad stuff. Like Tony's stories from days of yore. How things were done before all the MPS scandals, the twenty-four-hour news cycle, and the rise of citizen journalists.*

Of course, in Tony's days of yore, the discretion was only temporary, and the crime was still investigated to the fullest. Had he ever been leaned on to completely suppress a crime from the public and the Crown Prosecution Service? Surely not. It was unimaginable.

Kate followed Kincaid into no. 9, buzzing with curiosity. What she found inside apparently had the power to end a career, ruin a life, or both.

Mercifully, it was cooler inside. The townhouse faced north, air circulating well through the open windows. The stink of death usually functioned as a welcome wagon for coppers, but Kate didn't detect a sniff of it.

The front room was decorated in English cottage style: striped wallpaper with pink roses, harmoniously eclectic furniture, a chenille-upholstered sofa, and framed bits of embroidery. The coffee table book was called *Great Stately Homes of England*. In the built-in bookcase, Kate glimpsed Mary Berry, Chrissie Rucker, Delia Smith, and an extensive collection of vintage paperbacks from Mills and Boon.

"Who opened the windows?" Kate asked.

"That would be me." DI Deepal "Paul" Bhar emerged from one of the inner rooms, jerking his head to the side and putting a finger to his lips. That meant they couldn't speak freely; their interviewees were in earshot. "How are you, DI Hetheridge?"

"Never better, DI Bhar." She mouthed the words "Big Daddy" at him. Like her, he had an infant at home, and whenever they met, the talk immediately went to babies first, when it had once gone to murder.

"May I have a quick word with Kate?" Paul asked. "Excuse us, DC Kincaid."

After Kincaid retreated to the foyer, Paul leaned close and murmured, "If I weren't such a good person, I'd nick those tatty Mills and Boons for my mum. She'd treasure every one of them." His eyes raked Kate up and down. "So, you've squeezed back into your old wardrobe, have you? Only by the skin of your teeth, from the looks of it. Brilliant."

"That white streak in your hair," she replied, clucking disapprovingly. "Makes you old before your time, doesn't it?"

"I have a hair appointment this afternoon, thank you very much."

Her jibe about hair wounded him far more than his remark about her post-baby body wounded her. After years of playing by society's rules, she'd decided obsessing over numbers on the scale was pointless. Since becoming a father, Paul had eased up slightly on his sartorial obsession —he hadn't bought himself so much as a new tie since Evvy was born. But he still found the stubborn white streak in his hair unbearable.

Kate asked, "Where are our witnesses?"

"Dining room."

"And the body?"

"Kitchen."

"I want to see it before them. Are you thinking gas leak?"

"At first blush. That's why I had all the windows opened. Now, I think it was an overabundance of caution."

He led her to the kitchen, which was magazine photo shoot ready. Although Kate had no time to read women's magazines, she guessed the style had a name like Retro French Farmhouse. There was a shabby-chic table, probably upcycled from a boot sale, mismatched ladderback chairs, and a midcentury fridge in pale mint green. From the dented copper pans hanging on the walls to the ruffled calico curtains over the sink, it was the sort of genteelly haphazard, imperfect effect that only the well-off could manage.

"Mrs. Cathleen Maitland-Palmer," Paul said, indicating the corpse. The door between the kitchen and, presumably, the dining room was closed, but he still spoke softly.

"Wow." Kate stared at the corpse. "We should all look so good when we're dead. After the front room, I expected a pensioner with a blue rinse. This is Sleeping Beauty."

"Sleeping Beauty fifty years later."

She nailed him with a look. He put up his hands in mock surrender.

"No shade. Just a fact. According to her daughter, Marilyn, Mrs. Maitland-Palmer was seventy-six years old."

"Seventy-six? Witchcraft," Kate muttered, stooping for a better look. She was still capable of kneeling thanks to two surgeries and approximately ten thousand bed slides, but she no longer knelt without first seeking alternatives. Especially on a hard, cold marble floor.

As she lay supine in the middle of the kitchen, Catherine Maitland-Palmer's face had settled into a peaceful, almost line-free, wrinkle-free mask. Honey-blonde hair fanned out around her face and head like the halo of a secular martyr: St. L'Oréal, our lady of perpetual conditioning.

Kate resisted the temptation to touch it. "D'you reckon that's real? Or a wig?"

"Extensions, maybe? But I don't see any clips."

"There's such a thing as fusion extensions. They're top tier. I'm frankly shocked that there's a beauty treatment that's escaped your notice."

"Yes, well, whatever it is, it's longer, thicker, and brighter than yours. Neatly coiffed, too."

"Shut it, Pepé Le Pew."

Closer inspection revealed that Cathleen Maitland-Palmer wore a full face of makeup—powder, blush, lipstick, eyeshadow, eyeliner, and mascara. Her brow was smooth, her chin was firm, and her neck was the neck of a forty-year-old. She probably had tiny scars hidden along the hairline, but Kate cast no stone. Women were criticized, even reviled, for aging visibly, then pilloried for taking measures to look younger. Perhaps one day, people would learn to mind their own damn business.

As for the cause of death, none of the usual signs were present. Kate saw no divot in the skull, no broken limbs, no gashes or bullet holes. The only visible injury wasn't serious enough to be fatal: on Cathleen Maitland-Palmer's right hand, there was no index finger, just a dry stump. Two perfect drops of blood had dried on the marble. The missing finger was gone.

"Are there any other injuries?"

"No. If you repeat this to anyone, I'll deny it in the most stringent terms, but I had a look-see. Gloved up and lifted her upper body oh-so-gently. Skull intact. Spine intact. No signs of a stabbing or shooting. That cooker is gas, so I opened all the windows, just in case."

"I don't blame you. But she doesn't look like a carbon monoxide case. No cherry red spots on her cheeks."

"True. Which puts me at poison."

"Agreed. Provisionally," Kate said automatically. Earlier in her career, she'd worked with a superior who had a particular methodology. He stepped onto a crime scene, looked left, looked right, decided what must have happened, and tailored the rest of the investigation to fit his supposition. The frustration she'd experienced working with a man incapable of taking in new information made her wary of early theories. "What about the finger? I'd say it was severed post-mortem."

"Agreed. And no, Kincaid and I haven't found it. The cleaner and the daughter both claim they wouldn't touch it if they did find it. When the SOCOs take over, I'll ask them to check all the pipes, but we're probably out of luck if it was flushed."

Kate frowned down at the body. "The finger thing is weird. As for poison—she didn't vomit. Almost any poison worth its salt causes vomiting."

"Maybe someone put a bag over her head as soon as she passed out. Then took it away, along with the finger."

"Maybe." Now that she'd been in the presence of the dead for a few minutes, the stink of death was making itself known at last.

"Smell that?"

Paul nodded.

"Care to guesstimate time of departure?"

"Nine hours."

"Yeah. The eight-to-twelve zone feels right." A long and varied association with the deceased had taught Kate and Paul a thing or two about fixing time of death, a data point not even an ME could determine absolutely. "Meaning she was probably killed last night, somewhere between nine o'clock and midnight. Considering how she's dolled up, she must've come home from a party. Or a date." Kate turned to Paul. "Did the cleaner or the daughter have anything to say about what Mrs. Maitland-Palmer was doing last night?"

"The cleaner hasn't said anything worthwhile. But the daughter, Marilyn, is raring to go. She even has a theory about the finger."

"Wow. Let's meet her, then."

Chapter Three

Paul led Kate into the room where the interviewees sat waiting at the dining room table. The cleaner was huddled with her knees against her chest like a little girl. The victim's daughter, a middle-aged woman in huge black-framed specs, sat with arms folded, staring at the wall. DC Kincaid hovered nearby—ostensibly to fetch anything they needed, but actually to make sure neither woman did a runner. People who happily sat down with Scotland Yard detectives after a sudden death in the family were rare indeed.

Paul made the introductions, then said to Kincaid, "Sean, take Ms. Botezatu upstairs. Find a spot, close the door, and wait with her. I'll sing out when we're ready to—"

"She can stay," Marilyn announced. She sounded knackered but resigned, with no sign of tears. "It will be more efficient if you interview us together."

"That's not how it's done." Kate signaled for Kincaid to lead the cleaner out. "This is a serious inquiry. Proper procedures must be followed."

Marilyn stared at Kate. Those square black specs were so big, the face behind them was almost canceled out. Unlike her mum, she was a tall, broad-shouldered, and robust woman. Her short brown hair was uncombed, and she wore no makeup or jewelry. Blue jeans and Crocs were paired with a shirt that read, I SEE DUMB PEOPLE.

"Didn't have being treated like a murder suspect on my bingo card," she muttered. Her accent sounded like North London.

Paul sat down at the head of the table, adjacent to Marilyn. As he expected, Kate took the chair directly across from her, a power move that set many interviewees on edge. And teetering on the edge was the best place to put close family members after a murder. Almost ninety percent of British women were killed by someone they knew. When the death occurred in the home, the murdered woman's relatives were instantly de facto persons of interest, whether this was formally communicated to them or not.

"Right." Paul put his secure mobile on the table, pressed record, and rattled off the MPS boilerplate they were obligated to disclose before every interview. After identifying himself and Kate, the location, and the time, he told Marilyn, "State your name, please."

"Marilyn Maitland-Palmer." It was indeed a North London accent, a strong one. "Maitland" came out more like "may-lan."

"Place of residence?"

"17 Filbert Street," she said, fixing him with what seemed like tiny eyes behind those giant specs. "Brixton, London. England. United Kingdom. The world. The solar system. The bleeding universe."

"Do you live alone, Ms. Maitland-Palmer, or with a partner?"

"Partner."

"Named?"

"Bonkers. He's a cat." Her tone suggested Paul really should have guessed.

"Your occupation?"

"Cyber monkey."

"Excuse me?"

"You heard me."

"Where is your place of work?"

"Cyber Monkeez. M-O-N-K-E-E-Z. We repair laptops, desktops, mobiles, you name it. And we fling poo," she added rather menacingly.

"All poo flinging is metaphorical, I'm sure." Paul tried one of his charming, man-about-town smiles on her. Her blank reception was less than encouraging. Clearing his throat, he continued, "What is your relationship to the deceased, Cathleen Maitland-Palmer?"

"What do you think?"

"State your relationship for the record." Kate sounded stern yet serene.

"She's my mum." Marilyn sighed. "If I say I'm glad she's dead, will you arrest me? I can put on the grieving daughter act if you insist. But that's all it will be. An act."

"No need to put on any special demeanor." Paul was startled by her candor. "Nothing but good of the dead" was an enduring societal expectation, as true now as it had been a hundred years ago. When it came to mums, the expectation was even more potent. "How did you become aware of your mother's death?"

"I already told you. I said it when you walked in."

"For the record."

"Fine. It's my day off, and I was having a lie-in, or trying to. Dacy rang me at about half-seven. I was—"

"Witness refers to Daciana Botezatu, the cleaner," Paul said quietly for the recording.

"That's right. Daciana Botezatu, spelled D-O-Z-Y-B-O-Z-O. I thought the silly doughnut was calling in from work and was afraid to ring Mum directly. I picked up. She was babbling—more than usual, I mean. Getting her to speak plainly enough for me to follow took a few tries. Once I understood she thought Mum was dead, I hopped on the tube and came straight here."

Kate asked, "Why did you refer to her as 'dozy bozo?'"

"Because she's flighty. Off with the fairies."

"Was she intimidated by your mother?" Paul asked. "Afraid to displease her by calling in sick?"

"She behaves like she's intimidated by everything. Maybe it's an act, so everyone pities her. Or maybe she really is scared of her own shadow. Either way, she's a right numpty."

"You said, 'She thought Mum was dead.' So, you didn't believe her?" Kate asked. "Had to see it for yourself?"

Marilyn sighed. "Listen. I know this silly song and dance is mandatory, but I can't think straight. I haven't had a ciggie today and I'm gagging for it. Let me smoke and I won't fling poo, I swear."

Kate nodded. Marilyn dug into her handbag, or what she carried as a handbag: an insulated zip-top carrier meant for groceries.

"Don't bother looking for an ashtray, there isn't one," she said as Paul, ever the good cop, tried to oblige. "Mum didn't permit smoking here. Even when she hosted parties, she flung the smokers out into the arctic blast rather than let them pollute her precious air."

Locating a light blue packet of Sovereigns, she shook out

a cigarette and allowed Paul to light it. "Thanks, doll. My ex-husband looks a bit like you. What's it like being a Paki in the Met, working with blondie over there? Is she racist to your face, or just behind your back?"

"That counts as poo," he said. Kate didn't react. They'd both survived the Lady Margaret Knolls insults-over-tea program, and they'd both been taunted by Sir Duncan Godington, a master of devastating *bon mots*. Minor needling from witnesses no longer pierced the skin.

"Sorry." Marilyn took a deep drag, closed her eyes and had another. "Oh. That's better." Her smoker's rasp put a serrated edge on each word. "What were we talking about? Oh, did I believe Dacy? I don't know. I suppose I thought Mum would never die. Or if she did, she'd come back as a zombie and terrorize the countryside.

"But anyway, when I turned up," she continued, "I found Mum on the floor just like Dacy said. Dacy was going on about a murderer breaking in. Climbing in through a window or something. But the door looked fine, and the ground floor windows don't open enough to let a person climb through. They just tilt, as you already discovered." She looked at Paul keenly. "Are you thinking gas leak?"

"Nothing's off the table."

"Well, maybe not, but I don't see it," Marilyn said. "Didn't get a whiff of rotten eggs when I came in. I think it's obvious Mum did herself in."

"How do you figure?" Kate asked.

"I don't mean she topped herself. I mean killed herself by accident. You have to understand, Mum couldn't cook, or bake, or sew, or knit. She had zero homemaker skills. Lived on frozen food and protein shakes to keep her figure. Her domestic goddess, last-of-the-glamor-girls reputation was bull." Turning, she seized a bouquet off the sideboard and yanked out the flowers, heedless of their dripping stems. Placing the vase in front of her, she tapped her cigarette ash into the empty vase. Grim satisfaction gleamed in her eyes.

"Oh! Aren't I the bad girl? I keep expecting to hear shuffling footsteps behind us." Marilyn playfully glanced over her shoulder at the door between dining room and kitchen. "If I needed any proof Mum's gone to the big debutante ball in the sky, there it is. She couldn't play possum with me breathing carcinogens in her *sanctum sanctorum*."

"Anyhow," Marilyn continued, breezily blowing smoke at the ceiling, "Dacy said that when she left last night at half-six, Mum was getting tarted up for one of her society dos. She probably brought a man home, unless she couldn't find a single Y-front to say yes. And she probably decided to fix a little something, charcuterie or the like, to impress him. I can see her cutting off her finger whilst slicing cheese or salami. Especially if she'd had a few. And when she saw what she'd done to herself, she had a heart attack. Dropped dead on the spot. Her man friend took it in, got weak in the knees, and skedaddled."

"That's a rather developed theory," Kate said.

"I knew my mum."

"Let's break it down. Did your mum often go out at night alone and return to an empty house?"

"She often went out alone. Never came home alone if she could help it. There's a reason my father divorced her, and it wasn't because she couldn't cook."

"Father's name?"

"Joseph Palmer. Dead," Marilyn added. "Cancer."

"Did your mother have any particular male friends, like a serious boyfriend or fiancé?"

"Nope."

"What about more casual male friends who knew where she lived, or visited?" Paul asked.

Marilyn snorted. "I can try to make up a list."

"That would be helpful," Kate said. "Did Mrs. Maitland-Palmer have heart problems?"

"She had a heart attack ten years back. As soon as she woke up in hospital, she *demanded* to know what caused it," Marilyn said. "The doctor said lots of stuff factored in—family history, sedentary lifestyle, too many cream teas. Mum asked if secondhand smoke could do it. The doctor said, possibly. And just like that, I became an attempted murderer."

"She blamed you?" Paul asked.

"You'd better believe she did. And I see you there, scribbling something in your little book, despite the bloody mobile recording every word." Marilyn looked him in the eye. "Let me see what you wrote."

"My observations are professional. And confidential."

"Uh-huh. I know what you must think of me," Marilyn said. "I resented my mother because she was this pretty princess and I'm as common as dirt. Because she cheated on my father, who I loved—" Her voice caught, and she took a moment to compose herself. "Loved very much, and broke his heart, and kicked him into an early grave. And I'm a mess, and I'm hateful, and someday I'll look back on today and be ashamed of how I behaved.

"I own it. I'm rude, unkind, uncaring," she continued, pausing only to flick cigarette ashes into her mother's vase. "Write this in your little book. Mum didn't want children, but she had me because it was expected. And I didn't go down a treat because she couldn't vicariously relive her youth through me. She didn't care for me, and I didn't care for her. So, if you think that makes me a killer, do a little detective work. My mobile's GPS will tell you I was home last night. My browser history will tell you I've been researching how to find a cheaper home in London, not how to get away with murder. It's true, if I'd been here when she cut off her finger, I probably would've laughed my arse off. But I would've rung 999 all the same." She stabbed her half-smoked cigarette in Paul's direction. "I mean it! Write it down."

Paul wrote,

There is a nutter in every. Single. Case.

"All right. Let's think about your theory a bit more critically," Kate said, still on that higher plane of stern serenity. Paul thought there was something different about her, about how she sounded, but he couldn't decide exactly what. "If Mrs. Maitland-Palmer died because of a simple kitchen accident, why isn't a knife and cutting board out? And where is her missing finger?"

Marilyn shrugged. "Dacy probably tidied up, then took it."

"Why would she do a thing like that?"

"For the ring Mum always wore."

"So, it was valuable?" Paul asked.

"No, it came two-a-penny at a boot sale. Of course it was valuable. And Mum loved it. She never took the bleeding thing off. I mean—maybe I have no business accusing Dacy. That's like fingering a muppet for the crime of the century. Fingering," she added, smirking. "Whoops."

Kate said, "What if I told you it's quite likely the finger was cut off after your mum was already dead?"

"I'd say Dacy isn't quite the muppet I think. Flush the finger down the pan, cry us a river, hold onto it until things cool down, then pawn it for cash. A little bonus, now that her job's gone." Marilyn shrugged again. "Mum was seventy-six. If it wasn't her heart, maybe she had a stroke. There isn't a scratch on her."

"That doesn't automatically make it a natural death, I'm afraid," Paul said. "We're quite serious when we say a list of her known male acquaintances would be helpful. Is there anyone else we should know about? Someone in her life who might have wished her harm?"

"Everyone at Annabelle Carter." Marilyn dug in her bag for another cigarette. "Mum got on with the old janitor, but he was male, so go figure."

Paul and Kate swapped glances. "What's Annabelle Carter?"

"Google it. I need more nicotine to stomach talking about it."

The very first result was the right one. Paul had expected a woman's fashion boutique, or perhaps an upmarket jewelry company, but he got a school's slow-loading, non-mobile-friendly website instead. The building on the landing page was quintessentially English—gray stone, climbing ivy, small sash windows, a turret. Mature trees suggested a vast campus, but the picture was so tightly framed, Paul suspected there might be less exalted properties looming on either side. A website banner proclaimed:

TIMES CHANGE. STANDARDS DO NOT.
ANNABELLE CARTER.

He passed his mobile to Kate, who looked it over.
"Is that a culinary school?"
"No. So, then. You've never heard of it." Marilyn's softened tone suggested ignorance of the school was a point in

Kate's favor. "And why should you? You're a proper career woman, aren't you? Besides, if you'd attended someplace like Annabelle Carter, they would've beaten that accent out of an East End girl like you."

"You're one to talk," Kate said, smiling.

"Don't be offended. It's quite soft. 'His that ha culinary school?'" Marilyn repeated. "Very gentle h-sounds before your vowels. Otherwise, you're winning the battle. As for me," Marilyn said, suddenly taking on the plummy tones known as RP, or Received Pronunciation, "I was reared to enunciate properly, on pain of spending two hours with the hand mirror and the bone prop. I started talking like this," she added, dropping back into her strong North London accent, "just to fit in with my ex-husband's people. And to put the customers at ease. Cyber Monkeez caters to down market clientele, which is just how we like it."

"And because talking this way made your mum mental?" Kate suggested.

"That, too."

"But what *is* Annabelle Carter?" Paul asked.

To his surprise, Kate answered. "A finishing school. You know. Like in a Sharon Lacey novel."

"Sharon Lacey" was the Anglicized nom-de-plume of Paul's mother, Sharada Bhar. Paul had skimmed enough of his mum's bestselling bodice-rippers to reassure her that he, a good son, cared about her chosen career. But secretly, he was appalled by it. Her books contained very frank on-page descriptions of men and women panting, heaving, and beyond. Sharada called it "spicy;" he called it a collection of images no good son wants connected to his mother.

"I thought finishing schools went out with the bustle," Paul said.

"They did. Except for Annabelle Carter," Marilyn said.

"Last woman standing. And I've read Sharon Lacey, you know," she said, noticeably warmer toward Kate. "Fun stuff. I read it aloud to Bonkers."

"Earlier, you told us that Ms. Botezatu left around half-six, while your mother, er..." Paul tailed off, trying to rephrase it.

"Tarted herself up for a society do," Marilyn supplied. "She was one of those people who never said no. She'd show up to the opening of an envelope. The more stuffed shirts and old men in baldrics, the better. Assuming Dacy didn't get it wrong—and let's face it, that's likely—Mum was at Cottlestone Manor last night."

"Location?" Kate asked.

"Hampshire. And here's something else. Mum didn't drive, didn't take the tube, and wouldn't even go by cab if she could help it. She insisted on being escorted. She arrived on a man's arm and exited on a man's arm without fail. Not that I think any of them would have the raw courage to hurt Mum, much less kill her," Marilyn added, as if realizing that what she'd said could be taken as an accusation. "Her crowd sticks to social assassination. And if it *was* an accident, which is still what I think, and Mum was trying to impress her escort when the knife slipped, I reckon the poor bugger did a legger."

"Really?"

"Don't you think that would be extraordinary behavior?" Paul asked. "For anyone, much less a cultured type who cared enough to see a woman safely home, to witness a horrible injury and leave without calling the authorities?"

"Not if it's the man I'm thinking of." Marilyn leaned back in her chair, a smile playing on her lips. "But I shouldn't be saying this."

"Go on," Kate said.

"Easy for you to say. You don't have to live with the consequences if he finds out. But fine—it's Patrick Bruce. The Earl of Dellkirk. He's one of mum's playmates, and he'd run a mile to escape another scandal, now wouldn't he?"

Chapter Four

Kate may have been in the dark about an elocution training device called the bone prop, but she knew all about the Earl of Dellkirk's scandal. And not just because she shopped at Tesco and browsed the red top tabloids while in queue. It had been front page news not only in Britain but worldwide: how Patrick Bruce, wealthy owner of the L + P discount retail chain, was granted a peerage by a recent ex-Prime Minister. Apart from buying a storied old heap in Hampshire and using it to host massive Tory fundraisers three times a year, he'd performed no particular service to the nation that anyone knew of.

It wasn't that the handing out of life peerages was a spotlessly clean, above-board process, or that it ever had been. Even its beginnings were cynical. In the early twentieth century, when socialism was catching fire and revolution seemed all but inevitable, the nation's great minds had hit on a patriotic scheme: to flatter some of the most dangerous agitators and revolutionary sympathizers into joining Team Status Quo.

This, they reasoned, could be achieved by handing out

special honors or lifetime titles. By praising the organizers and agitators, the government could effectively herd them back into the fold. The scheme worked brilliantly. The recipients generally became far more forgiving of how the nation was run, and of the old boy network that ran it, now that they, too, directly benefitted. And even if the recipient's political philosophy remained unchanged, accepting a life peerage from the nation's top men utterly destroyed their reputation with revolutionaries still in the field. Mischief managed, indeed.

As for Patrick Bruce, not a single soul across the length and breadth of England cared about him receiving a lifetime earldom, even though he was the first commoner to be elevated higher than knight, baronet, or baron in a very long time. It was the PM's secret fee schedule, somehow obtained by the press, that touched off a hue and cry. £500,000 for a lifetime knighthood; £1,000,000 for a lifetime baronetcy, £5,000,000 for a lifetime barony. (This detail had prompted Tony to muse aloud about selling the barony of Wellegrave to the highest bidder, a joke that his manservant, Harvey, considered in rather poor taste.) Lifetime earl wasn't on the menu, yet Patrick Bruce had received it, leading chat shows and scandal rags to speculate endlessly on how much "Lord Poundland" had paid for the honor.

"I understand Mr. Bruce might be desperate to escape negative publicity," Kate said. "But that would be outrageously callous, leaving a woman lying on the kitchen floor, don't you think?"

"Maybe." Marilyn shrugged. "Maybe he dropped her off and she keeled over while she was home alone. Or maybe it was some other Y-front. There are so many men who might have run out on the scene. Then Dacy turned up, sawed off the finger, hid the ring, and simulated a meltdown."

"Cards on the table." Paul leaned forward earnestly, his body language suggesting openness and empathy. Kate always enjoyed watching him play good cop. He was brilliant at it.

"My theory isn't accidental death or natural death. I think your mother was murdered. In which case, the finger may have been taken as a trophy."

Marilyn stared at him. "That's mental. You're mental."

"Serial killers are known to take trophies." Kate was intrigued by Marilyn's visceral reaction. Either this cyber monkey and self-proclaimed poo flinger was a great actress —as good as Mr. Good Cop Paul—or she was genuinely appalled to think somebody kept her mother's finger as a memento of his big night out.

"Most serial killers are male loners with mummy issues," Kate went on. "For one of them, Mrs. Maitland-Palmer might have seemed like a perfect stand-in for the real mum he can't or won't confront. We'll know more after the postmortem, but there's no rule that says murder has to look violent. Certain poisons, suffocation, forms of strangulation—they can leave a peaceful-looking decedent."

"Then there's theft. A junkie will steal anything from anyone to get his next fix," Paul said. "Putting aside the issue of Ms. Botezatu and whether or not she had the motive or opportunity to take your mum's ring, I'll say this: people have been murdered for less. Do you have a picture of your mum wearing it?"

Marilyn produced her mobile. "Give me a sec. The Annabelle Carter website takes forever on a phone. It's as much of a relic as its curriculum." After a lot of swiping,

Marilyn found the correct image. Pinch-zooming to magnify it, she passed the phone to Kate.

There was Cathleen Maitland-Palmer in her official faculty portrait. Hands folded in a ladylike pose, the ring was front and center, straddling the line between luxurious and vulgar.

"Is that a sapphire?" Kate's gaze automatically flicked to her engagement ring, a vintage cushion-cut diamond nestled between two deep blue stones.

"No, it's semiprecious. A London blue topaz," Marilyn said. "Your sapphires are sort of electric in color, see? That's what makes them precious—the purity of the hue. London blue topazes are darker. Almost inky. Look closely and you'll see that Mum's stone had some respectable diamonds encircling it. Good cut and color. Set in platinum. I don't know how much the materials and labor cost together, but the finished product was several thousand pounds, without a doubt."

"Well worth stealing, then," Paul said.

"Materials and labor," Kate repeated. "I take it your mum ordered it bespoke?"

"No. Lady Griselda Bothurst ordered it bespoke. Actually, she ordered two."

"Lady Bothurst is...?"

"The headmistress at Annabelle Carter. At a faculty Christmas party, she bestowed the rings on her favorite instructors: Mum and the cookery teacher, Ginny Braide. The other teachers almost died of envy. Ruined some friendships. Which was probably what the venomous old bat intended."

"I'm surprised the center stone is semiprecious," Kate said.

"For the school colors," Marilyn said. "Dark blue and silver."

"You seem to know a lot about gemstones. Does it come up much at Cyber Monkeez?"

"Never. I told you, I matriculated at Annabelle Carter," Marilyn said. "I can arrange flowers, sew my own knickers, and appraise jewelry at a glance. When I decided to get a computer science degree, I attended Open University. Mum was not best pleased."

"Is it fair to say that despite your strained relationship, and the fact that you live in Brixton, you maintained good communication with Mrs. Maitland-Palmer?" Paul asked.

"She couldn't go a week without ringing me, if that's what you mean."

"Did your mum ever confide that she was afraid? Or mention someone who might have wanted to hurt her?"

"Wanted to hurt her? Or wanted to hurt her *and* had the bollocks to go through with it?"

"Both, but start with the bollocky ones." Paul's pen hovered above his notebook.

"Well, there's Mrs. Dankworth. She's the deputy head-mistress of Annabelle Carter. Probably the person angriest about not getting a bespoke ring.

"Then there's Lady Hattersley. She's about twenty-five. Not that long ago, she was a student at AC. Now, she's teaching art and flower arranging. Mum didn't care for her as a student. They had a heated row in the faculty lounge when she got hired."

"Define heated row."

"Mum called her a jumped-up student, and Lady Hattersley dumped a cup of tea in her lap. After that..." Marilyn puffed thoughtfully. "There've been plenty of disgruntled students over the years. Lord knows my class hated the entire faculty, Mum in particular, but none of us had the raw nerve to do anything about it. We had spirit, but only in secret. Over the last few years, the classes kept getting smaller, until the only girls signing up were sheep. Except..." She paused, considering.

Kate waited silently. She never liked to rush an interviewee, especially at a moment like this.

"Last semester, there was a girl Mum humiliated in class. Mind you, at Annabelle Carter, that's a daily thing. Only this time, one of the girl's mates videoed it with a contraband phone. She uploaded the video to YouTube, and it went viral. Every girl and mum who'd ever heard of Annabelle Carter watched it. Eventually, someone published a think piece in the *Independent* about the patriarchal tyranny of finishing schools, and all hell broke loose."

"The girl's name?" Paul asked, poised to write it down.

"Alexa Alexandretta Hicks-Bowen."

"Oh, go on."

"I'm being for real." Marilyn laughed. "Half the girls who attend Annabelle Carter have names like that."

"So, did posting the video satisfy her need for payback? Or is she suing Annabelle Carter, too?" Kate asked.

"What? That kid isn't suing anyone. Lady Bothurst is suing *her*."

"For what?"

"On enrollment, students and parents sign a pledge. The document starts with all the usual stuff: no drinking, no smoking, no mobiles, no slipping off the premises, no hookups, and so on. Then, there's a warning about publicly defaming the school. If you do, you'll be subject to legal action. If Alexa wanted more vengeance than a video, her only option was to get physical."

"Is that right?"

London Blue

"Not that I feel especially sorry for her," Marilyn continued. "At the end of the day, Annabelle Carter is a voluntary experience. If a student feels mistreated, nothing is stopping her from packing up and storming out. But it never happens. Like I said—sheep. There's something you never hear about. Sheep attacks." Stubbing out her cigarette, she yawned and said, "We've been at this a while, haven't we? If it's all the same to you, I'd like to pop home and change into something decent."

"I'm afraid we must ask you to stay a bit longer." Kate's tone didn't hint that "a bit longer" meant anywhere from thirty minutes to several hours, if a breakthrough was made. "We need to interview Ms. Botezatu, and she may say something we need to discuss with you. Therefore, we'll ask you to wait in the front room while we interview Ms. Botezatu upstairs."

"Upstairs, eh?" Marilyn snickered. "Be sure and have a good look around."

* * *

Number 9's carpeted stairs were rather steep. Once upon a time, Kate would've bounded up them without a second thought. These days, she ascended with a firm grip on the handrail.

"Marilyn loved the idea of us going up here," she whispered over her shoulder. "What d'ya think we'll find?"

"Sex dungeon."

Kate stifled a giggle. "I'm imagining a room crammed with antique dolls. The ones with the awful, staring faces. But sure, maybe it's a sex dungeon. Should we take the tour before we tackle Dacy?"

"Definitely. Between you and me, Marilyn isn't wrong about her. She's an absolute melt."

'Melt' must be the new 'wally,' Kate thought. London was rich in new slang; the wise woman strove to keep up.

"Great." On the upper floor, Kate saw three doors. They visited the first room on the left, which turned out to be a pleasant if over-rose-budded and over-chenille-fabricked bedroom occupied by DC Kincaid and Daciana. She looked as wan and infantile as she had been earlier, when they'd sent her away so they could interview Marilyn —knees hugged to her chest, eyes red, expression somewhere between muddled and maudlin.

"We'll be back directly," Kate called, leading Paul to the second room. It was a pink-tiled loo with a pink Jacuzzi bath, pink toilet, and pink pedestal sink. Kate didn't despise pink on principle, but this was the exact shade of a certain liquid antacid sold in chemists' shops.

"Third time's the charm," Kate said, opening the last door. "Master..." She tailed off. She'd meant to say "suite," but the totality of the room startled her into silence. Beside her, Paul whispered, "Would you look at that? I'm a prophet."

This was no English country bedroom or shabby chic boudoir. Three of the walls were deep purple. One was covered in mirrored panels. The floor was highly polished black tile. The bed—of a sort—was mostly constructed of steel and leather restraints that buckled. In an open wardrobe, if you could call a seven-foot steel cabinet a wardrobe, there were various whips and wearable accessories.

"This absolutely is a sex dungeon," Kate said. "Only thing missing is the smell."

London Blue

"I've been in a few that didn't smell. Apart from massage oils. And the corpse."

"Obviously. Now, then." Kate felt in her coat pocket for the fresh pair of blue nitrile gloves she always carried. "I don't plan on picking up any evidence, but I might sort of poke it. Gently."

"Same. Without the SOCOs to keep us at arm's length, I'm drunk on power." As Paul moved to inspect the bed, he added, "By the way—Marilyn obviously rang someone in authority before calling 999. Should we confront her?"

"Not yet. Save some ammo for later. And I'm pretty sure there'll be a later—I'm taking her entire interview with a grain of salt." Kate peered into a bedside table's top drawer. "You heard what she said about how litigious the school is. I'll bet she rang the headmistress. Anyone called Lady Griselda probably has connections."

"I'll be gutted if this turns out to be a natural death, a thieving cleaner, and an overabundance of caution about bad press." Kneeling, Paul looked under the bed's industrial-style frame. "Nothing stashed below. Mrs. Maitland-Palmer kept a tidy dungeon."

"Or cracked the whip over Dacy to keep it clean. Pun intended." Kate waited for a chuckle, received nothing, and went back to her day job.

"Do the mirror panels look strange to you?"

Paul studied himself in the left-most glass. "No." He moved to the next panel. "Still devilishly handsome." He moved over again and immediately scowled. "What? I don't look like that. Something's wrong with mirror number three."

Kate had a look. "Yes, but wrong how?"

"Some detective you are. My face looks rounder." He stepped to the side. "My face looks right. Rounder." He stepped to the side again. "Right. Back to perfection." He smiled at himself.

Kate made him demonstrate the perceived effect twice more. To her surprise, it was real. Subtle, but real.

"Maybe we're dealing with cheap glass. Still..." Kate placed the tip of her index finger against the mirror panel. There was no gap between fingertip and reflection. They seemed melded at the tip. "Paul. Kill the ceiling light, will you?"

That plunged the room into a respectable gloom, if not complete darkness. Switching on her mobile's torch, Kate ran the beam across the strange glass until she found what she was looking for: a tiny blue pinprick.

"Hah!"

"Top marks. To us both, mind you," Paul said. "If that two-way mirror hadn't besmirched my looks, we would have missed it."

"Besmirched. How do you know that word?"

"Mum's author vocabulary. By the way, Marilyn was right about you. You're starting to sound like a Beeb talking head."

"She's mental."

"You still drop a few *hatches*," he said. "And stick others in front of words like intel. *Hintel*. But face it. You're starting to sound like the chief. Don't want little Nicky to grow up talking like a Wakefield, eh?"

Kate jerked as if he'd slapped her. Their jibing banter was eternal, with no foibles off the table. But that particular question made her face go hot.

"What is it?" Paul's grin disappeared. "Hey. Come on, Katie. You know I didn't mean it."

"I don't think I sound like a Beeb presenter," Kate said. "To my ears, I sound just the same."

That was a threadbare lie, but Paul loyally accepted it without so much as a raised eyebrow. "Sorry. Never mind me."

"I'm not bothered," Kate lied. "It's just that the whole question of Wakefield vs. Hetheridge is my soft underbelly." Glancing in the mirror, she was relieved to find herself merely pink-cheeked, not turning the deep scarlet that took an hour to fade away. "Let's crack on."

In the rose-and-chenille explosion that was Cathleen Maitland-Palmer's bedroom, DC Kincaid was right where they'd left him, hands in pockets, looking like he would disintegrate from sheer boredom. Daciana was still a portrait of girlish despair.

"Hello, Ms. Botezatu." Kate didn't like to start with first names, especially with women. It struck her as an unearned familiarity most people would never presume if addressing a man. "I'm DI Hetheridge. You've already met DI Bhar. How are you feeling?"

Daciana wiped away a tear.

"I'm sure it was very upsetting, finding the body. But this is a serious investigation, and we must ask you a few questions."

Do I sound like Tony? Kate wondered. *Maybe I phrase things more formally now. How would I have talked to her three years ago? 'It must've given you a right turn to find your boss like that. But I've got a job to do, love, and that means asking questions, don't it?'*

"Please come with us," Kate said.

Daciana didn't move.

"Up you come, Ms. Botezatu," Paul took the cleaner's hand, half-pulling her to her feet. "We'll make this quick, I promise."

"I'll ask you the burning question right now," Kate said,

smiling as if she were doing Daciana a favor. "Did you know Mrs. Maitland-Palmer was filming her bedroom partners with a camera hidden behind the two-way mirror? We found it in there. My torch light bounced off the lens."

Daciana gaped at Kate in horror. Then she slid, boneless, to the floor to lay at their feet.

Kate looked at Kincaid. He shrugged. Rolling her eyes, she signaled Paul, who was always best disposed to tackle nonsense.

Obligingly, Paul knelt beside Daciana. Lifting her arm, he positioned her hand directly above her face, held it momentarily, and let go. In a genuine faint, the unconscious person will be smacked lightly in the face by their own hand, sometimes bringing them around with a jolt. In a sham faint, the person will involuntarily dodge the hand to protect their face while still pretending to be unconscious.

Daciana's head turned aside. Her hand lightly smacked her thick, dark braid instead of her face.

"Right. Get up, love," Kate said, deliberately channeling her Wakefield. "Lots to talk about, innit?"

Chapter Five

Breakfast was served upstairs in the nursery. Harvey had been kind enough to bring up the full English, serving it on a handsome cherrywood butler's table he enjoyed using. As he ate, Tony alternated between reading on his mobile and watching Nicholas amongst his pile of stuffies. The infant would select a toy, chew on it for a while, then toss it away and taste another.

Toward the end of the meal, Kate texted him one of her tantalizing murder non sequiturs:

> Ever hear of a crime connected to the Annabelle Carter school?

Intrigued, Tony had first gone about learning what Annabelle Carter was, then searched his long and excellent memory for murder or malfeasance at London's last finishing school. Nothing came to him, but he was still letting the topic percolate in the back of his mind. Even if the school had never been part of a criminal scandal, one of its teachers or benefactors might have been.

Harvey peeked in discreetly, coffee pot in hand.

"Shall I warm it up for you?"

"Just leave the pot. There's a good man. And thank you," Tony added, looking over the top of his reading specs to emphasize the words. "I appreciate all the accommodations. We'll soon be back to business as usual, I hope."

"Don't rush it. The only thing worse than injury is re-injury. I do wonder…" Harvey cleared his throat. "Is this the right moment to discuss a rather delicate topic?"

"By all means," Tony said. His tone was untroubled, but inside he thought, *If Harvey gives me his notice, I'll get down on my knees and beg him to stay, even if it puts me back in hospital.*

"Of course, having been with you a very long time, and being quite cognizant of how things are done in your service…"

Tony steeled himself.

"…I dislike finding myself in this position. But—would you consider choosing a special menu? To celebrate your birthday, that is?"

He sagged, relieved. "Kate put you up to this?"

"She insisted."

"I thought after last year she understood my view on birthday parties, birthday dinners, birthday lunches—and any other variation that may have metastasized while I wasn't looking."

"This time last year, you were both at Briarshaw. All expectations were suspended, I believe," Harvey said. "I didn't even present you with your yearly cigar."

"I missed that cigar," Tony admitted. He'd quit smoking almost twenty-five years ago, but still enjoyed a fine cigar on his birthday. Harvey, with his extraordinary genius for doing the right thing, always gave him Cubans.

"Lady Kate is quite determined to mark your sixty-second birthday somehow," Harvey said. Before Tony could say, "Nothing's stopping her," Harvey added, "*With* your participation."

Harvey continued, "I told Lady Kate you have no patience for that sort of thing and specifically instructed me never to bring it up. I said you can lead a horse to water but can't make it drink. And she said, 'You can lead a horse to water, and you *can* make it drink. You can't make it enjoy the situation, but that's the horse's problem.'"

Tony smiled in spite of himself. The next time they were at Briarshaw, he'd let her try it with a farm horse. There was truth in the old saying. And he could be every bit as stubborn when he wanted to be.

"A special menu means what? A meal of my choosing? Or some sort of dinner party?"

Harvey cleared his throat again. "The latter, I fear."

"Right. Well. Thank you for telling me. I'll handle it from here."

"Yes. And, well." Harvey sighed. "While I'm delivering information of a dissatisfactory nature..."

"What?"

"I finally reached the Society's executive secretary," he said. "Next year's meeting will be in Lisbon."

Tony perked up. "That isn't so bad. A three-hour flight, I believe."

"Yes. But I fear only the Chinese military historian, Dr. Wu, will attend. Dr. Joyce Fox is writing a book and has turned down all invitations for the next three years. Dr. Gerstein's secretary told me he would now only attend American conferences. Specifically, West Coast meetings. And Dr. Paulson has..." He sighed. "He's retired altogether."

Tony let the bad news sink in. Worse than bad—a

crushing disappointment, if he were being honest. The AWMHS, or Ancient Warfare Military History Society, had come to Tony's attention during the course of his reading. The acknowledgements in a Pulitzer Prize-winning book on Genghis Khan by Dr. Leonard Wu had directed him to the AWMHS website. There, he'd discovered books by other historians, including a handful by Dr. E. Edwin Paulson.

Paulson's books were, in Tony's opinion, the finest work on global military history, full stop. Therefore, he was delighted to discover that the next annual AWMHS conference would be held in London, and immediately bought tickets for himself and Henry. The notion of a weekend's immersion in ancient warfare had inspired him to prepare questions for Dr. Paulson. But then his knee gave out, baby Nicky narrowly escaped serious injury, and Tony chose to put off the conference. Forever, as it happened, though he hadn't guessed it at the time.

"Yes, well, thank you for looking into it, Harvey," he said, doing his utmost to hide his disappointment. "Can't be helped. Mustn't grumble. And don't worry about Kate. I won't stomach a party or a dinner, but if she's determined to mark the occasion, she can buy me a book."

Tony returned to watching Nicky sleepily drooling on a stuffed rabbit. Harvey, gathering the breakfast dishes, paused to answer his mobile.

"Wellegrave House, how may I help?"

Surprised by the silent interval that followed, Tony looked over at Harvey curiously.

"I see. Madam, if you allow me to put you on a brief hold, I shall be back with you directly." To Tony, he said, "A lady called Dame Ingrid Hazelhurst is at the gate. She'd like to see you."

He stared at Harvey. "Really? This is...unexpected." He'd caught himself nearly issuing a Kate-ism: "This is gobsmacking!" His wife's manner of speech was beginning to wear off on him.

"Shall I ask her to make a regular appointment?"

"No. If she came to speak to me in the middle of the day, she must have a very good reason. Particularly since she's always despised me." He tucked reading specs into the breast pocket under his jumper. "Please show her into the living room. Offer her tea. I'll put Nicky in his cot, then come down to meet her."

Distracted by Dame Ingrid's sudden appearance, he pushed aside the tray table and stood up—or meant to. His post-op knee straightened, but the pain was like a cricket bat to the joint. Staggering, he grabbed for his crutch, but he was already toppling in the opposite direction.

"Tony!"

Harvey Sixsmith wasn't large, but he was wiry. He was also determined. Arresting Tony's fall, he maneuvered him back to his chair.

"Thank you, Harvey. Well. Bit of a disappointment, that. I've explained to Nicky, and I hardly need tell you, what happens between gentlemen stays between gentlemen."

"Of course. I wouldn't dream of telling Lady Kate. Shall I help you get Nicky in his cot?"

Tony swallowed his pride. "Please. I'll wait while you give our guest today's gate code."

* * *

"Good afternoon, Dame Ingrid."

The former police commissioner occupied her living

room chair without any outward sign of impatience, but no one could accuse the woman of making herself at home. Her teacup was mostly full; her shortbread biscuits were distinctly unnibbled. Dame Ingrid, now in her second career as a victim's rights advocate, was all business.

"Good afternoon, Lord Hetheridge." Rising to meet him, she gave his hand a brief, firm shake. Tall and thin, with a heavily lined face and pallid blue eyes, she looked like what she was—a seventy-year-old woman obsessed with helping the victims the system had failed to protect. Although she'd received the honorific, Dame, for distinguished service to the West Yorkshire Police, Ingrid Hazelhurst was as down-to-earth as she was professional. She expected to be treated with the respect due to a retired police chief and knew her value well. If the King and the PM ever asked her to luncheon, she could easily hold her own.

"Terribly sorry to keep you waiting," Tony said. "We have a new baby who had to be put down for his nap. Then there's this." He indicated the crutch. "Takes a bit longer at present, dragging my carcass from point A to point B."

"The apology should be mine, my lord. I dropped by your home on impulse. I had no idea you were recovering from surgery."

"Come, now, Ingrid. Don't 'my lord' me in my own home. I'm Tony. I realize we've never been friends," he added lightly, addressing the elephant in the room head-on, "but we've also never been enemies. At least not on my part." To spare her the obligation of pretending to agree, he asked, "Are you quite finished with tea?"

"Yes, thank you, my—er. Tony." She picked up her carryall, a black leather affair capacious enough to hold dozens of files. It looked heavy.

"Then please, come through."

His office was a comfortable room, as large as his old digs at the Yard but more warmly decorated in burgundies and greens. He placed Dame Ingrid in the client's chair opposite his desk, then made his way to the other side, careful not to bang his knee as he sat down.

"Rather Spartan, isn't it?" Dame Ingrid regarded his desk with approval. "But in the modern age, what does one need besides a laptop and a phone?" Studying the framed black-and-white pictures decorating the walls, she asked, "Are those your compositions?"

"No. My executive assistant, Mrs. Snell, is a rather good amateur photographer. One day, I'll prevail upon her to enter her work in a competition."

"I rather expected to see all your accolades hanging from the picture rail."

Tony shrugged. Boxed away in the attic were those framed commendations he'd received for dedication, service, and bravery; a Queen's Medal for Gallantry; and a couple of Lucite trophies awarded by the borough of Westminster, granted in recognition of his contributions to public safety. "I prefer not to get bogged down by ephemera. Age has its perks. One of them is not feeling a need to hide behind props."

"You mentioned a new baby," Dame Ingrid said. "Allow me to congratulate you on becoming a father."

"Thank you. I should also mention that I have a grown-up daughter and an eleven-year-old son. And as you may have guessed, I didn't expect to have an infant at this time of life. There are no words for the experience."

Dame Ingrid smiled weakly. Thirty years ago, her beloved only daughter had been kidnapped and murdered. That still-unsolved case had pushed her to excel as a copper, protecting other people's children. After retirement, it had transformed her into a victim's advocate. And even then, Tony suspected, she knew no peace. He changed the subject.

"Now, as for your visit. I must confess that my curiosity is piqued. To what do I owe the pleasure?"

"Lord He—Tony. If you will indulge me, I must begin by getting something off my chest. From the first time we met," Dame Ingrid said, lifting her chin and looking him in the eye, "I treated you with suspicion. At times, even contempt. I made no secret of my belief that you were Michael Deaver's acolyte. Worse, his willing accomplice in stitch-ups, cover-ups, and God knows what else. I grievously misjudged you. Please accept my apology."

"Past is past. Now. Dare I hope you've brought me a case?"

"I have. Scotland Yard considers it cold. As sometimes happens, certain affected parties called my office and asked me to audit the investigation personally. Having done so, I'd like you to reinvestigate the case as a private detective. In aid of that, I've brought you this." She lifted that heavy carryall with both hands, placing it upon his desk with a *thud*.

"In those files, you'll find every single piece of information the Met has released publicly about the investigation into Will Wilkinson's death," Dame Ingrid continued. "It also contains press clippings about Wilkinson's career, and interview transcripts with his colleagues in the aftermath of his death."

"These are all freely available? I'm surprised the man's name doesn't ring a bell with me if he was so well-known."

"Only within his industry. I erred on the side of completeness," she said. "His colleagues included some moderately famous people, so three of the files are devoted to those individuals. Take as long as you need to acquaint yourself fully with the case. Then, I'd like your honest opinion. If you agree that further police investigation is wanted, I'll see that Scotland Yard grants you consultant access. Heaven knows what information they've held back."

"Will Wilkinson," Tony repeated, trying to prompt his memory.

"Perhaps the name Damselfish will do the trick?"

"Damselfish. Musical, I presume, and not aquatic," Tony said. He thought for a moment, and it came to him. "Yes, of course. Their tour bus exploded in the middle of a Manchester concert, right? The performers were all on stage and got off unharmed. A few passersby were injured, but only one person died. Their manager," he finished, mildly triumphant.

"Their producer, actually, although in his relationship with the band, lines were blurred." Dame Ingrid opened her carryall, withdrawing the first file, which was two inches thick. "Forgive all the paper. My office is going digital, albeit slowly. If you'd prefer all of this on flash drives, I can have an assistant scan the lot, but that could take a week. We're overloaded with cases."

"I imagine so." Anyone desperate for job security had only to become a victim's advocate; the inboxes, email and otherwise, would never be empty. "Don't worry about scanning all this. Paper's fine."

Opening the file, Tony was confronted by a black-and-white portrait of Damselfish's late producer, seemingly at work. At any rate, he was posed next to a proliferation of knobs, slide switches, and electronic keyboards. His curly dark hair was artfully unkempt; his mouth had a petulant cast, as if someone had promised him ice cream and forgotten. He wore a designer tracksuit, a thick gold chain, and a pair of Nike Phantom Luna 2 boots with gold-tone cleats. Aviator shades hid his eyes.

"How old?"

"Forty-nine."

"Married?"

"Technically, but he was in the process of getting a divorce when he died. Three children, the youngest of which is seven years old."

"So, he was the band's producer, not their manager. Yet he was inside their tour bus while they were onstage. I had the idea producers were more hands-off. Why was he at the arena?"

"You'll want to read this." Dame Ingrid searched through the folder until she found a *Rolling Stone* article, tapping it with her finger. She didn't varnish her nails. Several were bitten down to the quick. "It's about four thousand words, which is rare for a profile of someone who isn't a household name. I rang up the reporter to ask about the experience of interviewing Wilkinson. He said the man was so obnoxious—and told so many untruths—that what was meant to be a one-page article turned into a sort of state-of-the-music-industry exposé."

Tony skimmed the article. "Family money...rapid promotions...spoke on condition of anonymity...fears of retaliation..."

Dame Ingrid handed him another photocopy, this one of a single paragraph in a music magazine's "blind item" column called "Guess Who, Don't Sue." It read:

For weeks, we've been hearing that a certain very successful act is done with their handsy, interfering, delusions-of-competence producer. And like a soon-to-be

ex who sees the writing on the wall, that producer has been begging, pleading, and promising a better future. The act says it's time for a change; the producer says they're damn selfish.

Tony chuckled. "Couldn't resist giving it away at the end."

"From what I've gathered, everyone in the industry expected Damselfish to sack him come the first of the year. Instead, he was blown to bits halfway through their Christmas Eve show."

"You've amassed so much about him," Tony said, marveling at the folder's girth. "Is any of it complimentary?"

"Only the press releases sent out by the label. Most of what's contained in the file are interview transcripts with Wilkinson's family members. Also, his subordinates at the record label."

"May I see what the Met declassified regarding the explosion?"

Dame Ingrid passed it over. It looked extensive until he dug into the particulars of each interview. Most were rule-out discussions with Damselfish's road crew: thirty-seven people responsible for everything about the tour, apart from climbing onstage and performing the music. There was the stage manager; the guitar, bass, drum, and keyboard instrument techs; the merchandiser manager and crew; the bus drivers; the caterer; the lighting team; the pyrotechnician. This last roadie had been interviewed first, and most formally, in the presence of a Manchester detective, a Scotland Yard detective, and a person from EOD—Explosive Ordinance Disposal.

Tony reviewed that interview carefully. The professional assigned to the explosion was a methodical man with twenty-five years' experience handling explosives for the entertainment industry. In the EOD man's opinion, a ticketed guest couldn't have brought the device into the venue. Security was reduced for VIP guests and persons with backstage passes, but he didn't believe one of them could have managed the feat. Even if all the security checks had failed, there would still be CCTV footage of that person entering the bus.

"The detective who interviewed Damselfish's pyrotechnician struck him off as a person of interest," Dame Ingrid said. "In part because no direct evidence tied him to the explosion. In part because two dozen people associated with the tour signed affidavits swearing that his behavior was normal, and his presence accounted for."

"Yes, I see that. I should perhaps mention, Dame Ingrid, that the detective who performed many of these interviews is a close friend. DI Bhar."

"I know. During the Gulls case, I seem to remember him becoming flustered and babbling at me. You manufactured a coughing fit to make him stop."

"Yes, well, that's Paul."

After leafing through the interviews, all of which ended with the crew member duly eliminated as a person of interest, Tony moved on to the basic facts of the case.

On 24 December of the previous year, Damselfish had been playing its year-end concert at the Motorpoint Arena in Nottingham. The incident occurred just after intermission, when they'd returned to the stage to perform their second set. Two minutes into the song, their tour bus exploded in a yellow-orange fireball. There was extensive property damage to the facility, vendor kiosks, and parked vehicles. Six concertgoers who'd been out of their seats received minor injuries, earning them official MPS interviews as well as settlements. They were cleared of suspicion by CCTV footage, which showed them drinking and dancing, not planting a bomb.

Tony pushed the file aside. "How much was Wilkinson worth when he died?"

"Ten million pounds, according to initial reports," Dame Ingrid replied. "His ex-wife, children, and siblings all anticipated significant legacies as described by the terms of his will. Then the executor contacted them. He explained that none of the legacies would be paid out. Wilkinson's actual worth turned out to be thirty thousand pounds. That didn't even cover his debts."

"Are you quite serious? Thirty thousand pounds? He must have been addicted to gambling," Tony said. "Or living far beyond his means. Assuming he didn't commit some kind of asset concealment. You mentioned he was in the midst of a divorce."

"Yes. His wife suspected concealment, full stop. She hired a forensic accountant to pore over the books on behalf of her and her children. In the end, the accountant certified that in his opinion, there was no sign of criminal activity." Dame Ingrid regarded Tony shrewdly. "An old copper like me naturally comes to one conclusion."

"He was being extorted. And when he reached the point that he could no longer pay, his life became forfeit."

"Yes. If true, it might explain some of his general unpleasantness. His meal ticket, Damselfish, was giving him the keys to the street right when he needed them most."

Tony returned to the pyrotechnician's interview, checking if the EOD agent had made any preliminary guesses about the means. He hadn't.

"Was the cause of the explosion ever determined?"

"Not absolutely. The lab declared that it was probably

commercial-grade Semtex. That's why Wilkinson's death is presumed murder."

"There's another possibility. Wilkinson might have obtained the ordnance himself. Perhaps he accidentally killed himself whilst rigging up the bus to kill the band."

Dame Ingrid rewarded him with one of her rare smiles. "That's my pet hypothesis. Alas, there's no evidence to back it up. For all anyone can prove, Wilkinson might not have been the intended victim. Just a man in the wrong place at the wrong time."

Tony digested that. "Not to sound churlish," he said at last, "as I maintain the old-fashioned belief that each person is entitled to their life. But this case doesn't strike me as your sort of advocacy. What am I missing? Do Wilkinson's putative heirs feel hard done by, since the expected legacy never came?"

Dame Ingrid gave a dry chuckle. "Money? Tony, I can promise you this: if I come calling at your door, it will never be to recover money. No, I've come on behalf of three young women: Zoë Schultz, Elodie Queen, and Miranda Griffin. In a word: Damselfish."

Chapter Six

"Miranda Griffin," Tony repeated. "I've been in rehab hell, frankly, but I know the name. The story was everywhere last week. How are her bandmates involved?"

"In July, Damselfish returned home to London from their second world tour," Dame Ingrid said. "On 27 July, Zoë Schultz survived a knife attack. Around the same time, Elodie Queen acquired a stalker. If not for the fact she never leaves her flat except in the company of a large Rottweiler, there probably would have been a knife attack on her, too. As for Miranda, she was found dead on 26 August. Strangled and locked in her car's boot."

"Has there been an arrest?"

"No. But certain factors have muddied the water."

"Right. Start with Zoë Schultz, then. Just give me a moment to google her."

Tony's search me turned up hundreds of pictures of the same young woman, pretty and pouty, usually dressed in tatty jeans and a velvet blazer. Her signature hairstyle was tiny twin ponytails, one above each ear, uneven and mussy.

Black lipstick and multiple piercings completed the glam girl rocker look.

"Zoë's a fit girl—sorry, woman," Dame Ingrid said. "I occasionally slip and say 'girl' because at my age, they often seem like absolute fetuses. Anyway, she's quite fit and in the habit of a daily morning run."

Bypassing the publicity photos, Tony examined the selfies and candid pics by paparazzi. There was Zoë, pictured in running gear on a narrow lane, sandwiched between tall wrought iron fences and mature trees. She'd posted an Instagram selfie in front of Strawberry on the Vine Beauty Clinic, whose famous all-pink exterior was visible from orbit. In another pap snap, Zoë exited a yoga class, head down and green nutrition shake in hand. There was a banner behind her, and though out of focus, the words "South Bolton Gardens School" were perceptible.

"On the morning of 27 July, at around seven A.M., she was ambushed by a man wielding a chef's knife. He grabbed her by a ponytail and attempted to slash her throat. Fortunately, he only cut her chin before she twisted away. After a brief struggle, she ran for it, but he overtook her. Stabbed her in the chest and legged it."

"Chef's knife," Tony repeated. "Forgive me, I'm not much in the kitchen. That's the thick one with the small point, yes? Meant for dicing veg?"

"Right."

"What a ridiculous weapon for a mugger. Did her sternum stop the point?"

"Yes. As I said, after he stabbed her, the attacker ran off, probably thinking he'd left her to bleed out. Zoë rang 999 on her mobile. She was transported to Casualty, received a couple of sutures, and was released the same day. I've been more badly hurt in my kitchen making Christmas lunch."

Dame Ingrid shook her head. "You've been a copper too long when your first response to news of a young woman stabbed in the street is contempt for the choice of weapon."

Tony concurred. In films, desperate people often pick up a chef's knife to defend themselves. In reality, even the thickest mugger soon learned that bone is an excellent defense against a blade, especially if that blade is a big veg knife with a fine point. True, a strong and highly determined person might force a chef's knife into his victim's chest deeply enough to kill her—but not, in Tony's opinion, when she was upright and fighting to get away. Fatal knife crimes were usually carried out with something practical and concealable, like a double-edged titanium handyman's knife.

"How did Zoë describe her attacker?"

"He wore a red tracksuit, gloves, sunglasses, and a balaclava. He never spoke. He dropped the knife, but there were no prints."

"Is there any possibility this was staged? As publicity for the band, I mean." It was an ugly supposition, but he was in the business of ugly suppositions.

"If this event happened in a vacuum, I'd be forced to ask the same question," Dame Ingrid said. "But in reading Zoë's file, you'll see it was the culmination of a harassment pattern that started three weeks prior. A threatening note slipped under her door the day she returned to her flat. It said, 'Won't be long now.' After that, she got strange phone calls and letters containing gruesome images. Blood-spattered crime scenes taken from the internet. Her local police chief suggested she consider moving, but she was attached to her place. It's a very nice building in—"

"Kensington," Tony cut in.

"Yes. How did you know?"

"Google. I don't know precisely where she lives, but I suspect the attack occurred in Holland Park. Lots of lonely lanes there where a man might ambush a woman, especially in the early morning."

"Well. Yes, it happened in the Holland Park area. Top marks."

Tony was tempted to suggest she needn't sound so surprised, but as they'd only just managed a cordial half-hour, it was probably too soon to introduce her to his dry sense of humor. Instead, he asked, "Where is Ms. Schultz now?"

"In hiding, per the advice of her Scotland Yard liaison, DC Kincaid."

"Toff Squad. Yes, I suppose a band with Damselfish's profile would qualify. What about the second young woman? Ms. Queen, I believe?"

"Yes. Elodie Queen. By the way, I did ask if she chose her stage name because it sounded like Ellery Queen. She hadn't the faintest notion what I meant. A gifted performer, and on her way to becoming a shrewd businesswoman. But an absolute fetus nonetheless."

Chuckling, Tony consulted his mobile to see what results Elodie's name would bring. Unlike Zoë, Elodie wasn't a glam girl rocker. Still, she was striking, with short, artfully disheveled green hair. She wore heavy eyeliner, a septal nose ring, and two studs by the outer corner of her left eye that resembled tears—tears of steel.

"Now, this is encouraging. My search turns up nothing but headshots and concert photos," Tony said. "Did you advise her to take control of her internet presence? Perhaps through an online reputation doctor?"

"I didn't have to. The day after Zoë's attack, Elodie initiated that step herself. Like you, she believed Zoë scattered too many breadcrumbs for her own safety."

"Yet Elodie's also been stalked and harassed. What's the timeline? Concurrently with Zoë's troubles, or after the stabbing?"

"There's some confusion. After Zoë removed herself from public view and Damselfish announced that touring was on hiatus, Elodie had a run-in with a typical London bag-snatcher. Or so she assumed at the time. As she was walking past Burlington Arcade, a man bumped into her. She thought he tried to take her bag. Then her Rottweiler bit the attacker, who fled. It was a confused scene. Dozens of eyewitnesses, all of them useless, so we have no description. Elodie came away with a rip in her sleeve and a scratch down her arm. Whether it was a garden-variety crime or an attempt on her life, we don't know.

"The next week, a letter was slipped under her door. The writer claimed to know an embarrassing secret about her. He threatened to go public unless paid off." She passed a photocopy of the printed note to Tony.

> **Miss Queen,**
>
> *I know all about your school days. A story like that would be terrible for your image. Bright Star would pay top price for the intel. There's nothing worse than a poseur in rock and roll.*
>
> *Meet me this afternoon at two P.M. sharp in Hampstead Heath. Sit on a bench by pond no. 1 and watch the swans. You will receive further instructions there. No need to bring cash just yet. I only want to come to an understanding. Do not involve the police or authorities in any way. At the first whiff*

of indiscretion on your part, I will auction your secret to the highest bidder.
   A Friend

Tony handed it back. "Don't tell me she went to the park alone."

"No. She rang her local Met station straight away, told the police everything, and turned over the letter."

"Then the fetus accusation must be retracted. That was wise beyond her years. Did another threat follow?"

"No."

"Did the secret come out?"

"Yes. The next day, Elodie gave *Bright Star* an exclusive interview that contained the news. The press foamed over it for a day or two. Then, the PM was a silly arse during Question Time and the matter was forgotten."

"So, Zoë was stabbed and went into hiding. Elodie had two run-ins, probably but not necessarily related to Zoë's experience, and rescued herself both times."

Absently, Tony rubbed his post-op knee, which had begun to ache. If not for the TKR, he wouldn't have needed Dame Ingrid to recite the details of Miranda's murder. He certainly knew her face after seven days of wall-to-wall news coverage. Zoë was a glam girl rocker and Elodie was a soft punk *artiste*, but Miranda had been a glossy pop star. She'd worn her honey blonde hair in spiral curls; her fashion taste ran to pinstripes and polka dots. Her grin for the cameras was sparkling, almost wholesome. The headlines blared,

MELODIC MIRANDA, DEAD AT 24

TAKEN TOO SOON: THE DAMSEL OF DAMSELFISH

'MUSIC KILLED MY GIRL' SOBS MIRANDA'S MUM

"It began with a kidnapping, yes?"

"That's right. There were eyewitnesses," Dame Ingrid said. "Miranda was driving alone in the city. On Lynwood Road, waiting to turn onto Upper Tooting, a man near a Lyca Mobile shop approached her car and asked her to lower her window. I suppose Miranda didn't find it as off-putting as most of us would." Reading his mind, Dame Ingrid added, "I know, it beggars belief that a woman with an international following and all the usual messages from stalkers and nutters would lower her window for a strange man. But according to Elodie, Miranda loved being recognized. She never said no to an autograph or selfie.

"At any rate, for whatever reason, the poor girl complied. Instantly, he lunged and hit her hard enough to stun her. The Met acquired CCTV footage of the event from a Barclays nearby. It's rather poor—the angle is wrong, with the assailant's back to the camera. But from the speed of the blow and the way she collapsed, I'd say he seriously injured her."

"I do hope some sort of E-FIT or useful description came from the eyewitnesses," Tony said without much hope.

"We know he was bald, wore glasses, and had a black beard. Beyond that, no one agrees. He's been described as white, Spanish, and Arabic. Twenty-five, thirty-five, and forty-five. Fat, average, and fit.

"Before any pedestrians could intervene, the assailant pushed Miranda aside, got behind the wheel, and sped away," Dame Ingrid continued. "This was on 22 August. The Met searched for Miranda discreetly. No appeal to the public."

"Probably wise. A media circus might make the kidnapper panic and kill her," Tony said. "But this wasn't a kidnapping, was it?"

"No. There were no demands. On 26 August, in an outer borough—Bexley—a man in a car park clocked a bad smell. It was coming from Miranda's car. She'd been stuffed in the boot. Death by manual strangulation."

"Bexley," Tony said thoughtfully. "The Bexleyheath Ripper."

"Precisely," Dame Ingrid said. "I believe Miranda's killer picked Bexley to dump her because there was a serial killer in the area last year. One who was never caught and, therefore, might be assumed to have made a resurgence. In my view, dumping her in Bexley successfully hindered the investigation. Exploring two radically different theories can create chaos. Moreover," she said acidly, "my personal belief —that Wilkinson and Miranda were killed by the same person that stabbed Zoë and tried to lure Elodie to Hampstead Heath—has been met with polite disbelief by Scotland Yard."

"It's a stretch," Tony said.

"Is it?"

"Respectfully—yes, and that's for any murder squad, not just the Toff Squad. Arranging the bus explosion required a certain amount of sophistication. Either technical expertise or connections to get it done as a contract job.

"Contrast that with Zoë's stabbing, which was amateurish. It could have been done by a nutter fixated with the band. Elodie's apparent run-in with a bag-snatcher might have been exactly that. As for her blackmail threat, celebrities receive that sort of thing all the time. I don't mean to suggest these events are insignificant, or don't belong under the purview of Serious Crimes. But there's no clear-cut connection to hang your hat on. As for the Toff Squad—it's called in when an investigation is likely to mortify someone up the social food chain."

"Is that so? I thought it was all to do with money."

"That, too."

"And Miranda? Can you dismiss her death as merely a kidnapping gone wrong?"

"No. I dismiss none of it," Tony said, sitting up straighter. "Speaking as a private investigator who has no obligation to convince the Crown Prosecution Service of anything, I believe this is a campaign to annihilate Damselfish. The idea that four people could individually be so unlucky in the span of a year doesn't sit right with me. Now, getting back to filthy lucre. I take it these young women are not yet millionaires?"

"They should be, but no, not yet. After Wilkinson's death, Elodie engaged a forensic accountant to review the band's books. Turns out he'd been embezzling royalties all along. She said it would take eighteen months of touring non-stop to earn back the money."

"She can prove that? Her accountant attested to as much?"

Dame Ingrid blinked. "Presumably. Perhaps I should've put Elodie under oath before believing her description of her band's troubles."

"Forgive me. It's just interesting that the man was apparently embezzling from his cash cow yet still went to his grave a pauper. Yes—interesting." Turning over the possibilities, Tony unconsciously pushed away from the desk, intending to lean far back in his chair, as he'd often done at the Yard. The resulting jolt of pain in his post-op knee brought him sharply back to the here and now.

"My goodness." Dame Ingrid looked alarmed. "Are you quite all right?"

"Fine," he croaked. "A reminder for me to bloody well keep both feet on the floor."

"I'm assuming you had a TKR. In which case, take my advice. Do all of your prescribed exercises, and then some."

He nodded. "Thank you, Ingrid, for bringing this case to me. I'm quite happy to take it. As for the data you so kindly provided," he added, gesturing to the thick files deposited on his desk, "I'll review them, of course. But I won't take any of it as gospel until I've interviewed the major players. It's just how I work."

"I'd expect nothing less." Dame Ingrid appeared cautiously optimistic, which was the equivalent of outright jubilation for her. "Alas, there is one remaining barrier, and I fear it's a rather large one."

"What?"

"Your fee. Elodie and Zoë have agreed to pay you if you solve the case, or at least dig up enough new evidence to put the Met's nose to the grindstone. But after losing so many royalties last year, they can't stomach the fact that private detectives are paid by the hour, not by results. Should you uncover no significant findings, I fear they'll refuse to reimburse you."

"Bugger that. My fee is negotiable, depending on how much a particular case interests me. This one is intriguing. And much of the legwork, so to speak, can be done sitting down—which certainly suits my present circumstances."

Dame Ingrid thanked him warmly, then insisted on showing herself out. Her hand was on the doorknob when a loose thread occurred to Tony.

"Ingrid, forgive me, but there's one last thing. What was the secret Elodie's blackmailer threatened to expose?"

"Oh, that." She looked amused. "You must understand, Tony, young women's lives are different than in my day. Authenticity is everything now. So, Damselfish in general, and Elodie in particular, cultivate what my niece calls 'in-your-face, girlie-punk, burn-it-down rage.'"

"Ah." He was tempted to ask how burn-it-down rage fitted in with cheesecake photoshoots and corporate sponsors but tactfully bit his tongue.

"Elodie keeps her private life under wraps to protect her image. She especially didn't want it known that in her early twenties, she attended a ladies' finishing school."

Tony stared at her. "You don't mean Annabelle Carter."

"I do."

Well. That's quite a coincidence, thought Tony, who did not believe in coincidences.

Chapter Seven

Daciana Botezatu looked like a guilty woman. She behaved like one, too. In his baby copper days, Paul would have taken that as proof he was onto something. Now, in his detective inspector days, he simply took notes on her demeanor, agnostic as to whether they would prove helpful or not. After all, some people simply couldn't be in the same room as a police officer without remembering unreturned library books or a pack of sweeties they nicked at age six. Guilt complexes were epidemic in modern Britain.

"I am sorry I faint," she said for the fifth time. It was her turn in the hot seat Marilyn had vacated, and neither a glass of water nor reassurances that she wasn't in trouble had put her at ease.

"I say to myself, Daciana, be strong. But poor Ms. Cathleen is dead." She crossed herself in the Orthodox manner: top, bottom, right, left. "I pray for her."

"Of course. Let me just get this out of the way," Paul said. Into his mobile, he began, "Interview with Daciana Botezatu at No. 9 Bulwer Street on—"

"No! No recording!" she cried.

"It's standard operating procedure," Kate said.

"Turn it off or I say nothing."

Paul complied, leaving his mobile screen-up on the table so she could see for herself. "This is a voluntary interview, so we'll honor your request. Tell us a bit about yourself, Daciana. You're Romanian by birth, yes?"

"Yes. Father come on settlement scheme," she said, referring to a now-defunct European Union policy. "I was being in school and living with Mother. Then Mother die, and I come to be living with Father on family visa."

"Have you always worked as a cleaner?"

"Yes. I apply for care worker visa but they say no. Romanian care not like UK care." She stared at Paul with big, dark eyes that reminded him uncomfortably of his mum, Sharada. Specifically, Sharada when she was putting the screws to him, guilt-tripping him into doing things her way.

"You not take away family visa," Daciana said urgently. "Please, please don't take away family visa. Father need me here."

"We're not taking away anyone's visa," Kate interjected coolly. "*Unless,*" she added, heartlessly staring Daciana down, "we find you've committed some sort of crime that forces our hand. Obstruction of a lawful inquiry comes to mind."

The cleaner shifted her gaze to Kate like a field mouse locking eyes with a kestrel.

"At home in Romania, were you ever in trouble?" Kate asked.

"No," Daciana whispered.

"What about here in Britain? I'll check, so I suggest you tell the truth. Cautions? Fines? Parking tickets?"

The cleaner shook her head.

"Did you do anything to harm Mrs. Maitland-Palmer?"
"No."
"Do you know who harmed Mrs. Maitland-Palmer?"
"No."
"There. See how easy that was? No need for you to be so frightened. Just answer the rest of my questions honestly. Starting with this one. Did you know about the hidden camera set-up in your employer's master bedroom?"

Daciana's eyes dropped. "No."

A glance from Kate cued Paul, as the good cop, to steer the interview in a friendlier direction. As the bad cop, Kate was like a great white. She tended to circle her victims, bumping them once or twice before opening her jaws for the kill.

He asked, "When did you begin working for Mrs. Maitland-Palmer?"

"As soon as I come. Father arrange it."

"Yes, but when was that?"

She paused to consider. "One year ago."

"How did he know the victim?"

"From school."

"The school Mrs. Maitland-Palmer worked at? Annabelle Carter?"

"Yes."

"Did he work there?"

"Did. Is old now. Retire."

"What was his job?"

"Janitor. Janitors are what Botezatus are in UK. Clean. Mop. Sweep," she said sullenly.

"Right. Take us through your discovery of the body again."

"I come. Regular time. On time, always on time. Light in kitchen on. I think, Ms. Cathleen up? Want breakfast? I look. See her on floor with white face. Cold." She crossed herself again. "Finger gone. I was sick. Then I ring Ms. Marilyn."

"Right. You said you don't know who hurt Mrs. Maitland-Palmer. Do you know who wanted to hurt her?"

Daciana gaped at him like he'd asked when she planned to ride Virgin Galactic to the edge of space. "No. I don't know people. Not Ms. Cathleen's kind of people."

"He means, can you identify them. Face. Name," Kate cut in. *Bump*.

"For example," Paul said, all gentleness, "as you cleaned rooms and prepared meals, did you see or hear something we should know? Perhaps you witnessed a guest behaving toward Mrs. Maitland-Palmer in a threatening manner? Shouting at her? Telling her she'd be sorry, or raising a hand to her?"

"No." Daciana shook her head excessively.

Kate lifted an eyebrow. "Simple as that? In the last year, Mrs. Maitland-Palmer never had a heated exchange with anyone who visited here? Ever?"

Daciana directed her answer to Paul. "First rule for cleaner: discreet. No gossips."

"Answering our questions truthfully isn't gossip, and it isn't indiscreet. It's the only thing you can do now for your employer, to try and help her get justice," Paul said. When the cleaner seemed unmoved, he added, "Telling us the absolute truth protects your immigrant status on the family visa, too."

"But I need new job. If I have bad name, no work."

"I see. It almost sounds like you know something, but you're afraid to tell us," Paul said. "Are you thinking of someone important? Somebody with the power to blackball you?"

London Blue

Daciana said nothing.

"We can be discreet, too. There won't be any confrontations," Paul assured her, hoping his statement didn't turn into a bold-faced lie. Odds were, whatever information Daciana was sitting on would be of little or no interest. But if she coughed up something significant, a confrontation *did* lie ahead—the kind with her sitting in the witness box facing the accused standing in the dock.

"Ms. Marilyn," Daciana said, so low Paul strained to hear. "She row with Ms. Cathleen. Threaten. Say she should be put away."

"Was this row a one-time thing? A blowup?" Kate asked. "Or did they shout at each other every time Marilyn came to visit?"

"Every time," Daciana said, again directing her response to Paul.

He said, "You used the word threaten. Explain what you mean. Did Marilyn get violent? Push her or slap her?"

"Not that. Ms. Marilyn wanted to put Ms. Cathleen in home. Care home for"—Daciana jabbed her temple—"dementia people."

"I see. Give us your opinion of Mrs. Maitland-Palmer's health," Paul said. "Was she in need of dementia care?"

"I think, no. But she always…how you call it… *eccentric*. So many parties. So many men in house. I ask Father. He say Ms. Cathleen only trying to be young again. Ms. Marilyn cross. So they fight."

"Daciana, this interview will not end until you tell us the absolute truth." Kate's dorsal fin surfaced, cutting through waves on a collision course with the cleaner. "Did Cathleen Maitland-Palmer take men up to that room and secretly film herself having sex with them?"

"I clean. I cleaner." Daciana tapped her chest. "Only cleaner."

"So, you cleaned up afterward, is that what you're saying?"

Daciana shot Paul a desperate look, clearly hoping for a heroic lifeguard to save the day. When he gazed back impassively, her face crumpled like a little girl's. She began to weep, shoulders shaking, hair falling over her face like a dropped curtain.

"Let me explain something to you," Kate said. Daciana tried to drown her out by sobbing louder, but Kate only raised her voice. "If you think DI Bhar and I are bad, think again. We're your best hope of coming out of this in one piece. Ever watch *Traces*? If you have, you know how it goes.

"First, the SOCOs will turn up. They'll dust and swab and photograph every inch of this house. They'll pull down that two-way mirror and lift fingerprints from the camera rig behind it, and they'll test every knife in the kitchen. If your prints are on those knives, you'll be arrested on suspicion of murder.

"While you go into remand," she continued, "your father's place will be rumbled. We'll search for Mrs. Maitland-Palmer's missing ring, and who knows what else we'll find in the process? Most people don't lead completely blameless lives. If you or your father have something to hide, it will come to light—meaning more charges."

Kate was playing hardball, stretching the facts. While the Crown Prosecution Service might theoretically agree to banging up someone with such flimsy evidence, Paul had never seen it happen. Unless Daciana confessed or was revealed to have the missing finger tucked in her pinnie, the worst she'd get from the Met was a lengthy back-and-forth in one of their windowless interview rooms.

As for her family home, it couldn't be searched without a court order, which required probable cause. But if Daciana were half the dutiful daughter she claimed to be, she'd balk at the notion of coppers swarming over her father's house. New immigrants tended to be wary of law enforcement. The idea of being cautioned for typical Magistrate-level offenses—watching telly without a license, computer software unlawfully shared between users, cannabis possession—produced outsized dread.

"What do you say, Ms. Botezatu?"

Daciana lifted her head. She wasn't shaking; her eyes were dry. "I smell fags. Give me fag," she said, smoothing her hair back. "Then we talk."

"PC Kincaid, could you scrape up a fag for Ms. Botezatu?" Kate called.

Kincaid appeared with a loose fag and an ashtray. Closing her pink, well-shaped lips around the cigarette, Daciana waited for him to light it. Then she took a slow, sensual drag, holding Kincaid's gaze until she blew smoke in his face. His pale, Anglo-Irish complexion reddened. He looked half offended, half turned on.

Paul wrote in his notebook:

Sex trade cautions for D.B.?

It was an avenue that might be worth looking into. In the UK, prostitution wasn't illegal if it was conducted privately between consenting parties and wasn't affiliated with an organization, i.e., a brothel. "Privately" meant silently—no saucy ads, placards stuck to nightclub walls, or curbside solicitation. If Daciana had openly dabbled in sex work, as newcomers to London often assumed was permitted, she would probably have cautions on her record.

Daciana waited until Kincaid retreated before she took up the interview again. "I mention Ms. Marilyn because they did row. But she never hit Ms. Cathleen. She was only, you know, hide face..."

"Mortified?" Paul supplied.

"Mortified. Because how Ms. Cathleen carry on. So many parties. Not for married people. For single friends. Men. All night, she flirt, flirt, flirt, and call me to pour wine. Then people get together. Sex," she clarified matter-of-factly.

"Drugs?" Kate asked.

"No. Mostly wine. Some was special wine."

"Meaning what?"

"During party, Ms. Cathleen serve wine from bottle. But I bring carafe wine to special men."

"I see. And what was in the carafe wine?"

"Benzo." Daciana, puffing calmly, looked Kate in the eye. "Roofie. Or similar."

"How did Mrs. Maitland-Palmer get her hands on roofies?"

"From me. She say not a crime if you do it for boss. I do it for boss," Daciana said, still matter of fact. "Never take it or sell it. My boss say do it. Compel me. That is word. Compel."

Paul thought, *She's no thickie.*

"Did the drugged wine work?" Kate asked. "Get the special men into bed with your boss?"

Daciana laughed coquettishly. "No. Benzo loosen up men, not make them hallucinate. Ms. Cathleen still old. Pretty, but old."

"Daciana, are you aware of prostitution laws in the

UK?" Kate asked. "If Mrs. Maitland-Palmer hired you to entertain guests—to procure their interest for her—it probably wasn't illegal. Even if it was, it's not our concern. We're looking into a suspicious death. You can speak freely about sex work to us."

"This is no brothel. Ms. Cathleen no pimp," Daciana announced, looking pointedly at Kate's secure mobile, which was face down on the table. "Turn that over and I'll say it louder."

"I promise we're not recording you," Paul said. "Just talking. So, you say Mrs. Maitland-Palmer asked you to serve the drugged wine. What else?"

"I was the young, pretty *soubrette*. Make party fun."

"Soubrette?" Paul asked.

"Black and white dress. Feather duster."

"A French maid costume," Kate said. "Right. I'm still waiting to hear how the two-way mirror and camera came into play."

Daciana paused, considering. Rising cigarette smoke curled around her face, like a scrollwork border around an old lithograph. She might have been an Edwardian tart, waifish on the outside, hard-nosed on the inside, answering police questions with contempt rather than fear.

"Ms. Cathleen had stable. That her word. Stable, like horse. Men collected over the years. She would test them. If they still want her, fine. If not, I give them special wine. Extra friendly. If they tell me no, they pass test. If they say yes and go upstairs with me, they fail test."

"So, you slept with them, knowing the camera was recording everything," Kate said.

"Compel is word," Daciana repeated. "So I can pay rent."

"What happened next?" Paul asked.

"Ms. Cathleen take the film."

"What did she do with it?"

"How would I know?"

"Take a guess."

She shrugged. "Maybe she confront them. Maybe she say give me money, or I send to wife."

That admission raised the stakes. Now, Daciana probably *was* on the hook for a criminal offense. It depended on how she answered the next question.

"Did the men pay you before sex, or after?"

"No pay," Daciana barked. "Am gift for men, they think. Ms. Cathleen pay me to be *soubrette*. After man leave, Ms. Cathleen says, good job, *soubrette*." She rapped the tabletop for emphasis. "Here is your money for being *soubrette*."

Kate maintained a stern expression, but Paul saw she was fighting back laughter. "Thank you, that's incredibly specific. I don't suppose Mrs. Maitland-Palmer paid you by check?"

"Cash only."

"What about a receipt that said, 'Given in exchange for *soubrette* services?'"

Daciana puffed away, unmoved by sarcasm.

"Right. Well, Ms. Botezatu, I must caution you that filming a sex act without a person's knowledge and using that film to extort money are two separate, serious offenses."

"Extort!" she cried.

Paul, who'd located the relevant statutes in his Met app, read, "The Criminal Justice and Courts Act 2015. It prohibits, and I quote, 'sharing, or threatening to share, private sexual images of someone else without their consent and with the intent to cause distress or embarrassment to that person.'

"Section 21 of the Theft Act 1968 also applies," he continued. "Making unwarranted demands with some kind of threat, to gain something for yourself or to harm another person. The penalties are severe. Fines. Prison..."

"Ms. Cathleen broke law. Not me." Daciana stubbed out her cigarette. "I tell what I know. Try to hurt me, I lawyer up."

"No one's trying to hurt you," Kate replied serenely. "But look at it from my point of view. This morning, you arrived at work and discovered your employer dead. Someone cut off her finger, and an expensive ring was missing. DI Bhar and I come in and find out your dead employer was an extortionist. And you were the linchpin of the blackmail scheme. That gets my mind working.

"Maybe you truly were compelled," Kate continued. "Trafficked, in a sense. Maybe you wanted out, but Mrs. Maitland-Palmer said no. Maybe you only saw one way out: get rid of her, pawn her ring, and live off the proceeds until you found a new line of work. Maybe even one you could tell your father about."

"Tell Father?" Daciana looked baffled. "Didn't I say already? He give me to Ms. Cathleen for this job."

Paul was startled by the admission. Maybe being a new father was making him go soft. But Kate took the revelation in stride. Her sister, Maura, had once been on the game, as old-timers called it, and their mother, Louise, had shown her the ropes.

"Thanks for clearing that up. We'll drop in on Mr. Botezatu next," Kate said. "If he doesn't mind pimping his daughter, I reckon he's good for a drug bust and a weapons charge. Maybe extreme pornographic images on his laptop. Vices are like birds of a feather. They flock together."

The cleaner and the detective inspector stared one

another down, neither blinking. Then, Daciana yawned pointedly.

"So tired. Up late last night, in early. Let's make deal."

"What kind of deal?" Paul asked.

"You leave me alone. Leave Father alone. I tell you names of men who failed Ms. Cathleen's test."

"Names aren't enough for a deal," Kate said. "How about the location of her film collection?"

"I don't know where is."

"Too bad. I suppose she might have asked a friend to keep it for her. Mr. Botezatu, perhaps?"

Daciana bit her lip. Paul held his breath, sure she was about to demand a lawyer.

"Right," she said at last. "I can tell you if I get deal. Now, give me another fag."

"With pleasure." Paul rose to fetch it as Kate, looking quietly triumphant, picked up her mobile to ring CPS. If she received verbal authorization to promise Daciana immunity, they were in business.

Chapter Eight

"Next round's yours." Kate put down her glass in front of Paul with a thud. The pint was reduced to nothing but thin foam lace. "Unless you're halfway pissed already."

"I am, and I don't care. God bless the Tube." He raised his glass. "Preventing drink-driving charges for over a hundred and fifty years." Glancing around the Peregrine, a Southwark gastropub that had become a copper hangout since Scotland Yard's move to Victoria Embankment, he added, "I haven't had a night out since Evvy was born, do you realize that?"

"Oh, go on. You've been to our house a million times without Evvy."

"A night out is strictly defined as getting pissed down the pub in the company of your mates," Paul insisted. "And I've earned this. Last week, while I was beavering away on the Radley Mews case, getting nothing but a royal rogering from MI5 and two fingers straight up from CPS, I know for a *fact* that Em scarpered off to a hen do. My own mum lied and told me she was consoling a sick friend. Right.

Consoling her with Jell-O shots and pin-the-junk-on-the-hunk."

"Not to take Em's side," Kate began.

"Except you are."

"Well, she did carry Evvy for nine months while you breezed about, sipping lattes and pretending to work. And she did push Evvy out while you were—what were you doing?"

"Squeezing her hand. Which was pure torture. I'd forgotten, till you asked. Thanks for that."

"All part of the service. Anyway, my point is, don't pretend like Evvy's holding you back. If you didn't have her and Em, you'd be crying in your bitter right now, whinging about always picking the wrong girl."

"True." Paul indicated the table tent, which advertised a Wiltshire ham, egg, and chips plate. "I'm famished. Even that looks good. When I go up for drinks, should I order us some?"

"Hard no. Fish and chips," Kate said. "That's all this place can manage without bungling it."

"What about the sign that says, 'Try Our Famous Chicken Bites?'"

"Chicken frights, more like. Fried in the same oil as the fish."

"Fine."

As Paul picked up their empty glasses and headed for the bar where punters were waiting three deep, Kate couldn't resist checking her email. Not her MPS inbox, but the new account Tony didn't know about. It was connected to the personal bank account, also unknown to him, that she'd recently opened. Thus far, the inbox had received only seven emails, and two were bank advertisements shilling fund management companies.

London Blue

Squealing over a new reply, she scanned it rapidly, hardly daring to get her hopes up. The email was extended and a bit rambling. But in the end, the answer was yes.

She voice-texted Harvey,

> We're in!!!

> What about the box?

> Go for it.

"What are you whispering into your phone?" asked Paul, returning with a pint in each hand. "Sexting the chief?"

"Harvey. And not sexting him," she added before he could pounce. "Greenlighting Operation Horse-to-Water."

"That horse is going to kick us in the face. But cheers."

"Cheers. Hey, guess what I forgot to tell you. This afternoon, while we were recording Daciana's formal interview at HQ, Nicky rolled from his tummy to his back and then back again. Can you believe it?" Kate sipped her pint. "Sometimes, I feel like it's all happening too fast. He hit another milestone, and I wasn't there to see it."

Paul made a vague noise of assent.

"Don't tell me you're pouting because I nixed the chicken frights?"

"No, you were right. If it's going to taste of haddock, I'd prefer it is, in fact, haddock."

He seemed to have unaccountably sobered up. Kate hoped he didn't use his first night out in seven months as an excuse to go to the dark side. Before Em and Evvy, that happened occasionally, especially when Paul ruminated over past mistakes. But his hasty marriage, which Kate had secretly feared would end in a quickie divorce, seemed to be going strong. As for his career—if she was being honest with herself, it was humming along better than hers. She had a lot of ground to make up.

"Anyway, enough about Nicky the wonder boy. Let's talk about Evvy. The most beautiful little princess I've ever seen."

"Thanks for that. Generous," Paul muttered, staring into his pint.

She kicked him under the table.

"Ow!"

"'Thanks for that. Generous,'" she mimicked, sounding like Eeyore. "What are you on about? Evvy is a living doll. She could model for adverts if you were mad enough to try it."

"I know." He knocked back more beer.

"Then why are you such a gloomy Gus?"

"No reason. Beauty is everything, right? You and Tony have some kind of prodigy, and we have—a girl we love more than anything," he finished, choking up.

"Bloody hell. Don't chug that." Kate took the pint out of his hand. "You'll do yourself an injury. Tell me exactly what's going on. Now."

"It's her milestones. She isn't meeting them." He dashed away a tear. "I mean, she's met a few. She can sit up by herself. I think she's getting ready to crawl. And she watches everything happening around her, so it's not a vision thing."

"You're sure?"

"It was the first thing we checked. The pediatrician said it was normal, then sent us to an ophthalmologist to be sure. They flashed grids at her retinas and measured the electrical response. She passed with flying colors."

London Blue

Reaching across the table, Kate took his hand and squeezed it.

Paul said, "She knows my face and Em's, of course, and Mum's. She turns away from strangers. That's all to the good. But she doesn't care about her toys. She should be chewing on them, tossing them around, but she doesn't. And she's so quiet. I've heard Nicky babbling. And Henry probably said a few words by seven months, didn't he?"

Kate nodded.

"What about..." Paul tailed off, took a sip of beer, and tried again. "What was Ritchie like at seven months?"

There it was. Kate squeezed Paul's hand again. She decided to be frank but gentle.

"That's hard to answer. Ritchie's my elder brother, so I wasn't around to witness his milestones. And neither was Louise or Maura, in the practical sense," she added, meaning her estranged mother and troubled sister. "If you really want to know about Ritchie's early pediatric assessments, I can request his case notes from social services. But I think the difference between him and Evvy would be stark."

"Really?"

"Yeah. When I was little, Ritchie couldn't bear loud noises. If something upset him, he would scream blue murder and curl up in a ball. He ate the same dinner every night. He liked telly but would get up and walk away while you read a story to him. He didn't relate to other kids."

"And they made him pay for it, didn't they?"

"Of course. I mean, his own mum and gran called him the r-word all the time. Imagine what people on the street called him. He didn't understand. But I understood, and I shut up those kids with my fists. Or took a beating trying to shut them up. Not because I was a saintly little girl who wanted everything sunshine and roses. I was ashamed of him. I don't think I came to terms with Ritchie until I was twelve or thirteen. Until then, I prayed he'd get better."

Paul put his hands over his face. Kate feared he might break down, but fortunately, a kitchen porter interrupted the tension by arriving with their fish and chips.

"You all right there, mate?"

"Fine." Clearing his throat, Paul picked up the malt vinegar and began squirting everything in sight, including the ceremonial bit of kale.

"If you've had a bit too much, your next one's a soda, yeah?" said the kitchen porter, looking at him suspiciously. "And if you're gonna be sick, take it outside. I've mopped enough vomit this week to last a lifetime."

Kate produced her warrant card with a practiced motion. "We're discussing police business. And we're both sober. Now, off you go."

"Not sure that's true," Paul muttered after the porter had gone.

"Then eat to help the booze metabolize."

Kate shook vinegar on her chips. They ate silently for several minutes, Paul half-heartedly at first, then picking up speed. When his plate was empty, Kate asked,

"What does Sharada say about Evvy?"

"Not much."

"I don't believe you."

"I mean, she talks about Evvy all the time, but she refuses to get negative. She just keeps trying to entice Evvy into playing with her toys or playing peek-a-boo and whatnot. And she's always emailing articles to us. 'Ten Ways to Enrich Your Infant's First Year of Life' and so on. They're just adverts for formula companies, but she thinks the advice might contain a pearl that will turn things around."

London Blue

"What does Em say?"

"Nothing. She pretends everything's fine." He sighed. "When I insisted on taking her to the eye specialist, we had a blowout fight. And then another one when the vision tests came back normal, and I suggested a pediatric neurologist."

"How long have you two been agonizing over this?"

"I don't know. Weeks, now."

"Why didn't you say something?"

"Because you're Sister of the Year to Ritchie," he burst out. "More like Sister of the Decade. How could I whinge to you about intellectual disability"—the phrase seemed to leave his lips with difficulty—"when you're his number one champion?"

"Paul," Kate said in her most serious tone. "You've always whinged to me about everything under the sun. This is no time to go cold turkey."

He didn't even crack a smile. "I just didn't want to seem disrespectful. I like Ritchie. Most of the time, I can't relate to him, if I'm being honest. But I like him."

Kate pushed her plate aside. "Look, I get it. People are sensitive these days. Especially online. There's probably an unwritten rulebook of things you can and can't say or feel without kicking up a hue and cry. I wish I could tell you what a caregiver is *supposed* to say or feel. I can't. But I've spent my whole life taking care of Ritchie, and I can tell you this: Sometimes, having an intellectually disabled person in the family is the worst. Full stop.

"*Other* times," she continued, smiling, "we have amazing little moments that make it all worthwhile. I love Ritchie. I respect him. Loving and respecting him doesn't mean I don't dread his meltdowns. I wish he could look after himself better. He *burned down our house*, for God's sake." She paused to eat her last chip. "Of course, he didn't mean to. I suppose Henry might have done the same thing—when he was two.

"But Henry gets smarter and more independent every year. He progresses. It's only natural to want to see progression in the people we love. It's human. So, if you're beating yourself up for it, stop."

"Wish I had a crystal ball," Paul said.

"But you don't. So don't obsess about the future. Maybe Evvy will be diagnosed as delayed. Or autistic. Or something else. It's the same with Nicky. There are no guarantees for any of us."

"Nicky's bright."

"I adore him. He's everything. But if we're talking milestones," Kate said, "Henry was far ahead of him. Henry is what they call gifted. And you see how easy and perfect his life is."

"I don't want Evvy to be different," Paul said plaintively. "I would do anything, pay any price, to keep her from being different. And that makes me no better than your mum."

Kate snorted. "Please. Understand my beef with Louise. She was sad about Ritchie's limitations. She felt trapped by him. I never resented her for that, Paul. She had a right to feel what she felt. We all do. But Louise didn't *do* what she needed to *do*. She disappeared for days at a time. She slapped him about when she got frustrated. She only treated him well when it made her look good to someone in authority. To Louise, Ritchie was never more than an object. But Evvy will never be an object to you."

Paul seemed to take that in. "Right. Thanks. Let me chew on that. Let's talk about the case," he said, switching gears with obvious effort. "Thoughts on Daciana? Do you like her as the killer?"

Chapter Nine

"As the killer," Kate repeated thoughtfully. The pub was loud, with periodic outbursts from patrons watching a footy match on telly, but she spoke softly, just in case. London was packed with people getting on with their lives, talking, laughing, seemingly unconcerned with a stranger's business. That made it easy to overshare in public places accidentally. Even Tony, of all people, had once made a driver's day by saying too much in the back of a cab. "No."

"Because she didn't do a legger?"

"That, and because the finger was chopped off. Even if the ring was stuck, she could've greased up the finger and taken all the time she needed to work it off."

"Maybe she was afraid someone might see her hunched over the body?"

"In that case, she could've said she was rendering aid to CMP."

"CMP? I like that. So, how do you fancy MMP as the killer?"

Kate shrugged. "We know she wasn't close to her mum."

"True. Didn't tear up once. Maybe it would have hurt her image. The tough-as-nails gal from Brixton."

"Right," Kate said contemptuously. "'We fling poo' is something Henry used to say. When he was six."

"Oooh, no one's as tough as our Katie. By the way, have you ever looked into matricide?"

"Not since I joined the Met. Why, is Sharada skating too close to the edge?"

He chuckled. "I mean the stats. I checked them today. Matricide is rare. Most of the perps are male. There's a high correlation with schizophrenia, too."

"Uh-huh. Know what's not rare? A man killing the woman in his life. Especially an ex-lover he perceives as a problem."

"If one of my exes blackmailed me, I'd call it a problem."

"Yeah. MMP pretended to be worried about mentioning Lord Dellkirk, but I think she enjoyed dropping his name."

"He can definitely afford to pay off an old girlfriend."

"Or pay someone to silence an old girlfriend, which guarantees she'll never ask again."

"What do you know about Lord Dellkirk?"

Kate shrugged. "Posh wanker."

"Yeah. Strikes me as a perfect muppet," Paul said. "I suppose it's not impossible that he sent his groundskeeper or whoever to knock off CMP. Said bring back the finger as a souvenir."

"It's one possibility. First, we need to make sure he was the last person to see CMP alive. I rang his office to ask for an interview."

"I'm sure he's happy to assist the police with their inquiries."

"His secretary hung up on me. I had to call again from

my iPhone and introduce myself as Lady Hetheridge to get her back on the line. Then, I explained in no uncertain terms that while remaining incommunicado might work with tabloid reporters, it doesn't work with the police."

"So, when do we administer the white-glove treatment?" Paul asked, using one of Tony's phrases for managing suspects who were rich and powerful.

"I haven't got an appointment yet, just the promise of one. But that's fine. It will give our team the weekend to determine if he appears in one of Dacy's home movies."

"I think she coughed up their location in the locked filing cabinet too easily," Paul said. "Wonder if she's holding the hottest ones back to take over the blackmail game once this all blows over."

"Maybe. Anyway, I put Sean in charge of matching faces to names. And I authorized facial rec," she added. "He's already scanned a few movies and didn't find any famous people. Then, again—could you identify all of Britain's government ministers if they stood in a lineup?"

"Sure. Just check for the trail of slime."

"How about I tell your ministry pal, Neera, you said that?"

"Go ahead. Actually, don't." Paul grinned. "The chief taught me never to burn a possible future source."

"You'll be waiting a long time," Kate predicted. "If she ever gives you info, as opposed to trying to get it, I'll buy you dinner at Juno's. Including drinks and dessert."

"I'll hold you to that. I'm surprised you're okay with using facial recognition, though. There's a high rate of false positives on people of color."

"Yeah, but it's fine for government doughnuts and rich gits," Kate said airily. "The new software scraped images off *Bright Star's* entire publication run. I watched the demo. It picks up society column faces with ninety percent accuracy. Besides, it's a starting point, that's all." Kate regarded him keenly. "Have you sobered up?"

"A bit."

"Told you, you just needed some nibbles on your tum. We're practically next door to the tube station—I can see you home if you need it. One for the road?"

"Please. Better make the most of my night out."

"Right." Rising, Kate glanced at the crowd at the bar to see if the queue was still three deep. Immediately, her eyes were drawn to a very tall woman with broad shoulders and long black hair. Standing near the cocktail garnish caddy with a pink girlie drink in front of her, she was chatting animatedly to a seated man. In Kate's opinion, she wasn't a pretty girl—she was coarse-featured, with a big nose and heavy brows. But her purple specs were jaunty, there was a sparkling pin in her luxuriant hair, and she looked like a woman having the time of her life.

Bugger me blind, Kate thought, mouth falling open. *That's Octavia Chakrabarti.*

During her last month of pregnancy, Kate had been on strict bedrest. Meanwhile, Paul and Tony—in his occasional role as consultant to Scotland Yard—had investigated the murder of a beautiful young woman called Valeria Chakrabarti. Pulling on that thread had unraveled half of the MPS, or so it felt to the public. Solving the case had exposed unforgivable corruption in high places, including the murder of DC Amelia Gulls by a superior officer.

Kate had never met Octavia or her brother Antonio, but she'd seen them interviewed on programs like *Good Morning Britain*. Their billionaire father, Parth Chakrabarti, had been charged with murdering their mother. Naturally, a man of his power and influence had

London Blue

dispatched fleets of lawyers to defend him, but he couldn't control his rage. Just a month after his arraignment, Parth Chakrabarti keeled over from a massive heart attack. No one, except possibly the legal team that had billed him by the hour, missed him. Least of all, Octavia and Antonio, who refused to attend the funeral. On telly, she'd seemed particularly somber; tonight, she positively glowed.

Probably from inheriting all that dosh, Kate thought.

Instantly, she disavowed that snarky sentiment, which came from the unrefurbished, Wakefield-era parts of her brain. She herself had married a rich man, and if anyone dared suggest it was Tony's money that made her glow, she would've stood up and punched them out.

Besides, didn't Paul tell me Octavia was completely disinherited? Kate thought. *She's a social reformer—anti-institution, anti-government, anti-police. Whatever you think of that, it's no shortcut to wealth.*

Still, it was odd to find her in a pub full of coppers. Peregrine's was the kind of "thin blue line" place Octavia would surely avoid like kryptonite. Unless she was picketing it, issuing demands through a bullhorn.

The bloke beside Octavia threw his blond head back, roaring at something she said. Then, he swiveled to check the footy score, and Kate saw a man who, as she'd once heard someone say, was as pretty as gilt-edged Irish china. None other than DC Sean Kincaid, out on the town in the company of his one-time informant.

Striding to the bar, Kate wedged in between a couple of MPS analysts. "Sorry, kids. Will you let a DI jump the queue this once? I promise to repay the favor."

The analysts, both young and a bit overawed, readily let Kate position herself beside the garnish caddy. "Two more guest cask," she called to the bartender.

"Guv!" DC Kincaid practically fell off his stool. "Hiya, guv. Wow. Reckoned you'd be home with the baby by now. Not—not that you should be."

"I thought you said you'd be in the bullpen till at least eight. Analyzing those home movies," she said more coolly than intended.

"Yes, well, just popped in for a bite and a quick one. But I'm going back soon. Or, that is to say, I can go back now, if—"

"Don't do that," Kate interrupted, annoyed with herself. She didn't doubt Kincaid's dedication to the job; on the contrary, she'd been more than a little worried he might burn himself out. Since Amelia's murder, he'd become paler and quieter, often working two or three weeks in a row without taking even a half-day off. She'd been afraid he would lose his taste for policework, sublimating all that grief.

Sublimated it pretty well, laughing it up in Peregrine's, Kate thought. *And here's Octavia wearing a dress, of all things, when she never appeared on national TV in anything but a T-shirt.*

"I mean it, Sean. You have a right to your downtime. God knows you've earned it." Forcing a smile, she stuck out her hand to Octavia. "Hiya. I'm Kate Hetheridge."

"Octavia Chakrabarti." The woman's glow had fizzled out. Meeting Kate's eyes, she lifted her chin and squared her shoulders as if preparing for a blow.

"Nice to meet you, Octavia. I like your specs. Pretty color."

"Oh. Um...thanks? My brother picked them out."

"Two guest cask," said the barman, placing the pints before Kate.

"Cheers. And one for yourself," she said, handing the

barman a note. "Well. Enjoy the game, Sean. Nice to meet you, Octavia."

Sean still looked vaguely horrified, but Octavia managed a timid wave. Flashing them a quick smile, Kate scooped up her ales and hurried back to Paul.

"Back already? Don't tell me you pulled rank to jump the queue."

"Never mind that." Kate nearly splashed him with the weekly special in her haste to sit down. "Sean is here. On a *date*."

"Do me a favor."

"I mean it."

"Where? The bar? Tell me when it's safe to look."

On Kate's signal, he rose slowly, head rising out of the partitioned booth like a meerkat peering from its burrow. Then he dropped back to his seat looking amused. "The only woman I see him talking to is Octavia Chakrabarti. The anti-date."

"They're beside each other. Right beside each other."

"By that logic, all twenty people at the bar are heading for an orgy."

"But did you see how she's done up? Dress, lipstick, the full monty."

"Maybe she saw herself on telly and decided to get a makeover."

"Listen, I might be an old married lady, but I still have instincts. She was smitten. And she looked at me funny, like she knew what I was thinking."

"What were you thinking?"

Kate was ashamed to say it aloud. But she forced herself, because it was the truth.

"That she's a bloody far cry from Amelia. Amelia was a wonderful person. And so little. So pretty. Perfect for him."

"Oh. Well. I doubt Octavia telepathically picked up any of that. She probably just expected you to mean-girl her."

"What? Why?"

Paul put his head to one side.

"*Why?*"

"Because you look like you, and she looks like her."

"Oh, come on. I'm not like that."

"Octavia doesn't know that," Paul said. "And...just at the moment...you kind of *are* like that."

"I spent half the night consoling you for this? A knife in the back?"

He grinned. "The consolation was very much appreciated. And I'm not saying you're wrong. I'm the one who called her the anti-date."

"Right. Didn't you say she hates coppers?"

"She does. She did. Maybe when we arrested her dad, she got back a little faith in the system? Besides, no one can hate Sean."

"True," she said a touch morosely.

"Face it. When the time is right, Sean will start dating again, and neither of us will think his new girl is half as good as Amelia. That's a given," Paul declared. "But right now, he needs friends. Pure friends who can't turn around and pull rank or write him a bad eval. That's not us, obviously. But maybe it's Octavia. So let him have a friend, Kate."

"Fine." Pretending to let the topic go, she listened with half an ear as Paul sketched out their agenda for the next few days. Until they had Cathleen Maitland-Palmer's confirmed cause of death, they couldn't begin aggressively interviewing potential persons of interest. By Monday, the medical examiner they knew best, Dr. Trevor Stepp, would have a preliminary conclusion; most toxins, all traumas, and many natural conditions would be evident.

As for Cathleen's missing finger, it was evidence of nothing on its own because it occurred post-mortem. Kate had always found it odd that the UK lacked a clear "abuse of corpse" statute; unlike their US cousins, UK lawmakers preferred to merely frown on the practice, unless removal of a decedent's body parts was done illegally for DNA collection. If it seemed likely that Cathleen had died of a stroke or heart attack in the presence of someone who stole her London blue ring, Scotland Yard would probably issue a theft report for the insurance company and move on to the next case.

When Paul ducked off to the men's, Kate dared another glance at the bar. Sean was no longer there. Despite receiving permission to stay, he'd probably returned to the Yard—only a five-minute walk along the Embankment—to burn the midnight oil. But Octavia Chakrabarti stood beside the garnish caddy, pink drink forgotten, lips curved in a secret smile.

Chapter Ten

Henry Wakefield Hetheridge felt his mobile vibrate for the tenth time in two hours and groaned aloud. It was a weird sensation, being aggravated by his phone.

Recently, his starter mobile had bit the dust. Instead of accepting a refurbishment, he'd campaigned for an upgraded mobile and won. Of course, Kate had selected a smartphone rendered almost dumb by typical parental spyware. Nevertheless, he'd soon unlocked it and could now jump on the internet whenever he chose, thanks to a couple of pointers from Paul, who was the coolest grownup he knew in terms of rule-breaking.

That was, apart from his biological mum, Maura. She was okay with any and all rule-breaking. Kate had warned Maura never to ring Henry when she was drunk or high. But she ignored that rule, and lately, her constant calls and texts almost made him want to fling the phone into traffic.

It was early afternoon under a cloudy London sky, and Jenner's Fencing Studio was under invasion by the beginner's class, ages five and up. Henry, who'd already had his lesson, showered, and packed his gear, had settled on the concrete steps outside the studio to wait for Harvey. He had been using his phone's web connection to research tobacco mortality rates—specifically, cigars—when Maura texted him. Then called him. Then texted him again.

Henry peeked at the latest message.

> So you don't care now it's all about money then

> Fine your killing me

He wished he'd never disobeyed Kate, who'd ordered him to block Maura's number as soon as it became obvious she'd once again fallen off the wagon. Worse, there was no one he could complain to. At home, if he mentioned the increasingly angry texts, he'd have to admit to disobeying Kate. At Highgate Junior School, he couldn't complain without destroying his new identity.

Henry Wakefield, the miserable, bullied kid at Dunwich Primary, Southwark, was no more. That Henry, who lived in fear of recess and being caught alone in the boys' washroom, was dead and buried. Highgate Primary School belonged to Henry Hetheridge, who'd grown up in Devon, in the village of Briarshaw. He'd transferred in after his mum, Kate, married Tony; Highgate was his first London school. Maintaining this ruse meant speaking *very* carefully, in a perfect imitation of Tony, but that had become almost second nature. Not once had he been called out on his Hs, either dropped or stuck in front of the wrong vowel.

He read the text again. It encapsulated drunk/drugged Maura's style of communication: no punctuation, no distinction between "your" and "you're," and a relentless focus on herself and her feelings. Sober Maura remembered to ask about his life, his grades, and what he wanted for his birthday. This year, the entire month of July, including his birthday, had come and gone without a peep. Then, she'd surfaced in August to bitterly complain to him about Kate: she thought she was posh, she thought she was a saint, she thought she could just ignore her big sister's calls…

Lately, it was more of the same and worse. She often bragged about getting a lawyer and suing for full custody. Once, that threat would have panicked him; now, he was old enough and wise enough to know how utterly hollow it was. Towards the end of each monologue, Maura typically unspooled a sob story about the latest bloke in her life, who only wanted her for sex.

"I'm telling you, Henry, and you'd better listen. You're a young man, and I'll train you up right," Maura had told him with the ponderous self-importance of someone minutes from passing out. "Never toy with vulnerable women. We have a lot of love and devotion to give. There's more to life than getting a leg over."

"Wotcha, Hen," said a familiar voice.

"Wotcha, Karlie." He played it cool, barely looking up as his fellow fencing student, a tall girl of thirteen, sat down beside him. He didn't have to see her to know she had light brown skin, long, curly hair, hazel eyes, and the face of an absolute angel.

"Your ride's late?"

"Just a little." Since Tony's surgery, the entire Hetheridge house routine had been thrown off. Once he could drive again, things would get back to normal.

"Mine, too," Karlie said. "I'd tell Mum to sack Kevin, but what would become of him if she did? He's, like, clinically depressed or something. Poor sod has one job, to drive me about, and still can't get it together."

The late, great Henry Wakefield would have asked, "Is he using?" But the more refined and somewhat innocent Henry Hetheridge would never jump to such a sordid conclusion.

"Maybe pull him aside for a quiet word?" Henry suggested. "If you tell him you know he's in a bad place, maybe he'll explain why he's always late."

"Aw, you're a good egg. I'd ask him, but I reckon he'd cry or something. He's scared of me. I swear to God, he is. Can you believe that?" She pushed him playfully. "And around Mum, forget it. Kev's straight-up bricking it."

"People are a little scared of my mum, too," he said, slipping the mobile back in his pocket.

"And so they should be. She's Scotland Yard. All my mum does is flog jewelry on QVC." Karlie chuckled. "By the way, I watched your match. Well done, you. Didn't I tell you being short is an advantage?"

Henry didn't like being called short, especially by the girl he was destined to marry. But today, he'd won his third match at Jenner's Fencing Studio, and she'd witnessed the glorious event. His opponent, a fifteen-year-old fencing novice, had probably expected to make quick work of Henry. He had the reach, but Henry had the speed. He wasn't the most physical student, not by a long shot, but during his brief time at Jenner's, he'd realized how many of Tony's lessons were about strategy. And strategy was something few, if any, of his fellow pupils seemed to understand.

"Thanks, Kar. You were good, too." He dared to look into her beautiful eyes.

"Liar!" She cuffed his upper arm. "That's a warning. Liars get a slap."

"No, I mean it," he said earnestly. "You would've won

if..." He tailed off. Was he meant to criticize the girl of his dreams? Or tactfully pretend not to notice her missteps?

"If what, Hen-hen? Spit it out. And don't lie," she added, hand raised as if poised for a slap.

"If you'd played to win," he said, hoping he wasn't putting his foot in it. "You defend too much. You're hung up on preventing touches, not scoring them."

Karlie beamed at him. Her smile did something strange to Henry's sternum. That, or he was coming down with a chest cold.

"My old fencing master told me the same thing."

"So did mine."

"Your dad, right? Think you'll go back to training with him once he's fighting fit?"

"I don't know." Henry felt disloyal saying it, but he didn't want to lie to Karlie. Healthy relationships were based on honesty and mutual respect; after picking up that lesson in a book about vampire-werewolf wars, he'd resolved to keep it top-of-mind. "I like fencing with my dad. We talk about stuff. It's our time. But here, I can fight matches with other kids."

And be near you, he added silently.

"That's nice about your dad. Mine doesn't see me as much since Hurricane Mimi blew into our lives. He totally caved on Christmas this year. It's his turn to have me for Christmas Day and Boxing Day. But he's giving it up to take Mimi to Greece."

She seemed to expect a reply, but Henry was stumped. Suggesting Karlie might be better off without her absentee father probably wasn't what she wanted to hear. As for saying her dad would surely dump his girlfriend soon and give Karlie his full attention, well, that was the kind of gormless lie that really did deserve a slap.

"Who cares about Greece? I'd rather go to Benidorm," he offered. It was true; he'd seen a bit of the comedy *Benidorm* on YouTube, and it seemed mint. The kind of place where anything could happen. Maybe he'd discover a talent for karaoke and serenade her till she fell in love with him...

"You're a riot, Hen. You know that?"

Judging by how she was chuckling, he'd probably said something dumb, but since she took it as a joke, he did, too.

Karlie's mobile pinged. "Right. This train is never late. It's the ape man."

"The what?"

"A guy who likes me. I call him the ape man because he's fourteen and shaves. Glandular." Karlie giggled at the message. Texting by voice she sent, "Banana emoji."

The whoosh of a response. "Wanker!" Karlie cried. Henry, leaning over, saw an orange peach and a purple eggplant.

"Oi! Don't look at that! You're too little. He's just gross. Forget it."

Too little? Henry thought.

As he struggled to process the violent destruction of all his hopes and dreams, a sleek sedan pulled up. The driver, a middle-aged guy with floppy hair, hustled out to open Karlie's door.

"Sorry. Sorry. You wouldn't believe the traffic. Don't tell your mum, will you? I'm really sorry. Please don't tell your mum."

"I'm not bothered, Kev. Calm down." Climbing into the backseat, Karlie waved at him. "Bye, Hen-hen!"

Hen-hen, he thought miserably. *She thinks I'm a bloody chicken. Not just a chicken. A girl chicken.*

He felt perilously close to tears, so naturally Harvey

chose that moment to roll up. He was driving Tony's gray Mercedes EQC 400 SUV, all-electric and exempt from London's congestion charge. Loyal to the family Bentley as he was, even Harvey was seduced by heated seats, satellite radio, and the ability to forego petrol stops entirely.

"Are you quite all right, Master Henry?"

"You can stop calling me that." Shoving in his gym bag and *epee* trolley case like so much rubbish, he got in and slammed the door.

"I thought you liked the sound of it," Harvey said mildly.

"I liked it when I was a little kid. It made me feel like Bruce Wayne. But I'm not little anymore."

"I see. Well, in that case, are you quite all right, Henry?"

"Yes."

"Fancy some McDonald's on the way home?"

"No." There was nothing he wanted more than a Cheese Bites Sharebox and a frozen strawberry lemonade, but he'd already been to McDonald's yesterday, and he was limiting himself to one visit per week. Then again—he'd been limiting himself because he hoped to slim down a bit for Karlie. And she'd just called him an infant.

"Sorry, Harvey. I meant to say, yes, please. Thank you."

The niceties were issued in a funereal tone but issued all the same. One of Tony's ironclad rules was to treat one's employees with unfailing respect. Harvey, like Mrs. Snell, was more or less part of the family at this point, but because they were also on the payroll, the rule remained in effect. Once, Henry had answered back to Mrs. Snell with withering sarcasm, only to go upstairs and find his laptop missing. It had taken seven days of good behavior to earn it back. Kate could be swayed by pleading, promising, and crying; Tony could not.

"I have news," Harvey offered.

Despite his enveloping gloom, Henry felt a twinge of excitement. "Really?"

"Operation Horse-to-Water is a go."

"Awesome."

"Yes. This being the case, Lady Kate says you'll need appropriate attire. Therefore, I'll be taking you to Savile Row on Saturday next. In the meantime, I suggest you do a bit of online browsing to see which styles and fabrics appeal to you."

The prospect of a fitting didn't worry Henry. His clothes were routinely tailored since being short and boxy made for a difficult fit. In fact, the idea carried a glimmer of hope. This would be his first visit to Savile Row, renowned the world over as clothiers to gentlemen. If he played his cards right, he'd emerge looking like a man instead of a boy. Then, if he could only manage to appear at Jenner's tricked out in his new suit, possibly a three-piece, with a watch chain...

His mobile pinged. Infuriated, he whipped it out. *What did Maura want?*

> You better not burn your bridges

> They have their own baby now

> Flesh and blood

> You think your the air?

It took him a moment to translate that. She meant, "You think you're the heir?"

> I'm the one who loves you

London Blue

> I'm all you really got kiddo

> Don't make me disown you

> I just need a loan

Of course she did. He knew Maura's cyclic thought processes when she ditched her psych meds and picked up street drugs. First, she insisted that she, and only she, loved him. Second, she threatened to disown him. Third, she revealed what she really wanted.

> I can meet you outside your new school

> Highgate poshie academy

> And you WILL give me something to live on right?

Was she lurking around Wellegrave House, watching him leave each morning? Following him to Highgate, Jenner's, and who knew where else?

Heart pounding in his chest, he blocked her number. How had she found out about Highgate? Her threat of showing up at his school, his *new* school—his refuge from the bad parts of his former life—made him so angry, he was tempted to go to Kate and confess to unlocking the phone. Then he could show her the messages and maybe, if he was lucky, hear what followed. Kate was nothing if not inventive when swearing down the line at her sister.

Fortunately, McDonald's was just around the corner, and the drive-thru was as quick as ever. Henry was halfway through his "Sharebox," which Harvey fortunately wanted no part of, before he remembered to taste what he was eating. Agitation over Karlie calling him "too little" made him suck frozen strawberry lemonade through his straw so fast, a thumping brain freeze followed. It hurt like crazy, but the pain seemed appropriate. His life would be all pain now.

Harvey, who'd parked the SUV so he could sip his coffee while Henry ate his sorrows, said abruptly, "How are you coming along with your father's birthday present? Are you still writing him a story?"

Fresh agony. Henry would've rolled his eyes, but the brain freeze still had him in its grip. "I don't know. It's easy to start a mystery. I already wrote the ending. But it's hard to make the middle part—well. Mysterious."

"I imagine so. I'm not without literary aspirations, you know."

"Really?"

"I fear so. Years ago, when I was still acting on stage, I tried my hand at writing plays." He chuckled. "It didn't go well. Now, I think I might like to try again. I have a notebook full of half-finished short stories."

"Can I read some?"

"If I manage to finish any, yes. But talking of mysteries— what sort do you like to read?"

"I don't."

"What, no Sherlock Holmes? No Hardy Boys?"

"Who're the Hardy Boys?"

Harvey sighed. "I'm past my sell-by. Never mind. If we visit Waterstone's, I feel certain we'll discover modern mysteries for young readers. And while we're there, you can browse through the history section and pick out a book for Lord Hetheridge. Just as a failsafe, of course, if your story isn't up to scratch in time." He sipped his coffee. "However,

London Blue

if your day was so terrible that you prefer to forego the bookstore, we can do it another time."

Had it been that bad? Yes, but Henry still wanted to go. Moldy kids' stuff from Harvey's old-timey childhood didn't interest him, but he was ready for the next book in the vampire-werewolf war series.

"Harvey, this might be a weird question. But did you ever fall in love with someone? Someone who didn't love you back?"

The manservant, caught in mid-sip, almost choked on his coffee. "Story of my life, Master Henry. Story of my life."

Chapter Eleven

"Aaaand he's out." Kate beamed down at her baby boy. Placing the empty bottle on the bedside table, she added, "He took six ounces before he fell asleep. Can't wait for his next weigh-in."

"He's ahead of Evvy in size," Tony said, eyes on his laptop.

"Don't compare." Kate placed Nicky on his back, then stood back to watch as he automatically brought his fist to his mouth. He was turning into a thumb sucker, but according to Sharada Bhar, it was nothing to worry about, and usually stopped as spontaneously as it began.

"I only mean, Evvy's dainty," Tony continued, looking up. "And quite an old soul. Always a pleasure to watch her if Sharada or Emmeline needs a break."

"Tony Hetheridge, child-minder. Who'd believe it?"

"I've had thirty years of child-minding detectives, thank you very much."

"*Whomp-whomp*. Hilarious." Heading to the bathroom for a pre-sleep pitstop, she asked, "What do you mean, she's an old soul?"

"Just different. Nicky chews on every toy within grasp, then flings it. Then cries to discover all his favorites have gone. I fetch them back, and the cycle repeats. Evvy likes watching the world go by. Makes me wonder what goes on behind those eyes."

Kate didn't answer right away. She was tempted to keep schtum about Paul's concerns; speaking aloud felt like tempting the universe to make them a reality. But that was pure superstition.

"Paul and Em are worried about Evvy. She isn't hitting her milestones," she called from the loo.

Tony didn't answer. Emerging, Kate found him slowly twirling his reading specs by one stem as he sat, contemplating.

"I don't suppose you've witnessed any milestones you'd like to share?" she asked hopefully.

"No. And she is a quiet one."

Kate began her nightly application of lotion. "Paul said she doesn't like to play with her toys. Doesn't babble. They thought maybe she couldn't see, so they checked her vision. It came back normal."

"Oh, she sees. Once, she noticed me writing and wouldn't stop reaching for the pen. I haven't heard her babble. Cries, now that she's teething. Last time she was here, she cried so much that I tried to distract her with stuffies, but she wouldn't have it. So, I put on a lullaby, and she calmed down. A budding music lover."

"Which playlist? Nicky's *CBeebies* nursery rhymes?"

"I never play that bloody racket when you're away. No, this was Bach—Piano Sonata no. 14. In C-Sharp," he added, as if that meant anything to her.

"If you can't soothe them, beat them into submission with culture. Anyway," Kate continued, getting into bed, "you seem like a happy man." She read aloud from his screen, "'Crime Against Households and People Aged 16 Years and Over: A Monograph with Data from Police-Recorded Crime, and the Crime Survey for England and Wales.' A little light reading before sleep?"

"Just cross-referencing the Met's official numbers against this." Toggling windows, he displayed a book chapter from Oxford Academic's website: *Stalking, Menacing, and Assaulting Public Figures: A Behavioral Analysis for Law Enforcement* by Lloyd P. McCauley. The chapter was called "Celebrities as Victims of Stalking."

"Vic and I handled a celebrity stalking case once," Kate said, referring to her unhappy pre-Tony days at Scotland Yard. "The woman was an actress on *Hollyoaks*. The stalker was your typical gaunt, intense, wide-eyed bloke with a mile-long digital trail."

"Did he harm her?"

"No, we arrested him in time. His computer convicted him. Something like fifty marriage proposals by email. At least a hundred nonspecific threats against her safety. Graphic death threats to the actress's mum if she didn't agree to meet him. The perp plea-bargained his way into a secure hospital, did a stretch, and hasn't been heard from since, as far as I know."

"Lovesick fans are the usual culprits," Tony said. "'Love' is the wrong word, and so is 'fans,' but you know what I mean. I'm searching the literature for cases of band annihilation, or attempted annihilation. With Damselfish, the band's manager was murdered first. Then, a few months later, two band members were attacked."

"And we all know what happened to poor Miranda. God, I hate that for Damselfish. They make good workout music, you know. Catchy and angry, all at the same time."

"There's an Annabelle Carter connection."

"Pull the other one."

Riveted, Kate listened as he described Elodie Queen's blackmail threat. "How about that? I had no idea there were alumni who were so desperate not to be named. Maybe Cathleen Maitland-Palmer didn't have to squeeze cash out of former boyfriends. She could've just blackmailed her old students."

Tony raised an eyebrow. "Does that possibility fit the facts?"

"Probably not. We can't even one hundred percent call it murder yet. That's why I'm taking tomorrow off—it might be my only chance for a while, if Dr. Stepp rings Monday with a murder verdict.

"But there was no sign of a break-in at Cathleen's townhouse," Kate continued, thinking aloud. "If she wasn't alone when she died, she let another person inside. Or her cleaner, Daciana, did. She wasn't a live-in, but she had keys, of course."

"And keys can be copied. Handed out to men who specialize in that sort of job."

"Yeah. But I can't imagine a graduate of Annabelle Carter mincing into Cathleen's house and killing her. Unless..." She tailed off thoughtfully. "They could have poisoned her drink, then put a plastic bag over her head. That usually leaves a peaceful corpse with no vomit. But then, after making things so nice, they go completely psycho and chop off one of her fingers like a *Godfather* movie. All to get a school ring."

"I presume the ring had some special meaning?"

"It was given to her as a token of appreciation from the school's headmistress, Lady Bothurst. Or, as you'd write in a letter, the Honorable Griselda Bothurst. How's that for a name?"

"Positively Dickensian. I've met her, you know. Many times, as a matter of fact. We support the same charities."

"What's she like?"

"Do you recall the cat that lived next door before we were married? Ancient, gray? Moved with a sort of painful grace, as though it had arthritis but refused to acknowledge it?"

"Sure. She yowled like a banshee when Henry tried to pet her. Scratched him up something awful."

"Yes, well, that's Lady Bothurst in a nutshell. Bony, brittle, but unbroken. I wouldn't advise trying to pet her against her will."

"Do you realize that every time you describe someone from your charities, they sound like an absolute pill?"

"Speak as I find."

"I'd expect the charitable to be more—charitable."

"I don't know why. Large-scale philanthropy is an expression of power."

Kate was tempted to say, "And you use your power for good, right?" But even now, discussing Tony's personal fortune—which he always called *their* personal fortune—made her squirm inside. She knew that if she asked for it, he'd direct his accountant and brokers to present her with all the sordid details: investment portfolios, the Briarshaw trust, the Devon properties, the Wellegrave House freehold, and so on. Kate didn't believe it was literally sordid, but thinking about all that money made her uneasy. By comparison, if the day ever came when he said, "I'm afraid we're ruined," she could've handled it with perfect calm.

Suddenly, she realized Tony was still talking but she'd lost the thread. "Sorry, love. Say again?"

"I said, if Elodie Queen's name comes up in the course of your investigation, do let me know. It's probably irrelevant, but I like to sweep up every little crumb."

From the bedside table, Kate's personal mobile emitted a specific tone: the one she'd chosen for texts from her sister, Maura.

"Here we go again." She forced herself to read the message.

"I don't suppose she's reaching out to say she's back in rehab?" Tony asked.

"No. She's complaining to me, of all people, because Henry finally blocked her. Maybe now's the time to confront him about unlocking his phone?"

"I don't think so. He clearly has no idea the software still transmits a report on his daily activity. This is a good experiment, finding out how responsibly he uses his mobile when he doesn't know we're watching."

"But I told him to block her a month ago, and he didn't. He disobeyed, and he's lying to us."

"Yes."

"What would your father have done if he caught you in that kind of lie?"

"Smacked me. He called it caning. He kept a beastly stick in his study as a remembrance of his school days, when getting 'whacked' was a rite of passage."

Kate, who'd been "corrected" by Louise via belt, hairbrush, and fist, didn't believe in corporal punishment. Knowing Tony had very different ideas about the proper upbringing of children, she asked cautiously, "Did being caned work?"

"If you mean, did it teach me to become a clever, careful liar? Yes, it worked a treat." Tony closed the laptop and put it aside, along with his reading specs. "It also taught me never to confess anything to him, under any circumstances."

"Right. Well, I don't plan on smacking Henry or Nicky, ever. But I do believe in consequences. Henry will want me to up his weekly pocket money soon so he can save for Christmas prezzies. That's the perfect time for us to say, unfortunately, you didn't keep to the terms of your mobile use, so your pocket money stays the same."

"I've been meaning to talk to you about that," Tony said, beginning a slow bed slide to work on his post-op flexion. "You're quite happy giving him £4 a week?"

"Yes. I don't think it's excessive," Kate said a bit defensively. "Not these days."

"I think the time has come to challenge him."

"Oh. How low do you want to go?"

"I propose..." He eased his leg back to the starting position. "£500 a month. We'll open a checking account for him. The sum will be deposited into his account on the last business day of each month."

"*What?*" If Kate had been closer to the edge of the mattress, she would've fallen off.

"To give my father his due," Tony continued calmly, with what for him was a cheeky smile, "he put me at £300 a month from age nine on. I was expected to use that money to pay for my school necessities; my days out; books, toys, etc. That first Christmas was a disaster. I found myself unable to afford presents for my friends or the usual sweeties for myself because I emptied my bank account prematurely."

"Buying what?"

"An electric guitar."

"An electric guitar?" She gaped at him. "*Who are you?*"

He chuckled. "I suppose I thought piano lessons were

boring. I certainly thought becoming a guitar player would impress my mates. But proficiency at the piano didn't transfer to proficiency at the guitar, at least for me. At nine years old, I suffered from the worst buyer's remorse of my life. I had an instrument I couldn't play, no sweeties, and I couldn't buy gifts for anyone, even my mum."

"Did your father take pity on you?"

"What do you think?"

Kate cuddled up to him. "Gimme another bed slide. Then tell me what happened next."

"I flogged the guitar at school. Got less than half my money back. Then, I went to the school library and found a book called *Investing for Young Men*. There were more spasms of idiocy along the way, of course. But when I entered Uni, my bank account was growing, not shrinking. And by the time I inherited, I was an old hand at dealing with money. Some of the lads I came up with were drunk on cash from the moment their trust funds paid out. These days, they don't have a pot to piss in."

"Right." She studied his face. "Got one last bed slide in you?"

"If I say no, will you show mercy?"

"Nope."

Groaning theatrically, Tony resumed the exercise with slow precision.

"I can't believe I'm saying this, but I agree with you. Your basic premise," Kate clarified. "But shouldn't we start him at, I don't know, £50 per month? See how it goes?"

"The entire point is to overwhelm him with possibilities. To tempt him into spending wantonly. The quicker he caves, the quicker he learns. Ninety degrees flexion," Tony added triumphantly. "That's it. Spent."

"Just think about it," he added, kissing her cheek. "The

day will come when Henry and Nicky have rather intricate responsibilities. To themselves, and their future families. To fail to prepare them would be a grave disservice."

"Yeah. Lights out," she ordered the room's smart system, which complied. "Are you tired?"

"Completely done in."

"Me, too." She fitted herself in his arms, careful not to jar his post-op knee. For a little while, she just lay there, her mind spinning plates on poles like it always did. Each whirling porcelain disc was a separate concern: Henry, Maura, Paul, Evvy, CMP, MMP, Daciana Botezatu, and Patrick Bruce, AKA Lord Dellkirk. Then, she heard the soft noise Nicky sometimes made from the crib while sleeping. She didn't know if he was dreaming or just enjoying his snooze, but the sweet little sound made her heart turn over.

"Tony, did you hear that?" she whispered. But like Nicky, he was deeply asleep.

Chapter Twelve

Putting aside his secure MPS mobile, Paul poured himself a cup of coffee. "Hey, babe. Preliminary cause of death for Cathleen Maitland-Palmer is established."

"And?" asked Emmeline, who was coaxing Evvy to eat her pureed veg.

"Cardiac arrest."

"So it was just natural causes?"

"No. Cardiac arrest due to pacemaker malfunction. Just before she died, CMP came in close contact with a powerful magnet."

"Ev-vee," Emmeline cooed at their seven-month-old, whose lips were resolutely shut. "One more bite of carrots, sweetheart. How close was the contact?"

"Dr. Stepp estimates six inches from her chest."

"I didn't know pacemakers were so sensitive," Emmeline said. "A fridge magnet or kitchen knife strip can do that?"

"No. He said the magnet would have to be industrial grade. In the realm of an MRI magnet. Apparently, it exerted enough force to pull the pacemaker out of its pocket, where it sits inside the chest wall. As it came out, a lead broke, and the device burst." Sitting down at the table, he picked up Evvy's ring of colorful plastic keys and shook it idly.

"Daddy, don't distract Evvy."

"Sorry."

"Never mind. I think she's done." Emmeline stroked Evvy's thick, dark hair. "Are you sure you've had enough, darling?"

Evvy reached for the golden locket at Emmeline's throat, hooking a finger on the chain and tugging clumsily.

"No, no." Tucking the necklace under her jumper, Emmeline said, "Shake the keys again."

Paul did. Evvy didn't react. He clacked them together more forcefully.

"She can hear it," Emmeline snapped in the tone she always used when he betrayed anxiety about their daughter. "She just doesn't care. Jingle your real keys and I bet she'll look."

Paul fished out his key ring and obliged. Ignoring him, Evvy reached for Emmeline's throat, felt under the jumper, and pulled out the locket.

"Oh! Don't strangle Mum, there's a good girl." Emmeline laughingly regained custody of the locket.

"More coffee, babe?" Paul asked, aware that his wife's must have long ago gone cold.

"Yes, please."

After refilling her cup, he sat down again, watching Evvy's wide eyes move around the kitchen, seemingly taking in everything and nothing. "Ev-vee," he called, waving. "It's Dad-dee."

"She's tired and cranky from teething. Leave off."

"Dad-dee," he repeated, moving directly into Evvy's line of vision.

"Leave off," Emmeline said sharply. "I'm with her all day. And if not me, Sharada. You think we don't encourage her to speak? Five-minute IQ tests at the breakfast table before you swan off to Scotland Yard don't make a difference."

Picking up his coffee cup, he drained what remained. It was bitter.

Emmeline reached across the table to squeeze his hand. "Sorry, love. Stir crazy. Jealous, if I'm being honest, because you get to go search for the magnet killer. But it sounds like a freak accident. Are you sure no one in the building was using magnets for maintenance or something?"

"Not six inches from her chest. Then, there's the ring that was taken, finger and all. Anyway, must be off." Paul carried his plate and mug to the sink, returning to plant a kiss on Evvy's sweet-smelling head.

"Will it be a late one?" Emmeline asked.

"Maybe."

"Right. Be careful. And come here. Mum needs a kiss, too."

He obliged, making it a good one. As he pulled on his coat in the foyer, he heard his wife say, "Evvy! Stop. You can't have Mum's locket. Let's go find your teether, shall we?"

* * *

"Burst? As in, exploded?"

Paul nodded. He and Kate were on the tube, taking the District Line from Victoria Embankment to South Kensington. It was an eight-minute ride, and by some miracle, they virtually had a car to themselves, apart from a woman seated far away, her head bent over her knitting.

"Dr. Stepp called it a catastrophic internal injury. CMP's heart stopped like it was blown open by a bullet. She never knew what hit her."

"Huh. Got any bright ideas about the super-duper magnet?"

"No, so I asked DC Baker to ring London University and ask the Chair of Science and Technologies where our killer might acquire such a thing. Daciana might be sharper than she pretends to be, but she doesn't strike me as the type to dismantle an MRI machine."

"DC Baker, eh? How is she?"

If someone else had asked, Paul would've shrugged. But since it was Kate, he felt obliged to put a positive spin on his reply. DC Corinne Baker now occupied the role DC Amelia Gulls once filled. She couldn't have been more different in temperament, work habits, or communication style, and Kate was transparently ambivalent—or worse—about mentoring Baker as she'd mentored Gulls.

"Baker's bright. Not one to write her own press releases or glad hand her superior officers. More self-contained," Paul said. "I think she'll be a good fit for the team once she loosens up a bit. There's some prickliness."

"Prickliness as in diva behavior?"

"No. More like prickliness because she isn't sure who she can trust. The way you were when you joined the Toff Squad."

Kate rolled her eyes. "Subtle."

Paul gazed back at her innocently.

"I'd rather have another you on the team, God help us, than another me. Anyway, I've been thinking about last week. How quickly we were called to the scene. Did the deputy headmistress email you that alumni list we asked for?"

"I have it here." Paul held up his MPS secure mobile.

"I assume it included the daughters of some heavy hitters in the Peerage."

"Yes."

"What about the royals?"

"Not our royals, at least in the last hundred years. But international royals, yes."

After a glance at the knitter to be sure she was still absorbed in her work, Kate asked softly, "And the government? MPs? Cabinet ministers?"

I knew keeping her out of the loop wouldn't work, Paul thought ruefully. *I predicted that our Katie could winkle it out of thin air even if I kept mum.*

Kate said, "Yesterday afternoon, I went through Gov.UK searching for women politicians. The Great Offices of Parliament. The PM. The Chancellor of the Exchequer. The Foreign Secretary. The Home Secretary." She was watching him closely.

"Two of those are women, but their public bios don't indicate taking time from their studies at Oxford or the Inns of Court to attend a twee ladies' academy. So, I went down to the next level of government. The people Tony calls 'administrative demigods.' None of those women cared to list Annabelle Carter on their bios. But one name stood out to me anyway. Neera Nausherwani.

"We were called in to the crime scene like lightning," Kate went on. "Told to keep things quiet, not tape off the street in front of CMP's townhouse, no sirens or flashing lights. Almost as if someone like Neera, who has a friend in the Met like you, already knew CMP was dead and wanted the whole thing wrapped up as quickly as possible."

"She's not my friend," Paul protested. "We're just a bit matey after what happened, that's all."

Neera Nausherwani, the Secretary of State for DEFRA (Department of Environment, Food, and Rural), had been in a bit of a scrape when they met. To wit: Neera, along with two colleagues, was tied up and sitting on enough high explosives to take out the top of a skyscraper and rain deadly debris on Westminster. Due to Paul's detective work, heroism, and sheer luck, he'd managed to help her and the others escape before they became a red mist hanging over the city.

In the event's aftermath, Paul—perhaps the only person who knew precisely how and why Neera and the two junior ministers found themselves tied to a bomb—held their careers in his hands. Simply put, all three had been offered a "consideration," or bribe, by "lobbyists"—actually terrorists—and let themselves be seduced by mammon.

After being celebrated by the British media as a hero who'd saved untold lives, Paul could've taken a second bite at the fame apple. By spilling Neera and company's ugly little secret to Parliament's ombudsman, he would have returned to the interview circuit and got his name splashed across the broadsheets again. But after what the four of them had endured during that brief but terrifying experience, the idea of grassing on the trio felt like betrayal. Their capture, humiliation, and near murder was probably punishment enough. Heaven knew, countless politicians had done worse and received only a slap on the wrist, if that.

Kate asked, "Am I right in assuming Neera attended Annabelle Carter?"

He nodded.

"How did she find out CMP was dead so soon? Make

that claim to find out, since from this point on, I consider her a suspect."

"It's not that nefarious," he said, irritation rising. "The daughter, Marilyn, gave her a bell, that's all. They graduated from the same class. Neera's had some political troubles lately, Marilyn knew about them, and wanted to give her a heads up."

"That reasoning makes sense to you? Mum's dead on the floor. Better call the DEFRA secretary in case her campaign's affected?"

"Stop hounding me," he burst out. The woman with the knitting looked up. She continued watching them until the next station, at which point Paul resumed the conversation in a calmer voice.

"I'm sorry. I'm just under a lot of pressure. After we lost DCI Jackson, I've been more or less running the Toff Squad. All the legwork, all the headaches, none of the perks," he said. "Everywhere I turn, somebody wants to nail me to the wall for someone else's cockup, and I just have to smile and say, 'Yes, sir.' I never missed the chief so much in my life. And you. I was counting the days till you came back."

Kate's indignation faded. "Yeah. I get it. Now that I'm back, I'll shoulder my half, I promise."

"And the situation isn't as bad as it looks," he continued, stung by the phrase "a friend in the Met like you." "Marilyn, Neera, and lots of the alums keep in touch. Fundraisers and whatnot. Marilyn said she didn't think it was a murder. She made it sound like she called Neera for support as much as to help her career."

"As far as I'm concerned, calling anyone before 999 is always suspicious. I wish you'd talked to me before you agreed to honor Neera's wishes."

"It wasn't like that." Paul wished the train would arrive so he could get some fresh air. "She called the assistant commander's office. The AC called me. He said, listen, it's a Toff Squad thing, it's why your team exists. Be discreet, say nothing to anyone else, and make the DEFRA secretary happy. Then Neera rang me up afterward to say thank you. And to promise she wouldn't try to influence the investigation in any way."

"Fine. Hopefully, she won't start asking for progress reports. Or, oh, I don't know, designate a culprit from her enemies list for us to stitch up."

Their train coasted into the station, where a sparse crowd was waiting to board. Paul and Kate disembarked, following the crowd through a colorful tiled tunnel and up into the late morning sunlight. Paul led the way since he knew Kensington better than she did.

"There's one thing I don't get," Kate said. "According to Neera's bio, she always intended to enter politics after uni. Why did she go to finishing school?"

"She was born in Mumbai and lived there until her late teens. Mum and Dad wanted her to present herself as a perfect Englishwoman. Behave and sound as if she were born here."

"Kind of gross."

"Maybe. Think of it the other way round. If you found yourself living in Mumbai at age seventeen, speaking only English and a little schoolbook Marathi, wouldn't you jump at an intensive course on how to fit in? Especially if you had aspirations?"

"When you put it that way, sure."

"I reckon her parents got a good return on investment. Neera married the vice president of Sky TV. Or maybe

TalkTalk. Their boys attend Harrow School, and she's only a few heartbeats away from Home Secretary."

"All right, you convinced me. So, why does she consider it a deep, dark secret?"

"Labour is supposed to be for ordinary people, not social climbers. The newspapers would spit-roast her. Every opponent would run commercials about the toffee-nosed chit who attended an ultra-exclusive school." He stopped to consult his mobile's map app. "Right. Cross here, then follow Graybar Street into that cul-de-sac.

"In any rational world," he continued, putting his phone away, "Neera's constituents would consider her parents' wealth and how she lives and not be *entirely* shocked that she attended finishing school. But people seem to enjoy suspending their disbelief for politicians. And God knows the press lives for proof of hypocrisy."

"Henry says we live in the stupidest timeline."

"He might be on to something. There it is. Annabelle Carter, in all its glory."

The house was a grand affair, peaked and gabled, with a domed rooftop pavilion on one side. Built of limestone, it ticked all the neo-Baroque boxes for an Edwardian institutional building: decorated keystones, Italianate columns, and a conservatory with an arched roof.

The front door was forbidding enough to be a façade, lacking a doorbell, post slot, and signage, so Kate and Paul veered toward the conservatory door, which was propped open. They were halfway down the path when a middle-aged man in blue overalls stormed out.

"I didn't say you could go." A pale woman with gray hair and a dowdy yellow dress started after him, but another woman, dark and stylish in red, put a hand on her shoulder to stop her.

"Consider yourself sacked!" the gray-haired woman called.

"Consider yourself an ugly old sack and we'll call it even." The man in overalls brightened to discover Kate and Paul in his path. "Maybe I'll go straight to the press. Say the pair of you cows are what done her in. And maybe you did! You lot *Daily Mail* or *Bright Star*?" he asked Kate hopefully.

"Scotland Yard." She held up her warrant card. "What's all this, then?"

"That there harpy in yellow is accusing me of thieving," he said, laying on the wounded innocence thick. "And the government lady is pretending to be on my side because she's a lying hack, like all her kind."

Government, thought Kate, giving the stylish lady in red a second look. *Speak of the devil and she appears. Neera Nausherwani.*

"You *are* a thief," the gray-haired woman insisted. "I have no doubt you rifled Cathleen's office. There was no one in the administrative wing but you and the two of us."

"Then you and the Iron Shady there best interrogate each other."

"Arrest that man!" the gray-haired woman cried, looking imploringly at Kate.

"For what?"

"For walking away from his employer's accusation of theft."

The man in overalls grinned unpleasantly. "What exactly did I steal?"

"Something from Cathleen's bookshelf."

"Oh, aye. And what did I take, exactly?"

"You might have taken anything. You must be searched."

Paul said, "We're not here to investigate petty theft. But

if something belonging to Mrs. Maitland-Palmer were taken from her office, it would be worth looking into. Would one of you tell me what this man is accused of taking?"

The gray-haired woman pursed her lips and did not reply. Neera, as poised and lovely as she was behind the podium, shook her head. "We don't know what happened. It's clear as day that Mrs. Maitland-Palmer's office was searched. We don't know what, if anything, might be on that gentleman's person."

"Gentleman," repeated the man in overalls. "I like that. You planning to run your fingers over this gentleman's person?" he asked Kate.

Her eyes narrowed. "Did you take anything?"

"No."

"If you can't even tell us what might be missing, and he says it never happened, there's no probable cause," Paul informed the gray-haired woman as Kate told the man in overalls, "Get off the property before we caution you for trespassing."

"My pleasure. Goodbye, Mrs. Dankworth. Enjoy scrubbing the toilets and swabbing the decks." Hands in his pockets, the man departed, whistling a jaunty tune.

"Scotland Yard," said Mrs. Dankworth, fixing Kate with a look of undisguised contempt. "Let's get this interview over with, shall we? You two look to be as useless as teats on a bull."

Chapter Thirteen

Eleanor Dankworth, Deputy Headmistress of Annabelle Carter, stood perfectly rigid, a mannequin with a steel rod up her backside. The Peter Pan collar of her drop-waisted dress suggested virtue—grinding virtue, in Paul's opinion, that wants to crush every carefree thing it touches. That was a heavy condemnation to put on a starched white collar. But given Mrs. Dankworth's cold gaze, pale face, and pursed red lips, Paul stood by it.

Neera Nausherwani, by contrast, looked ready to shake hands and make campaign promises. Like Kate, Paul was blindsided by her sudden appearance in a chic suit and matching hat. Had Neera learned about their appointment with Mrs. Dankworth and hurried over for a pre-interview chat?

"A key instinct in public life is knowing when to exit, stage right," Neera announced. "I dropped by to ask Mrs. Dankworth if there was anything I could do to make next month's fundraiser a success. With Cathleen gone, I thought perhaps we'd postpone it, but it appears we're going forward after all. Thank you, Eleanor."

Turning to Mrs. Dankworth, she offered the other woman a receiving-line embrace, complete with air kisses that were not, Paul noticed, returned. If anything, the ritual made Mrs. Dankworth stiffer. Treating Kate and Paul as a unit, Neera nodded pleasantly at them, slung her Tom Ford handbag over her shoulder, picked up her Prada briefcase, and departed.

"Good actress," Kate murmured in his ear.

"Well? Are you coming with me or standing there whispering like schoolchildren?" the deputy headmistress asked crisply.

"If you don't mind," Paul said, following her with Kate in tow, "would you tell us about that man? I presume he was the school janitor."

"Yes, but only for a short time. I fear the post will become like our groundskeeper's—a revolving door. It's the tragedy of our times. Men who'd rather be on benefits than put in an honest day's work."

"And it was Mr. Botezatu before him?" Paul asked.

"Yes." She sounded surprised. "Rasvan Botezatu. He was our caretaker from the day our headmistress reopened the school in this building. A diligent worker," she said, parceling out the compliment as if it cost her personally. "Foreigners are often one's best bet these days."

Paul wasn't sure if she meant that to sting him or compliment him, but he didn't let it slow him down. "Why did Mr. Botezatu leave his job?"

"Back trouble. A slipped disc," said Mrs. Dankworth, leading them out of the conservatory and into the school's cool, dim interior. The black-and-white checkerboard floors were cracked and chipped; some plastered walls were stained with rising damp. Paul saw no concessions to modernity like fire suppression sprinklers, emergency lights, or exit signage. Either the administrators skirted the law or had found a legal way around it.

"If you'll look at that picture of the ribbon-cutting ceremony," Mrs. Dankworth said, stopping in front of a framed photograph, "you'll see Mr. Botezatu. Off to the left, just there."

Most people in the picture were kitted out to the nines, the women in tea-length gowns, hats, and gloves, the men in suits. Rasvan Botezatu, a small, dark man in blue overalls, stood far to one side, a sour look on his face.

"He doesn't seem thrilled," Kate said.

"He always scowled like that when someone brought a camera out. Didn't like having his picture taken."

Resuming the tour, Mrs. Dankworth led them into the school's finest room, the parlor. It boasted well-kept Edwardian furniture, a magnificent Turkish rug, and a crystal chandelier. Over the fireplace hung an oil portrait of a forty-something woman in a scarlet ballgown. Painfully thin, with sharp cheekbones and blonde hair swept into a chignon, her two-dimensional eyes seemed to pick out Paul as an interloper in this feminine domain.

Nodding at the painting, he asked, "Is that the original Annabelle Carter?"

"No." Mrs. Dankworth sounded as disgusted as if he'd suggested it was Meghan Markle. "Annabelle Carter was a Victorian who died in 1899. That's our current headmistress, Lady Griselda Bothurst."

Someone giggled. Paul realized a young East Asian woman, perhaps twenty, was curled up in an overstuffed armchair. At the sight of her, Mrs. Dankworth stopped dead. The young woman instantly went from cheeky to downtrodden.

"Nayao, why aren't you in cookery class, helping Mrs. Braide with dinner?" Mrs. Dankworth demanded.

"Bad tum, Miss."

"I see. I happen to know tonight's menu includes broiled lobster. Step one of lobster prep is putting a knife through its brain. Did you prove unequal to the task?"

"I can't kill a living thing. I'm vegan."

"Nonsense. You ate buttered toast this morning. The butter was from cow's milk. The bread dough contained eggs. You're a skiver, and not a very good one. Put your shoes on."

Reluctantly, Nayao stood up and pushed her feet into her heels, which were higher than Paul would have expected for everyday wear. Her A-line skirt and plain cashmere twinset were more practical, though together they looked more like a period costume than something any modern woman would wear.

"Right," Mrs. Dankworth told the student. "Now smile, walk calmly back to the kitchen, and tell Miss Braide you're ready to kill and cut up your lobster."

"But she told me to get out."

"Yes, well, when the day comes that she is deputy headmistress and I am not, you can obey her dictates instead of mine. Until then, do as I say."

Looking as if she wanted to moan some more but didn't quite dare, Nayao exited the parlor. Although DI Paul Bhar was happy to continue without commenting, Paulie-the-mouth piped up to say, "I suppose it's vital for well-bred women to know how to kill and broil spendy seafood."

Mrs. Dankworth surprised him by actually smiling. She was accustomed to questions like this, he realized, and found them amusing rather than offensive.

"Killing and broiling a lobster is something Nayao may

London Blue

never do again after she leaves us," Mrs. Dankworth said. "If her life goes as one hopes, she won't even need to instruct her staff on the proper method, because her husband will hire only the best.

"The point of the exercise is two-fold. First, to develop self-control. I daresay no one wants to lobotomize wildlife, but everyone wants lobster. Our graduates must be able to push through discomfort or inconvenience in pursuit of a goal. The second point is self-discovery. Nayao arrived here a fainting flower, afraid of everyone and everything. Now, as you just witnessed, she tried to defy me. When she successfully cooks her lobster, she'll learn that she can defy her fears, too."

There was no retort even Paulie-the-mouth could devise for that, so he and Kate followed Mrs. Dankworth out of the parlor and into a short hall. The door on the right had a brass nameplate that read,

DEPUTY HEADMISTRESS
MRS. E. DANKWORTH

The door on the left said nothing. The white-painted wood bore pry marks where another nameplate would have been.

"Was that Mrs. Maitland-Palmer's office?" Kate asked.

"Yes."

"May we go in?"

Mrs. Dankworth blinked. "I don't understand why you would—"

"You just said your janitor rifled it," Paul cut across her. "We should take a look."

"Very well." Mrs. Dankworth ushered them inside.

For an office that was supposedly "rifled," Paul found it quite tidy. A shelf of framed photographs celebrated Cathleen's teaching career: smiling on the arm of a distinguished-looking man, posed next to a rose bush, beaming beside a round woman with a red face. She and the woman thrust their hands at the camera, showing off identical rings.

"That woman in the picture," said Kate, zeroing in on Cathleen's red-faced companion. "Who is she?"

"Ginny Braide. Our cookery teacher."

"A close friend?"

Mrs. Dankworth made a noncommittal noise.

"Did Mrs. Maitland-Palmer have enemies here?"

"I think you'll find we're all professionals."

"Can you think of anyone who might have wanted to harm Mrs. Maitland-Palmer?" Kate asked.

"Such a morbid topic," Mrs. Dankworth clucked. "I'm afraid I don't know what I'm expected to say. What happened to Cathleen is very sad, of course, but London has always been dangerous. To treat violent housebreaking like the crime of the century is rather naïve on Scotland Yard's part."

"Ooh, crime of the century! How exciting," said a chirpy voice from the open doorway. Paul turned to see a willowy young woman with light brown hair and a bright smile.

"Lady Caryn," Mrs. Dankworth said flatly. "Why aren't you with your students?"

"I popped out to gather asters," she said, holding up an empty basket as proof. "I told the girls to pick today's flowers, and they brought back the saddest collection of bedraggled greenery you've ever seen." If Lady Caryn was bothered by her boss's evident displeasure, she gave no sign. "Won't you introduce me?"

"Lady Caryn Hattersley, please meet DI Bhar and DI Hetheridge of Scotland Yard."

"Oh, my!" The young teacher dropped a deep curtsy, performing it with such ironic reverence that Paul and Kate laughed aloud. Mrs. Dankworth looked appalled.

"I just betrayed my training," Lady Caryn said. "One of the first things this school taught me was that introductions go according to rank. Since you two were introduced to me, I'm above you. Until the masses rise up to take back the country." She made it sound like a party she couldn't wait to attend.

"*Viva la revolución*," Paul said, smiling. It was good to be married. Now, when he met a pretty, charming, and almost certainly heartless creature like this, he didn't have to worry about falling for her.

"We're investigating the death of Cathleen Maitland-Palmer," Kate said. "If you have any information to offer, we'd like to hear it."

"Information." Lady Caryn's eyes roamed around the office, alighting on the bookcase. "Let me think... information..."

"Lady Caryn." Mrs. Dankworth seemed to be drawing on her deepest reserves of self-mastery. "Please. Return to your class."

"Just a moment." Paul produced his card with practiced grace. "As you're one of Mrs. Maitland-Palmer's former colleagues, we might like to speak to you in future. Here's my number if you think of anything that might be relevant to the case. Anything at all."

Lady Caryn looked delighted. "Why, thank you, good sir. And now, alas, I must be off. Farewell, DI Hetheridge. My pupils await."

Mrs. Dankworth didn't wait until Lady Caryn was definitely out of earshot to say, "I apologize for the interruption." To Paul, she added, "You'll come to regret giving her that card. She'll cook up some rubbish she thinks amusing to pester you with for a laugh."

Paul shrugged. "She wouldn't be the first. I recognized her name from an interview with Marilyn Maitland-Palmer. Apparently, there was some kind of staff room altercation between Lady Caryn and the deceased?"

"Yes. Very unseemly."

"About...?" Kate prompted.

"Animosity leftover from the schoolroom, I shouldn't wonder. Lady Caryn is, I'm almost ashamed to say, an alumna. Now, if you don't mind, I really must be certain that Lady Caryn has returned to her class. You may examine this room as long as you like," she added, and left.

"I came prepared." Fishing in her handbag, Kate produced blue nitrile gloves and clear plastic evidence bags. Nodding at the silver laptop on Cathleen's desk, she said, "That MacBook is going with us for sure. Oh, and that appointment book, too. If we dust them for fingerprints, think we'll find a certain politician's?"

"Maybe we'll find Lady Caryn's. She insinuated herself pretty readily, didn't she? Seemed interested in this bookcase, too." Gloving up, he added, "Why would you even imply that Neera tossed this place?"

"Mrs. Dankworth said there were only three people in the admin wing. That gives Neera a one-in-three chance."

Kate maintained her straight face for a beat, then grinned. "Mind you, I doubt she can be certain they were totally alone. Teachers like Lady Caryn can go where they please. Plus, there had to be students like Nayao out of class. When I was at school, I was always either someplace forbidden or trying to get there."

"I was a good child. That's why I became a policeman."

"I wanted to crack heads. I just needed a socially appropriate way to do it. Think she read any of those?" Kate asked, meaning the books.

To Paul's eye, the pristine top shelf appeared to be for display purposes only. Among the volumes, Paul found *Margaret Thatcher: The Autobiography, Princess Margaret: A Life of Contrasts,* and *I Reach for the Stars: An Autobiography of Barbara Cartland.*

"Nope. But we should probably see if she was in the habit of stashing things inside them."

Dutifully, he worked his way through half of the tomes as Kate took the opposite side. Nothing was stashed inside any of them, not even a bookmark.

The lower shelves contained Cathleen's preferred reading. Some well-worn, dog-eared paperbacks were Mills & Boon romances, some were old-fashioned bodice rippers, and some were advice books of a particular bent. *Getting What You Want Every Single Time* by Dale Reuter; *The 32 Rules of Persuasion* by Gal Gold; *Manipulation Isn't a Dirty Word* by K.N. Frye.

"There's space between the books and the back of the case," Paul told Kate. By removing some books, he revealed a minor mess: handwritten letters, opened envelopes, and discarded loops of ribbon with the bows still tied. "By the look of it, our rifler knew where to go."

"Maybe Mrs. D was right, and that janitor bounced out of here with some of those letters in his pocket."

Or Neera, Paul thought. He didn't believe it, but Kate had put the idea in his brain.

"These are ancient," he said, glancing at each letter and envelope before dropping them into the evidence bag. "Look, a Charles and Di stamp from 1981. Can you believe it? Not one of these stamps is over 14*p*."

"You could post a letter for 14*p*?" Kate also skimmed each letter before adding it to the collection. "As far as the contents go—are yours all blue?"

"Every last one of them. Must be how people entertained themselves before the internet." Paul cast a dubious eye over his evidence bag. "This is like breaking into a ransacked Egyptian tomb. No gold, no jewels, just papyrus scratchings by blokes long dead."

Kate giggled. "It *is* possible that Cathleen's newer love letters were taken."

"I doubt there was anything recent. People don't write letters anymore. It's all about sexting. But let's ask Mrs. Dankworth for the janitor's name and address, just in case."

"What's that you have there?" the deputy headmistress asked when they entered her office, evidence bags in hand.

"We found a cache of personal letters," Paul said. "It seems like you may be right about the rifling. Someone seems to have gone through them in a hurry." He held up his evidence bag. "Do you know anything about them?"

"Why would I? I wouldn't touch one without donning a hazmat suit."

"Sounds like you have some idea what they're all about," Kate said.

"Educated guess," Mrs. Dankworth sniffed. "I see you have her laptop, too."

"Be assured, we'll return it to Annabelle Carter if we find nothing helpful on it," Paul said.

"No need. That's Cathleen's personal laptop. She was never without it. She must've left it here by accident."

Detecting a stronger note of censure than usual, Paul asked, "Can you tell us what she used it for?"

"Zoom calls with her fiancé. He was in Sydney. The time difference is eleven hours, so his goodnight wishes invariably came when she was here, ostensibly earning a living."

"Right." Paul got out his notebook. "What's his name?"

"I really couldn't tell you. Robert Reynolds, or Robert Remington. Something like that. We on the faculty cut Cathleen off when she tried to brag about him. It was all too tedious," Mrs. Dankworth said. "If we mentioned him between ourselves, we called him Sydney."

"Marilyn Maitland-Palmer never told us her mother had a fiancé."

"Yes, well, she was skeptical of his existence."

"So, she thought Mrs. Maitland-Palmer was being catfished?" Paul asked. "Being catfished is when—"

"I know what catfished means," Mrs. Dankworth snapped. "I had the misfortune to walk in on one of Cathleen's Zoom calls. Despite what Marilyn thinks, the man was quite real. About sixty, reasonably attractive. An English expat."

"Right. Thank you for that," Kate said. "How long have you been at Annabelle Carter?"

"The span of my career. Thirty-three years."

"Were you hired by Lady Bothurst?"

"No, I was taken on by the deputy headmistress at the time. Cathleen Maitland-Palmer."

"Would you characterize your relationship with her as friendly?" Paul asked. "Unfriendly?"

"Strictly professional."

"Did your reversal of status create any friction? When you became her boss?" Kate asked.

"Not for me. What Cathleen felt, I really couldn't say."

"When was the last time you saw Mrs. Maitland-Palmer?" Paul asked.

"Yesterday."

"Did she mention any plans for the evening?"

"She'd been invited to a dinner party at Cottlestone Manor. And so was I, although I had to send my regrets. I don't like to drive from London to Hampshire and back again on a school night."

Paul asked, "You know the Earl of Dellkirk? Patrick Bruce?"

Mrs. Dankworth permitted herself a tiny smile. "My position of trust at Annabelle Carter takes me many places and allows me to mix in rather elevated circles. I was told about the party and Cathleen's behavior after dinner."

Intrigued by the gleam in the deputy headmistress's eye, Paul pressed, "And how did she behave?"

"Like a woman half her age. A vulgar, grasping woman half her age."

"Grasping," Kate repeated. "I don't mean to be indelicate, but in these inquiries, the victim's past is thoroughly investigated as a matter of course. Grasping usually means trying to advance socially. Is that what you mean?"

Mrs. Dankworth nodded.

"But Mrs. Maitland-Palmer seemed to have good connections, at least on paper." She read off her mobile, "Daughter of Tiffany Maitland, niece to an earl by marriage. Tiffany graduated from Annabelle Carter and met Sir Joseph Whitholt that same year. In the Swiss Alps, no less."

"Whilst burning his toast, presumably." Mrs. Dankworth still sounded disapproving, but her eyes gleamed happily. "Tiffany was in the Alps as a chalet girl, not a guest."

These are the things she wanted to say from the minute we turned up, Paul thought. *She was just waiting for us to open the door.*

He said, "Remind me, what's a chalet girl?"

"On a bender, under a stranger. Oh, don't look so shocked. I've dealt with young women my entire career. I know their ways better than anyone," Mrs. Dankworth said. "One presumes that's how Cathleen entered this world—the result of a chance encounter on the slopes."

"Then there's her late husband, Joseph Palmer. He seemed well-regarded," Kate said dryly. "Unless you have something to tell us about him as well?"

"I beg your pardon, DI Hetheridge. I can't quite place your accent. You are from...?" She tailed off expectantly.

Dropped an H somewhere, Paul thought.

"I reside in Euston Place. W1 J6LX."

Amused, Paul noticed how Kate allowed a beat for that exalted postcode to sink in before adding, "My husband is Lord Anthony Hetheridge."

Mrs. Dankworth stared at her. "Well. Good heavens. Well, well. That row with the janitor discombobulated me, I don't mind saying. I've forgotten my manners." Putting on a pleasant smile for the first time since their arrival, she said, "How do you do, Lady Hetheridge? What a pleasure to make your acquaintance."

Rising, she came around the desk to shake Kate's hand. Still more amused, Paul stuck out his hand, too, forcing her to repeat the gesture with a garden-variety Englishman.

"But getting back to Joseph Palmer," Kate said. "He seems to have been well-respected in his field."

"Yes. Well-respected... *in his field*," Mrs. Dankworth said. "He worked for a titled Scottish gentleman I shan't name. In those days, butlers were called butlers, not 'house managers,' and I daresay Mr. Palmer was proud to be a butler. When he retired, he took a teaching position with the International Butler Academy, a respected organization. Nevertheless," she added sweetly, "when Cathleen Maitland married Joseph Palmer, she married the help. Above her doors closed, never to be opened again."

"She still got invited to an earl's dinner party," Paul said.

"Yes. And that's down to the patronage of Lady Bothurst. If not for the support of our headmistress, Cathleen would have been brushed off like scurf wherever she went."

"Was Lady Bothurst at Lord Dellkirk's party?"

"Yes."

Kate asked, "Can you give us the complete guest list?"

"Not with absolute accuracy. I suggest you contact his office."

"We appreciate your honesty. I know we asked this earlier, but I'm going to ask again. Please be frank," Paul said, hoping Mrs. Dankworth would find a second chance irresistible. "Can you think of any reason someone might have killed Cathleen Maitland-Palmer?"

"There may have been some envy," she said demurely.

"Over the London blue rings that only she and the cookery teacher received?" Kate asked.

"Yes. There was also animosity over her behavior in

class. I'm afraid she could be rather abusive to our pupils," Mrs. Dankworth answered. "Write this down. There's a YouTube channel called *The Secret life of Lexie Lex*, created by a former student, Alexa Hicks-Bowen. She's an idiot girl, if I'm being honest, but her illicit video of Cathleen at the podium is genuine. And embarrassing. Lady Bothurst was appalled, but ultimately, one can only rise above it."

"Meaning, you found the publicity helpful?" Kate interrupted. "Or your brief advised you not to sue for damages?"

"I cannot speak on the school's legal matters. I can tell you that Cathleen considered it personally defamatory. She said she was consulting her solicitor, but I suppose that's all over now."

"Legal remedies can be expensive," Paul said. "According to Mrs. Maitland-Palmer's bank manager, her last direct deposit from Annabelle Carter was over six months ago. Yet it seems like she carried out her old job duties at the school as if still employed. Was she teaching here on a purely volunteer basis?"

"Yes."

"That's highly unusual, isn't it?"

"Yes, but it's up to the headmistress's discretion." After a moment's silence, Mrs. Dankworth checked her watch. "Ten minutes to lecture time. I'm teaching Cathleen's fashion classes this week until we can adjust the schedule. But even if I could remain with you all day, I cannot speak for Lady Bothurst. I fear you must take it up with her. Lovely to meet you, Lady Hetheridge."

Without a glance at Paul, she exited the office.

Chapter Fourteen

By Monday morning, Henry's gloom over Karlie's "too little" comment had lifted, and he once again felt optimistic about his chances to win her. In five days, he'd go for his Savile Row suit fitting. The clothes make the man, and he was determined not to leave without a suit that made him look at least ten years older. Then, Karlie would gaze at him with a new light in her eyes—he quite liked that phrase—and their love story would finally begin.

He was glad he'd heeded Harvey's advice and chosen one of those big history doorstops Tony liked to read as a birthday gift. The short story he'd hoped to write had crashed and burned over the weekend, and Henry was too much of a realist to believe any part of it was worth showing to another person. Except for the brilliant beginning he'd written:

> ***John K. Freeling didn't make mistakes. He was a good detective and a good man who never failed to catch the people who scoffed at life and believed they could hurt anyone and get***

away with it. He set traps for them. They could not evade his ways of making them give up the truth in long interrogations almost beyond human endurance. He loved no one except the one who got away, and unless she came back to him, he would be alone forever. Unless of course one day they met again and she gazed at him with a new light in her eyes. Then—who knows?!

By anyone's standards, that was a banger of an opening, and Henry felt justifiably proud of it. But expanding it into a five or ten-page story was surprisingly tricky. Freeling needed to be called in by Scotland Yard. (They knew he was the best, but resented his disregard for authority and insistence on working alone.) Just getting Freeling in the room with the corpse had taken three pages of increasingly boring prose, during which Henry had seriously contemplated tossing a werewolf into the mix. Then, he gave up, saved that primo opening paragraph to his password-protected secret file, and resigned himself to giving Tony the doorstop.

The school day was going well—top marks on his history essay and a passing grade in Maths. After second period came a break that he could use however he wished: pop by the school library, walk around the vast green lawn, or watch the older kids playing tennis. He and his mates opted for the latter. They were sitting on the concrete benches outside the court, listening to balls thump and discussing music, when a woman called hoarsely, "Henry!" In her East End bray, it sounded like, "Ennnreee." The second he heard it, he went cold.

Pretend like I don't hear, he thought. He couldn't

believe it was happening. Maura was ambushing him at his new school. *Pretend like she's calling for some other Henry.*

"Are you seeing this?" Declan elbowed him. "There's a mad old bat in the schoolyard."

"How'd she get in?" asked Henry's best mate, Kyle. "She couldn't have climbed the hill, could she?"

"Ennnree!" Maura cried. She was looking right at them but seemed afraid to approach the knot of uniformed schoolchildren. Instead, she beckoned for him to come over. "I know you eaaaarr me!"

"Dude." Declan elbowed Henry a second time. "She doesn't mean you, does she?"

The designers of Henry's new school had done their best to accommodate security without compromising the grounds' natural beauty. In his Southwark school, Henry's breaks had been taken in a paved rectangle enclosed by chain-link fences. It had felt more like a prison exercise yard than a playfield. At Highgate, sculpted tiers created barriers that only cats, foxes, and squirrels could easily overcome, rendering fences unnecessary. One side of the tennis court tier faced the street, but that steep bluff was covered in broken granite blocks. If the climb wasn't impossible, it was certainly daunting. Even the biggest, wildest older students gave it a miss.

"Look at the state of her!" Kyle crowed. "Ripped tights and bloodied knees. Go home, love, you're pissed!"

The tennis game stopped. The players stared at Maura. Her condition stunned Henry, who wouldn't have known her if not for her trademark red-burgundy hair with the inevitable gray roots. Dressed in a mini skirt and clingy top, she looked as if she'd lost two stone or more. Her face was haggard, and she'd lost a shoe during her climb up the rocky bluff.

"Ennreee Wakefield, you get over ere! Ow dare you block me!"

"She *does* mean you." Wide-eyed, Declan turned to Henry. "You know her?"

"No," he protested, thinking fast. "She, er, used to... I mean..."

"You got more money than God now," Maura bellowed, belligerently staring down the crowd of Year 6 and Year 7 kids. "Where's mine? Don't I deserve a piece? I'm your bloody *mum*, for God's sake!"

"Shit," Kyle whispered.

Henry's heart dropped. If he lost Kyle, he only had Declan for a best mate. And Declan swung like a weathervane according to prevailing winds.

"She's *not* my mother," he declared, lifting his chin. "She was our housekeeper for a little while. Then she started—" He almost said, "back on the hard food," but swallowed the phrase, remembering Henry Hetheridge didn't know drug slang. "Started taking cannabis, I guess. Or something worse."

"Taking cannabis? You smoke piff, you don't *take* it," Declan corrected wisely. "I reckon she's a proper junkie."

"Proper junkie," Kyle echoed.

"Yeah. Anyway, Dad sacked her," Henry said. "She's been looking for a handout ever since. I don't know how she found me here," he added in his best detached tone, as if Maura's unpleasantness had nothing to do with him personally. "Maybe she's stalking our family."

"Then who's Henry Wakefield?" Kyle asked.

Inspiration dawned. "Her son—her dead son. That's why she takes drugs, I guess. Because her son died. Since I'm called Henry, too, she gets us confused."

"Oi," shouted Declan. He watched a lot of crime

dramas, including *The Responder* and *Luther,* when his parents weren't looking. "Bugger off, you old scrubber! Go jab yourself with a rusty needle."

Maura, who was pacing expectantly, waiting for Henry to cave in and do as she said, began shrieking curses. Henry caught a word or two—"nancy boy," "poncer," "poof"—but mostly it sounded like the bellowing of a wounded animal. One with enough strength left to kill anyone foolish enough to venture too close.

A bigger crowd of kids formed around Henry, Declan, and Kyle. The air seemed to buzz; it was electric, dreamlike. Henry didn't remember going from sitting to standing, but somehow his mates were on their feet, and he was, too.

"She doesn't belong here. She'll scare the Year 3s." Picking up a rock, Declan flung it at Maura. It sailed over her shoulder, close enough to make her shout,

"Eeeees my son, you bloody prick! My son!"

"No, he's not." Kyle lobbed a rock. It hit Maura's midsection. Declan threw another that glanced off her chin. She clapped a hand to her face.

"All I want's a score!"

Henry, who knew that "score" meant twenty pounds, would've gladly given her the note if he'd had it on him. But he knew that giving her the money wouldn't make her leave off these appeals. It would only train her to reappear at Highgate again and again.

"Go away! *I don't know you!*" he roared, fist clenching over a rock. He didn't know how he came to have it. Maybe he'd stooped to pick it up; maybe Declan had pressed it into his hand. "You're not my mum!"

As he drew back to hurl the rock with all his strength, someone caught his arm and held it. It was a grownup: Ms. Weaving, one of the librarians.

"We needn't be cruel," she murmured. "Here come the coaches."

On cue, the Track and Field coach, a sternly imposing man, approached Maura from one side; his assistant coach closed in from the other. Maura fought them half-heartedly, then let herself be led away. All around Henry, kids giggled, crowed, and high-fived each other at the show's conclusion.

After the children were put into queues and marched off to their next classes, Ms. Weaving ushered Henry into the library. He was shocked to realize it was barely noon. The worst disaster of his new life had unfolded in under twenty minutes.

"Are you all right?" Ms. Weaving asked gently.

Her tone made his eyes burn. He looked away.

"I'm sure it must have been upsetting. But why was that woman talking to you, do you know?"

Henry repeated his story about the emotionally disturbed cleaner. Even in his numb distress, he remembered not to pile on extra details. In criminal interviews, Tony and Kate always listened for details that shifted and multiplied.

"Oh, dear. That's very sad. Of course, she had no right to trespass onto our campus or accost you and your friends. It doesn't surprise me that you resorted to throwing stones," Ms. Weaving said. "But I happen to think violence doesn't work. Especially against people who are mentally ill."

"Declan said she was probably a junkie."

"Perhaps she was. She might even have been both. I still don't think," Ms. Weaving said gently, "hitting her with stones was the right response. Next time, consider finding a grownup instead."

"You think I'm cruel?" He sniffed, still fighting tears.

"No. I think you're frightened. Henry, it's not your fault

London Blue

a sick woman mistook you for someone else. You've done nothing wrong."

"Will Coach throw her out?"

"He'll escort her to the gymnasium until the police arrive. After that, it's out of our hands. But you still seem a bit shaky. Would you like to go home early?"

"No," he said quickly, appalled. If he left school like a little baby, Kyle and especially Declan might conclude Maura's appearance wasn't a fluke. He had to present himself as unbothered, intelligent, well-spoken Henry Hetheridge until Maura's accusations were forgotten.

"All right, then," Ms. Weaving said. "I'll need to ring your mum, of course."

"She's at work. Ring my dad. He always knows what to do." Taking a deep breath, he added, "Thanks, Ms. Weaving. I can take myself to class."

On the way, he stopped at the boys' lavatory, which was mercifully empty. Locking himself in a stall, Henry put down the toilet lid and sat down to think.

Why does she always do this? She's had every kind of free help there is. Then Kate paid for rehab at a posh place. Three times at least, he thought.

It occurred to him that maybe his story about a confused woman with a dead son wasn't so far from the truth. Thank God his friends had laughed at the idea of Maura as his mother. He'd cooked up an explanation and sold it. The worst was over.

Opening his right hand, Henry stared at the rock he'd been clenching ever since the librarian stayed his hand. It was sharp on one edge; his palm was red. He imagined the betrayal in Maura's eyes if he'd thrown it, if it hit home. Part of him wanted to cry. The other part of him was done. Just done.

Chapter Fifteen

"Thank you for coming, Ms. Queen," Tony said. It went against the grain to greet her while standing behind his desk, forcing his guest to lean in to shake his hand, but it couldn't be helped. It was four o'clock in the afternoon, and his titanium knee was already screaming. He'd been too ambitious with his daily activities, especially while playing with Nicky, and would have to resume icing it the moment the interview was done.

Elodie looked smaller in person than her publicity pictures made her seem. She was also softer, with round cheeks and pouty lips. Edginess was achieved by piercings, green hair, and a charity shop ensemble—a vintage T-shirt, velvet bellbottoms, and a military surplus jacket. All in all, Elodie Queen seemed unimpressed: by him, by Wellegrave House, and by life in general.

"I didn't have anything better to do, if I'm being honest." She spoke with a touch of Mockney—not "the full *oi-oi-oi*," as Kate called it, but just enough "innits" to sound streetwise. Dropping into a chair, she glanced around. "Not very private detective-y."

"What would you suggest?"

"Magnifying glass. Violin. Deerstalker hat." She met his eyes. "Ingrid thinks you're Sherlock. Says you can find out who killed Miranda."

"I'll certainly try. I spent yesterday and most of this morning reviewing the relevant case notes. It made for surprisingly extensive reading, given the lack of conclusions. Thus far, no trends suggest themselves. Give me your perspective. Is Damselfish simply unlucky? Or is a person or persons trying to annihilate you?"

"I don't think Miranda's murder had anything to do with the explosion that killed Will."

"Why not?"

"Because the pinheaded wanker topped himself."

Tony leaned back in his chair. "Why would Wilkinson do such a thing?"

"He was pinheaded. And a wanker."

"Was he also a plonker?"

"What?"

"Never mind. You genuinely respect Dame Ingrid, don't you?"

Elodie looked up from examining her short, black-varnished fingernails. "Why wouldn't I?"

"No reason I can think of. She's not only an eminent victims' advocate. She's an exemplary human being. Therefore," Tony said slowly, "if I were in your shoes, I too might want to present my, shall we say, best self for her examination. In other words, I might choose not to reveal every wretched detail in what must have been a contentious relationship between you and the late Will Wilkinson."

Elodie tried to gaze back uncomprehendingly. She didn't do a very good job.

"There's no use playing innocent. I know what transpired at last year's Spotify awards party. The after-party, to be precise."

She groaned. "How?"

"Let me back up a bit. The fact that you attended Annabelle Carter interested me since it certainly goes against your public image. So, I looked into you slightly, using tools available to private detectives, and found your original name was Charlotte Couch. When you were known as Lottie Couch, you met Sir Malcolm Watson of Piranha Records, married him at age twenty-one, and divorced him at age—"

"Looked into me *slightly!*" Elodie cried.

"I'm afraid murder inquiries can go much deeper, even for the victims. At any rate, I learned that your mother, Helena Couch, sent you to Annabelle Carter in hopes of modeling you into someone who could..." He tailed off, searching for a phrase that wouldn't sound condescending.

"Make nice with the Christian pop gods," Elodie said. "That was Mum's dream for me. To be the Brit version of Nichole Nordeman. But I wasn't up to scratch when it came to the gospel recording world. Did you ring my mum?"

"No, I rang the Los Angeles office of Sir Malcolm Watson. We've met in passing, once or twice, so he seemed the better choice. His assistant told me Sir Malcolm had no comment whatever on Damselfish. When I said I urgently need to speak to Sir Malcolm about the safety of his ex-wife, Lottie, he came on at once and was quite helpful."

"The bastard."

"He cares about you," Tony said. "The marriage may have failed, but he made it clear that he wishes you nothing but success. Why didn't you tell Dame Ingrid about your connection to Sir Malcolm?"

"Because she'd think I was a gold-digger." Elodie glared at him. "Like you do now."

"Stones will not be cast on that topic. Not by me," Tony said, biting back a laugh. In his thirties, Malcolm Watson had risen to prominence as a record executive and entrepreneur, receiving a knighthood for his golden touch. In his fifties, he'd transitioned to global charities, moving to America and operating mainly from his Los Angeles office. In his early sixties, he'd met Lottie Couch at an ultra-posh London holiday do and been instantly smitten. When they'd gone to the altar, he was sixty-two, and she was twenty-one. Two years later, divorce had followed, which Sir Malcolm attributed to a communication problem: she thought everything he said was boring, and he thought everything she said was inane.

"I only wish to point out that your connection to Sir Malcolm is potentially significant information that Dame Ingrid should have received. Many people seem to think he was the person who advised you to give up gospel music and reinvent yourself as a rock singer. If Miranda's killer is behind all the other misfortunes Damselfish has suffered, he might be in danger, too."

"He lives on the West Coast in a gated mansion."

"It's a long shot. But my role is to review the case with fresh eyes, considering all angles. At any rate, Sir Malcolm spoke to me at length about Will Wilkinson. Apparently, Wilkinson was a former protégé early on, but they parted on shaky terms."

"All of Will's relationships ended in bad blood."

"In your case, that brings us back to the Spotify after-party. Sir Malcolm gave me his version of the event, but I'd very much like to hear yours."

"I don't see how it's relevant."

"Wilkinson's dead. You claim he died by suicide. Are you sure your cruel trick didn't factor into his actions?"

"It wasn't just me," Elodie protested. "Miranda and Zoë were right there with me. Some of the label execs, too. It was just a bit of fun. Anyone else would've sucked it up and moved on. But not Will. He tossed other people around like bean bags but expected to be handled like spun glass."

Tony said nothing.

Elodie tried to wait him out but lasted only half a minute. "Fine," she groaned. "Have you seen *Succession*?"

"On telly? An episode or two, I suppose."

"Right. Well, there's a rich old man with one smart daughter and three failsons. You know—golden boys that fail at everything and just keep getting second chances.

"There's this scene," Elodie continued, pink creeping into her cheeks, "where the oldest failson decides to perform a song at his dad's birthday party. A *rap* song. He's, like, a forty-year-old white dude in an LA Raiders jersey and a backward ball cap. And he's not even an amateur rapper. Just a guy who sings in the back of his limo. Will used to do that, too. His driver always looked like he wanted to shoot himself.

"Anyway, in the show, it's not enough for the failson to rap in front of three hundred people. It's a super lame rap he wrote *himself*. And because he's the rich old man's son, nobody can laugh in his face. They have to nod and fake-smile. When it ends, the failson drops the mic—I mean, literally—and bounces out in triumph. He never cottons on to how bad he bombed.

"After I showed the scene to Miranda and Zoë," she continued, "we decided to try it on Will. Of course, the Spotify party planners wouldn't let anyone get onstage and make such a fool of themselves. It had to happen at the after-party, where everyone's pissed and anything goes."

She paused, apparently expecting him to interject. Tony waited silently for her to take up the thread again.

"I don't think I said it, but Will wanted to be a star. He went into the money side of the biz for one reason—he couldn't buy his way into the creative side. Not as a headliner, anyway, and he wanted to start at the top. He was so bloody jealous of us. And we were supposedly his creation.

"Really, it was Malcolm who had the golden touch. He handled the auditions. He selected Zoë and Miranda to perform with me and named us Damselfish. After that, we were turned over to Will. He was good at scheduling appearances and creating buzz, I'll give him that. But the bigger we got, the more he wanted a piece of the audience. *Our* audience. He insisted on traveling with us, supposedly to be more hands-on, but really to convince us he was ready. He used to get up and rap during the soundcheck, and it was pathetic. He wanted us to bring him on for a guest performance, and we wouldn't."

"I wondered why he was on the tour bus in the middle of a performance," Tony said. "He couldn't force you to let him perform?"

"Not without watching us walk. So. The after-party." Elodie's pink flush had gone bright red. "At first, he wanted to cover a song by Biggie, but we convinced him to write and perform his first single. He called it...are you sure you want to hear this?"

"If it damages my sensibilities beyond repair, I won't hold you responsible."

"Fine. He called it, 'Go Down Hoedown.'" When Tony didn't react, she added, "It means—"

"I understand what it means. And I know the reception

to his performance was as bad as you described in the TV program, if not worse. Was the problem only the lyrics? Or his, er, vocal stylings, as it were?"

"Both. The lyrics were something a little boy would write. A nasty little boy, trying to shock his mum. And he performed it wearing velour trackies and a gigantic gold chain with a big, shiny W. Backwards hat. Black shades. Sneakers that cost thirty K. He made *such* a ginormous git out of himself. I almost..." She tailed off.

"You almost felt bad."

She examined her nail varnish again.

"You still feel bad. But in the end—he chose to perform his song his way. If he hadn't done it at the after-party, he probably would've done it at one of your concerts, even if it spawned a walkout and years of litigation."

Elodie's mouth twisted as she fought back tears. Tony waited until she seemed to have won the battle, then continued,

"Sir Malcolm told me the rest. On telly, the character's audience may have suffered in silence, but in real life, there were catcalls and objects flung at the stage. Wilkinson cut his song short, left, and returned in a suit and tie, hoping to play the whole thing off as a gag. But the mood was vicious. People he'd insulted or burned over the years finally got back some of their own."

"It got ugly," Elodie admitted. "Next day, we were all braced to have it out with Will. But he never said a word. Miranda said Will was so vain and so sure he was a born rapper, he'd probably convinced himself it was just a bad audience. Zoë said he seemed normal. But I could feel the difference. He looked distant but determined.

"Eight days later, the bus exploded with him inside. It happened during the one and only time it should have been empty. We were onstage. The driver and our support people were having dinner. Will should've been backstage. But for no reason, he got on the bus, and it blew up." Surreptitiously, she tried to dash away a tear without smudging her eye makeup.

"I'm inclined to agree that suicide is the most logical assumption," Tony said. "But I wouldn't call his public humiliation the only cause, or even the predominant one. He was financially ruined. In the process of losing his Westminster flat. In the middle of a brutal divorce. He may even have been under blackmail threat."

"Ingrid said that. She asked me if I could think of any way it might have been murder, because that would tie it to Miranda's murder," Elodie said. "I told her that Will wasn't clever with gadgets. He would have had to get his hands on dynamite or plastique or whatever and rig it to explode, and I can't imagine him pulling it off."

"I can," Tony cut in with a tight smile. "All he needed was a friend of a friend. I seem to recall that another artist Wilkinson managed, a rapper, was tried in the Old Bailey for ordering a hit on his ex-girlfriend."

Elodie's mouth fell open. "He got off."

"These things are difficult to prove. If he did it and provided Wilkinson with a number to call, and Wilkinson paid the requisite price, professionals would've handled all the details. It's bombastic, I'll grant you, orchestrating one's death via explosion. In my experience, people contracting their own murder generally want two in the head in a public place. It's quick, painless, and bulletproof—if you'll forgive the pun—as far as insurance claim denials go."

She stared at him as if seeing him for the first time. "I thought you used to handle garden parties. Posh stuff."

"That's right. You'd be surprised how creatively vicious

London Blue

the upper crust can be." Leaning back a little more in his chair, Tony said, "Now that we agree that Wilkinson probably killed himself, that begs the question. Who might want to punish Damselfish for purportedly triggering his suicide? And if not that, some other grudge?"

"Punish us for Will? I don't know. But I've been wondering—can't the police zoom and enhance the CCTV pics of the man who killed Miranda? Then compare it to the description of the man who stabbed Zoë?"

Tony resisted the impulse to explain that techniques regularly employed by fictional detectives were often exaggerated or entirely made up. "Please take my word for it: the available information has been thoroughly examined. And we shouldn't assume that the man who attacked Zoë is the same person who kidnapped and killed Miranda.

"Zoë's attacker," he continued, "was what we call a dilettante: someone who thinks they're ready for the big show but fails. Either Mr. Grudge himself, trying to commit his first hands-on murder, or a hired killer on his first go. Miranda's attacker was quite different in plan and execution. Possibly it *was* Mr. Grudge, wiser after his disaster with Zoë. Or perhaps Mr. Grudge fired the dilettante and hired a journeyman killer. One capable of finishing the job. Forgive me," he added more gently, seeing Elodie wince.

"It's all right. I still can't believe she's gone, that's all. So, you coppers have cute little names for every kind of hired killer? If Will didn't top himself—if he was murdered, too—what would you call the person who rigged the bus?"

"A master. No witnesses, no clues, no meaningful remains left to analyze."

"Since the stabbing, Zoë's afraid to show her face in public. She thinks a sniper will gun her down."

Tony said nothing.

"But that's bonkers, innit? Kind of thing that only happens in the cinema."

"I don't want to frighten you, Ms. Queen. But many hits are carried out that way."

"Then my life is over," Elodie cried. "Bad enough we can't tour. I can't even get Zoë to audition replacements for Miranda. So, what? I have two choices. Either go into hiding like Zoë or prance through the streets till my head's blown off? It's not fair! It's not bloody fair!"

"Do *not* throw a tantrum," Tony commanded, holding her gaze. "Do *not* indulge in hysterics. Giving yourself over to emotion will do no good. People gripped by emotion make mistakes that get them killed."

"But I don't—I don't know what to—"

"Listen to me now. I will work as fast as possible. If I find reasonable cause for Scotland Yard to believe your life is in imminent danger, you will receive round-the-clock police protection. But until then, I expect certain things from you.

"First. Dame Ingrid told me you go out with a dog for protection, but that's not good enough. If you don't have a professional security detail, get one. They will coordinate your excursions and make sure you're safe.

"Second. Contact Zoë and discuss every significant person connected to you, her, Damselfish, or Wilkinson who might want to harm you. Mr. Grudge knows your home addresses and habits. Either he obtained them directly from you, or someone in your life is feeding him information. Make a list of everyone who has access to those details and submit it to me as soon as possible. Highlight the names of those you and Zoë think could be Mr. Grudge.

"Third," he said more gently, pleased to see her tantrum

dissolve, "trust me. I'm committed to helping resolve this. And to keeping you and Zoë safe."

"Wait till you try and tell her that."

"I already have. We FaceTimed this morning."

"Really?"

"Really. She's rather fragile at the moment, just as you intimated. But she doesn't want to spend the rest of her life in hiding. She'll help you make that list."

"I do trust you," Elodie said. "But Ingrid warned me, don't hold my breath for a miracle."

"Quite right. I give no guarantees, ever. And yet, either Mr. Grudge or his hired killers have made significant mistakes. The knife attack on Zoë was foolish. Kidnapping Miranda in broad daylight was sloppy. And trying to lure you into the park with a blackmail letter screams amateur. You haven't had any other near-misses you've neglected to mention, have you?"

Elodie thought about it. "The week before Zoë was stabbed, a mugger grabbed me on my way home from a party. It all happened so fast. I was with my Rottie, Patience. I don't go anywhere without her, and all my friends know that if you invite me, you invite her. She erupted at the guy. Bit him, I think. One minute I was being manhandled, and the next, the wanker was running away."

"Dame Ingrid mentioned that. Getting back to the letter: I realize it may seem irrelevant, but let's go down the Annabelle Carter rabbit hole. I understand why you wanted to conceal your history there," Tony said. "A finishing school hardly suits your artistic image. Is it possible that Mr. Grudge is actually Ms. Grudge? That she attended Annabelle Carter around the same time you did?"

"I can't imagine any of those prissy princesses lifting a

finger to kill me. Might break a nail. But Mrs. Maitland-Palmer was murdered, wasn't she?"

Tony sat up straight. "How do you know about that? There's been no formal announcement in the press."

Elodie seemed surprised by his reaction. "There's a grapevine for AC alumni. News of murder travels fast."

"I happen to know her death wasn't officially classified as murder until this morning."

Elodie shrugged. "I only know what I hear. Either somebody killed her and took a finger, or she chopped it off in the kitchen and died of shock."

"That detail, the missing finger, was held back from the public. Who told you?"

"I'm not one to grass."

"Ms. Queen, tell me and be quick about it."

"Right. Sorry. I heard it from Caryn. Lady Caryn Hattersley."

"You don't mean an instructor at Annabelle Carter?"

"Yeah. I know it sounds mental, but she's a new teacher. Only been there six months. Before that, she was a classmate."

"You're close friends?"

"Well, sort of. Caryn was in Knight Club. That's AC's secret society."

Sensing the rabbit hole had forked into a deeper, possibly darker passage, Tony regretfully put off icing his new knee for a bit longer. "I'm listening."

Chapter Sixteen

"Finally! Out of my way. Need a wee. *Now*," Paul said urgently, shouldering past Henry and Ritchie, who'd met him at Wellegrave House's front door.

"That loo's seen better days," Henry called after him. "Remember to jiggle the handle."

"Fine." Hurling himself into the guest bathroom, Paul unwound his Canali cashmere scarf, unbuttoned his Simkhai wool-blend overcoat, and did what he'd needed to do since leaving the Yard an hour ago.

These days, gaining entry to Tony and Kate's London home meant navigating strict security measures. One was obliged to pace outside, grimly tempted to abuse the shrubbery rather than risk a mortifying accident while waiting for someone, usually Henry, to acknowledge a text. Once the gate code arrived, one still had to wait outside the front door —period wood layered over steel—for identity verification via CCTV. Sir Duncan Godington was no more, but his murder-infatuated acolytes, the Fan Club, were still a threat, at least theoretically.

"Thank you," Paul said, emerging to find Kate had

joined her brother and son. "Accept my compliments on the foaming hand soap. Eucalyptus spearmint. The perfect scent." He kissed his fingertips like an exuberant chef. "Now. Henricus Rex. Good to see you. Ritchie, my man. Always a pleasure. Katie-Kate. Why are you still in tights and earrings?"

"Because I walked in five minutes ago."

"You left Embankment an hour before I did."

"I know. Errand." Winking, she removed an earring, one of those sober gold hoops she'd incorporated into her work wardrobe on the advice of Lady Margaret Knolls. Back in the day, he'd liked what he thought of as Classic Kate—frilly suits, pumps, big earrings—but New Kate was a revelation. He saw her now, only her, rather than polka dots or towering high heels.

"I'm famished. When's dinner?" Paul asked. Ritchie cuffed him on the shoulder. "*Ow*. I did say, 'always a pleasure.'"

"Paul." Ritchie cuffed him again.

"He wants a handshake. He's into those lately," Henry said.

Paul obliged. Ritchie grinned, made him do it again, then turned and wandered away.

"He likes you," Kate said. "You hit it off with him from the start."

Paul didn't quite remember it that way, but he appreciated Kate's oblique nudge of support, even if it brought no respite from his fears for Evvy. All he could do now was throw himself into his work and hope against hope that his daughter would catch up to the milestones she'd missed.

"Dinner will probably be another hour," Henry said. Lowering his voice, he added conspiratorially, "The cat is out of the basket."

"Beg pardon?"

"The *cat* is out of the *basket*."

Paul stared at him. Laughing, Kate said softly, "He means Tony's out of his office. Careful he doesn't overhear us chattering about you-know-what."

"Gotcha. I'm gagging for a drink. I don't suppose…"

"C'mon," Kate said, leading him into the modern living room, which wasn't in keeping with a Grade II listed home, but had purportedly been approved by the entities who decided such things. In the corner, Ritchie sat at the table, working on his latest LEGO creation.

"Hen, could you…?" Kate asked.

"All right, Ritch. Time for telly upstairs," Henry said. With patience and a little repetition, he coaxed his uncle out of the room.

"Thanks, Hen! You're the best," Kate, now at the drinks trolley, called after them. To Paul, she added, "He's such a great kid. He looks soft and cuddly, but there's steel in there."

"What's going on with him?"

"He had a hell of a day. Maura's on another bender. The worst since Tony and I got married." Selecting the whiskey decanter, she poured them each a double, using tongs to fish two perfect ice spheres from the bucket and dropping one into each glass.

"Fancy." Paul paused to appreciate the effect before taking a sip. "At least she can't pester him here. You'd need a tank to get past the gate."

"Remember what I told you about him unlocking his phone?"

Paul, who may or may not have answered some questions about basic unlocking procedures, gazed back innocently. Yes, he was a father now, but he was still a fun uncle, and fun uncles are silent as the grave.

"I wanted to bust him right away," Kate continued, sinking onto the sofa, "but Tony said he'd only use his last Pax Wakefield." She referred to a Wakefield family tradition, in which each family member got three metaphorical pax, or "get out of jail free" cards to end rows. When the Pax was invoked, the incident stopped—no punishment, no further discussion, no grudges.

"Besides, even though he can use his mobile however he wants, the nanny spyware still reports on everything he does. Every text, every website, every purchase."

"Really?" Paul concealed his dismay. Fun uncles occasionally failed in their missions.

"So, we've been watching, and really, he's very responsible. Maybe a few Google searches that were out of bounds. You know what Tony said about that? Boys will be boys. He actually said that to me." She laughed. "Then, Maura started up again, and she was sending him awful texts before long. We told him to block her. He just carried on as if it wasn't happening. No crying to me and Tony, no acting out. When trying to reason with her didn't work, he finally did block her. How do you think she reacted?"

"Ambushed him at the fencing club, probably."

"Worse. Highgate."

"His new school?" Paul sat up straight. "How? That place is meant to be secure. Some of the pupils are kidnap risks."

"Henry's a kidnap risk, strictly speaking. Anyway, Maura made an absolute and utter arse of herself. Police were called."

Paul sighed. "That's too bad. He was so keen on making a clean start of it."

"Oh, he totally played it off. Made Maura out to be a nutter who used to clean our house. And he finished out his school day with his head held high, thank you very much. Is he resilient or what?"

"Too right. Where's M now?"

"Banged up for trespass, obstruction, and assault," said Tony, entering the living room on his crutch. He'd traded his suit coat for a jumper, which meant his office was closed for the evening. Pleased to see his old guv looking as fit as ever, Paul decided to take the mickey.

"*Chief.* You poor, poor man. Let me help you." He hurried over like a boy scout bent on intercepting a pensioner about to dodder into traffic. "Come, now, love, give me your arm. Gently does it..."

"Take your hands off me." Tony waved his crutch menacingly. "I'll put you in Casualty and call it self-defense."

"Oh, Katie, he doesn't recognize me. Heartbreaking when the mind goes. Chief, I'm Paul. *Paaaaul.* We worked together a long, long, *long* time a—"

The crutch's rubber-tipped end poked him hard. Laughing, he retreated. "In all seriousness, Chief, it's good to see you without the Zimmer frame. It made you look like Father Time."

"Paul," Kate muttered.

He pretended not to hear. He'd sensed without being told—and certainly, Tony would never say it aloud—that dependence on the Zimmer frame had made him feel hideously enfeebled, to the point where he'd risked injury to escape it. When a policeman senses unhealthy vanity in a brother officer, he is bound by the code of the thin blue line to mock that vanity in the most obnoxious way possible. With any luck, it soon melts away, destroyed by ridicule.

"I concede my age." Tony thumped his way to the drinks trolley. "I concede my temporary limitations. But I invite you," he continued, mixing himself a G&T, "to note the brass clock on the mantel and the rather nice Turkish rug beneath your feet. A crack on the temple, a quick roll-up in the rug, and you won't be found until the year 3000, when someone unearths you under a car park."

"That's me told. You'd make a ruthless crime lord."

"I know. So, tell me, how goes the Maitland-Palmer case?" Tony settled in the wingback chair by the fireplace. "Acknowledging up front that you can't tell me, and I didn't ask."

"We're still waiting on a day when Patrick Bruce will sit down for an interview," Kate said. "He takes the phrase 'at your convenience' quite literally. As for Lady Bothurst, she refused to set a date without consulting her brief."

"Do you like either one of them for your killer?" Tony asked.

"Not as the hands-on perp," Kate said. "But Sean Kincaid finished compiling his list of men CMP filmed, and Patrick Bruce wasn't one of them. But just because the cleaner gave us the films doesn't mean she gave us *all* the films. She might have nicked a couple, or Cathleen might have had a second hiding place."

"If she had a big fish like Patrick Bruce, keeping the master somewhere outside of her house makes sense," Paul said.

"And we know something was stolen from Cathleen's office. If not a film," Kate said, "maybe a key or a lockbox code. If, just as an example, Patrick Bruce hired someone to get rid of his Cathleen problem, he wouldn't consider the job done until he got the film back."

"Lady Bothurst had a Cathleen problem, too," Paul

said. "At one point, she appreciated her enough to give her a bespoke London blue ring. But by the end, she wasn't even on the school payroll anymore. Apparently, the only thing that saved CMP from the sack was the embarrassment it might cause Annabelle Carter."

"No nefarious boyfriend lurking about?" Tony asked.

"We heard CMP was planning to marry a businessman from Australia. A man she met over the internet," Kate said archly, "and knew exclusively over Zoom. Once his finances were healthy, she planned to emigrate to Sydney and live with him in a house overlooking the sea."

"Does this man exist?" Tony asked.

"It's iffy," Paul said. "And it's interesting that CMP's daughter, Marilyn, failed to tell us about the engagement. Then again, her background check came through late this evening, and it seems like she has a strange relationship with the truth.

"Oh! I knew it," Kate said. "What did Marilyn lie to us about?"

"A lot." Consulting his leatherbound notebook, Paul said, "When discussing how she learned about her mum's death, she said the cleaner woke her around half-seven, and she rushed over by tube. An odd choice, given that she owns a car. Today, her neighbor rang the tipline to say they'd seen it parked on Bulwer Street around half-eleven last Thursday night. He was out walking the dog and recognized the car as hers. She'd parked rather far away from her mum's place, but he still recognized it."

"Beyond a doubt?"

"It has a bumper sticker that says, 'Tell your cat I said *pspsps*,'" Paul said. "Anyway, that testimony puts Marilyn in the vicinity of her mum's townhouse around the time of the murder."

"What else?" Kate asked.

"She said if we checked her browser history, we'd find she was looking for cheaper homes in London," Paul replied. "Maybe that's true, but a credit check says she bid on a new-build in St. John's Wood last week. Someone else got it, but not because she was turned down. She met the requirements."

"She didn't strike me as well-off, but I guess you never know," Kate said. "Anything else?"

"Remember how she called me a Paki and then walked it back? Said her ex-husband was a man of color? Turns out, she's never been married."

"I would ask, why lie about that?" Kate said, kicking off her shoes and playfully touching her husband's leg with a stockinged toe. "But people lie about all sorts of things. Maybe she's just a liar. What about the cleaner? Daciana? Did Europol come back with anything of interest?"

"Not yet," Paul admitted. "One caution for solicitation in Paris. Otherwise, she's clean. But her father, Rasvan, isn't. He got into some tight spots in Romania. Twice tried for accessory to murder, twice acquitted."

"Good to know. As for Marilyn, somebody needs to call her out on her lies. Feel like tackling that tomorrow?"

"Sure. Just me?" Paul asked.

"Yeah. I'll be taking a page from Maura's book and ambushing Lady Bothurst. A little bird told me she'll be at Tower Hill for a charity board do at St. Ethelburga's Center."

"There's no saint called Ethelburga."

"Look it up."

"I suppose you want me to interrogate Neera Nausherwani, too?"

"What does DEFRA have to do with this?" Tony asked.

"Paul's friend at DEFRA is a former pupil of Annabelle Carter's," Kate said.

"Not my friend."

"Is she the one who called in the Toff Squad before the body was cold?" Tony asked.

"Yeah."

"Paul. Has she been leaning on you to do things you shouldn't?" Tony didn't sound judgmental. He knew the pressures exerted on the Toff Squad better than anyone.

"Not yet."

"What's her link to the case?"

"She's an active supporter of the school," Paul said. "Friends with all sorts of high and mighty types she met through Annabelle Carter. That's why the school exists—to help young women make the right sort of connections. She and Marilyn are friendly because they were in the same year. Marilyn called her to give her a heads-up about her mum because Neera's office has had some bad press lately."

"Or that's another lie, and Marilyn had some other reason," Kate said.

"Right. For whatever reason, Neera decided the whole thing needed to be handled discreetly."

As Kate sipped her drink and occasionally ran her foot along Tony's leg, Paul described the rest of their day: the interview with Mrs. Dankworth, the janitor accused of being a thief, Neera's surprise appearance at the school, and Cathleen Maitland-Palmer's cache of old love letters.

"You forgot to mention Lady Caryn," Kate said.

"Now there's a name I recognize," Tony said.

"Good God, you know everyone."

"Not quite everyone. And I didn't say we'd been introduced, I said I recognized her name. The client Dame Ingrid brought me is also an alumna of Annabelle Carter.

Today, she sat in my office and blithely recited privileged details about your victim. When I demanded to know where she'd got them, she said, Lady Caryn."

"In that case, I think you should add Lady Caryn to tomorrow's agenda," Kate told Paul. "Assuming you don't end up hauling Marilyn into HQ for formal questioning."

"I suppose the two of you already know about Knight Club," Tony said in the casual tone he often used when dropping a bombshell.

Paul and Kate swapped glances.

"Is the first rule of Knight Club, you do not talk about Knight Club?"

"Precisely. It's Annabelle Carter's secret society. Young women who belonged to it keep in touch indefinitely and see themselves as connected, even if they weren't contemporaries. The club's been around for twenty-five years."

"What do they do in it? Learn how to meet and marry a knight?" Kate asked.

"According to Elodie, they simply spelled 'night' with a K so if they were caught, they could claim they were brainstorming how to meet unmarried aristocrats," Tony said. "Oh, one other detail. The club's founder was Marilyn Maitland-Palmer."

"You realize you could at least speak dramatically when you announce these things," Paul said.

"Yes, but it wouldn't be as much fun. Anyway, Marilyn seems to be a bit of a legend inside the Knight Club. Its year-one purpose was for her to tutor her friends in digital trading."

"Why?"

"Because it was new and intimidating back then," Tony said. "Most people were uncomfortable with online trading, and thus at the mercy of their brokers. Marilyn taught the other girls to trade manually and avoid the fees."

"So, Knight Club is all about learning to take control of your finances?" Kate asked.

"Among other things. Elodie told me the students trade competencies. She learned the basics of contract law from a student whose father is a barrister. In turn, she tutored a student on ghostwriting song lyrics. Successful acts who are creatively challenged will pay a great deal for songs they can call their own."

"I wonder if Marilyn's still involved," Paul said.

"Elodie used to email her with financial questions. She considers Marilyn a sort of long-distance mentor."

"Well. To enterprising young women." Paul lifted his glass and knocked back the rest of his whiskey. "Shall we dive into the shocking *Secret Life of Lexie Lex*?"

Kate set down her drink, suddenly all business. "Now, before Harvey calls us for dinner? Absolutely."

She pulled up the video, which had over two million views and more than five hundred comments, on her laptop, positioning it so they could all see. Noting the run time, Paul said, "Brace yourself, Chief. It's fourteen minutes long."

"I'll try to endure."

Kate hit play. A blonde girl with a bob and a posh Sloane accent waved manically at the camera.

"Hey, guys. It's me, Lexie Lex, back again despite the haters. The wicked witch sent her flying monkeys after me, but this video is up again because *truth is its own defense.*

"Now, before I roll the video that some of you need to see before you do something mental, like let your parents pack you off to AC, here's some context. No, I'm not suing. No, I don't have a personal beef with the Honorable You-

Know-Who or any teacher except..." Lexie Lex tailed off meaningfully, batting her eyes. "The other You-Know-Who. The pensioner we hate to mention, Cathleen Maitland-Palmer."

She began reading a short disclaimer that simultaneously scrolled across the bottom of the screen.

"I, Alexa Alexandretta Hicks-Bowen, when a minor, did *accidentally* turn on my mobile during class at Annabelle Carter and *inadvertently* record part of a lecture by Mrs. Maitland-Palmer. Whilst still a minor, I uploaded it to this channel in the spirit of sharing my school experience. I make no accusations and ask no compensation. This channel is not monetized. Your experience at the school, which declined to formally respond to this video, may be different than mine."

A smash cut showed Homer Simpson drooling in his sleep, signifying how dull the legalese was. Then Lexie Lex reappeared, eyes snapping with glee. "All right, ladies, here it is!"

To Paul's eyes, the clandestine video appeared digitally optimized to improve lighting and sound, but it was still very much what it was: a secret recording filmed at a weird angle. Occasionally, the mobile shifted, briefly showing Cathleen at the podium. The rest of the time, she was either a torso or a pair of elegant legs. Still, her saccharine-sweet voice came through, crisp and clear.

"Are we Annabelle Carter ladies? Yes, we are. And what is it that Annabelle Carter ladies never do?"

Silence from the class, apart from some shifting feet.

"Annabelle Carter ladies never reveal their sell-by date."

Fourteen minutes, Paul thought. *Of retrograde nonsense at best, and a motive for murder at worst.*

Chapter Seventeen

"One's years on this earth are like battle scars," said Cathleen Maitland-Palmer, heels clacking softly as she drifted from one side of the classroom to the other. "I'm surprised that none of you are nodding. Some of you even appear uninterested. Perhaps you don't believe the day will ever come when a two-digit number will become your greatest detriment?

"Let's start by acknowledging an essential truth. Every young lady experiences a day of perfect freshness. She peaks, if you will. On that day, her face has no lines. Her hair is healthy and free of grays. Her skin glows. Her summit of desirability is reached. At what age does each young lady typically reach this pinnacle, do you think?"

The audience was still silent, apart from the shifting.

"When I ask the class a question," Cathleen said, the saccharine suddenly turning bitter, "I expect an answer."

"Twenty-one?" someone ventured.

"Twenty-one. Well, class, do we agree? You there, you may speak. What is your name?"

"Freya. My guess is nineteen."

"Nineteen. How old are you, Freya?"

"Eighteen."

Stifled giggles. Even Cathleen looked amused. "I don't blame you for wanting to believe the best is yet to come. But I'm sorry to tell you, one's day of peak desirability happens around age fourteen."

Voice distorted by its proximity to her device, Lexie Lex asked, "Are you saying girls are sexiest when they're still children? Because that's disgusting."

"Your name?"

"Lexie."

"Your Christian name?"

"Alexa."

"Well, Alexa, neither the natural world nor Western society gives a fig for your scandalized feelings. Fourteen is the year, whether you choose to believe it or not. Let me give you proof.

"In 1963, fourteen-year-old Jennifer O'Neill became the print and television face of CoverGirl cosmetics. In 1987, eleven-year-old Milla Jovovich was selected by Revlon as one of the 'Most Unforgettable Women of the World.' Why do you imagine billion-pound corporations choose such young ladies?" The video angle shifted from the floating torso to Cathleen's face, which wore a grimly triumphant expression. "Because men expect it. Women expect it. Our primal, animal natures expect it. And Mother Nature doesn't care what's politically correct according to this year's so-called wisdom."

"But if we've already peaked, why are we here?" someone asked. "What's all this in aid of?"

"Good question. I'm pleased to tell you that this course, Femininity for Our Time, is about regaining and maintaining a strategic advantage," Cathleen said. "Previous generations had it easier. The problem with Juliet's romance wasn't that she was thirteen years old. It was that she formed an attachment to an unacceptable young man. Had her life gone as planned, she would have been comfortably married, respected, and no doubt awaiting her second or third child at... well, at your ages, more or less.

"Oh, look at all these tragic faces." Cathleen smirked at the class. "Chin up, ladies. I will teach you stratagems, shortcuts, and best practices. Make no mistake about it. I want to help you achieve your destiny: meeting and marrying the right man. Not only that, but keeping him interested over the years.

"We can't all be beautiful, but we can all work to be striking. Stylish. Fascinating. And we can't be forever young, but we can strive for agelessness. Whilst at the same time, maintaining the goodwill of your husband's social set and endearing yourself to his family."

The video smash-cut to Lexie Lex, who goggled at her viewers.

"Can you *believe* the nerve of that witch? She married a butler! An executive butler, but still. Back of the house," she cried. "My mum would *die*. Keep him interested? They're divorced! Have two or three kiddies by age twenty? She popped out one in her thirties and waved the white flag. As for *agelessness*..." The girl cringed exaggeratedly. "She's the bloody Crypt Keeper!

"Anyway, guys," Lexie continued, "I edited out a stretch where you can barely see or hear her. But I got clear video of the last ten minutes, so strap in."

The hidden camera footage resumed with Cathleen asking, "Who here is pleased with their appearance today? Which one of you is the total package?"

"My goodness. Look at all those hands," Cathleen

clucked. "Well. Confidence is an admirable trait. But it must be earned. And if I'm being honest, I can instantly divide you into winners and losers at a glance."

Smash-cut back to Lexie Lex, who told the camera, "By that point, most of us had given up. We were just decomposing in our chairs, waiting for it to end. But one of us couldn't take it anymore. She answered back—and then it all kicked off. I pixelated her face to protect the innocent." The video resumed.

"You. Up." Cathleen gestured imperiously at a student in the front row. "Stand beside me. Chin up. Now, class. Compare and contrast our attire, please."

Slightly muffled voices came from all sides:

"She's wearing jeans."

"Your clothes look more posh, Miss."

"Her crop top shows her belly ring."

"You're feminine, Miss."

Cathleen pounced on that answer. "Exactly right. My femininity is my armor. My calling card. My identity. One sees me and instantly sees a lady, equal to any occasion, from dinner with Sir Richard Branson to tea with His Majesty the King. She"—Cathleen pointed at the student beside her—"is dressed for quiz night down the pub. The sort of place where scrubbers go to get a man, and possibly a disease."

"You have no right," the pupil cried. "I'm feminine."

"You're female. Not feminine. And the difference between those words is the difference between a country house in Hampshire and a shared flat in Putney."

"But why aren't I feminine?"

"Your hair is too short. Your makeup is garish. As for that midriff-bearing top with some kind of slogan written across it... you might as well wear a sandwich board that reads, 'Get It Here.'"

"It's Balmain, for God's sake. My mum paid two thousand pounds for it."

"Then I pity your mum. It's hideous. As is that piercing."

"It's a *diamond*."

"Oh, dear. Think about it. When it's a fat tummy, does it matter which stone is poking out?"

The pixelated student ran out of the room. Cathleen called after her, "If you hurry, you can get to Wetherspoon's whilst the builders are still lunching. One might like what you have on offer."

Lexie Lex returned, looking as serious as a young woman hosting a revenge video can look.

"There you have it. If you've seen one lecture by Cathleen Maitland-Palmer, you've seen them all. Annabelle Carter is a Stepford bride factory. It has one message: all women are in competition, and it's kill or be killed out there.

"So, you might ask, did I actually learn anything at AC? Hmm, let's see. AC taught me how to eat a wedge salad without making a spectacle of myself. How to dance the foxtrot. And, oh yes, how to sew a button. Woo-hoo. But it wasn't all bad. My friends in the *secret society*"—flashing lights and dramatic music—"showed me how to acquire international real estate. I took my first trust disbursement and bought a hotel in Da Nang. All it needs is a flip, and I'll sell it for three times what I paid for it. So, did I exit Annabelle Carter better prepared for the world? Yes. Special thanks to M. She knows who she is, and she's awesome. Lexie Lex out."

Kate closed the laptop. "So. Marilyn Maitland-Palmer is

a known liar. But she also seems to have helped a lot of young women by founding that club."

Paul flipped through his notebook. "In her interview, Marilyn referenced Lexie Lex obliquely. She said she didn't feel especially sorry for her. And she didn't think a former student could have killed her mum before they're all sheep, and you don't hear of sheep attacks."

Tony chuckled. "Spoken like someone who's never left the city."

"You have attack sheep at Briarshaw?"

"On rare occasion. An isolated sheep, separated from its flock, will rush a man in sheer desperation."

"Well, I don't like Lexie Lex as the murderer," Kate said. "She got her revenge by posting the video. All her frustrations were worked out in public."

"She gave her surname as Hicks-Bowen," Tony said. "If memory serves..."

"It always does," Kate stage-whispered to Paul.

"One of you should google Archie Hicks-Bowen."

"Sure, Chief." Paul obliged, whistling at the wealth of hits. "Bullseye. Archie Hicks-Bowen has been in the news a lot lately. When the press started barbecuing Patrick Bruce for buying an earldom, it came out that Archie Hicks-Bowen was the MP who accidentally circulated the price schedule in an email. He's also—huh." Paul stared at his mobile. "This is quite a coincidence."

"We don't believe in them," Kate said.

"But this case may necessitate a change in opinion," Tony said.

"Well, either something's up, or this case will make you a believer. Archie Hicks-Bowen works for DEFRA. He's the Minister of State—second only to Neera."

London Blue

* * *

When Paul unlocked the door to his flat at half-eleven, he expected darkness. Now that Evvy was sleeping through the night, Emmeline positively gloried in putting the girl to bed no later than eight P.M. and turning in soon after. Though her plans to return to the office as an estate agent were very much up in the air, she'd resumed her old routine of early to bed, early to rise, hoping she could work part-time in the new year.

Instead of darkness, he found all the front room and kitchen lights burning. The telly was on but muted. Sharada Bhar sat behind her laptop, balanced on an ancient TV tray she'd brought from home. She was in full author mode: reading specs halfway down her nose, fizzy drink close to hand, baby monitor beside the soda can. The way she scowled at the screen meant she'd hit a rough patch.

"Mum. Why didn't you text me? I would've cut dinner short if I'd known you were babysitting."

She silenced him with a raised index finger. That meant the word she wanted was "right on the tip of my brain," as she said, and any nattering from him would cause her to lose it.

Accepting the rebuke, Paul unwound his scarf, shrugged out of his coat, and hung them both on pegs near the door. The flat was so small, and the furniture Emmeline had contributed was so large, that he always felt slightly claustrophobic in their living room. Finding a home in London that was both affordable and comfortably sized was as difficult as finding an honest mechanic.

Except honest mechanics exist, Paul thought. Emmeline's connections had already found them properties in Bexley and Hounslow, but either choice would mean (1)

187

moving houses and (2) quadrupling his commute time. *I'd rather make peace with the fear of tight spaces.*

Sharada, her sentence apparently completed, said, "I didn't text you because I didn't need you. I wanted time alone to write. Buck's sleeping over at home, and you know how he snores. Like Kahlil Gibran said: 'Let there be spaces in your togetherness.' I need spaces. I need Buck to go back to Texas. If he's not out by tomorrow, I'm calling the locksmith."

"Yippee-ki-yay." Paul restrained himself from asking precisely how much of an arse Buck had made of himself this time. Maura Wakefield wasn't the only one wrestling with the bottle. Buck Wainwright, the six-foot-five rancher with whom Sharada had an on-again, off-again relationship, could be a standup guy. On good days, he doted on Sharada and called her "little lady" in a corny but sincere tone. His mum's surname would already be Wainwright if not for one thing: Buck couldn't stay dry for more than a few months at a time. Even being briefly jailed for a murder he didn't commit hadn't shocked him into long-term sobriety.

Hoping his mum would resume writing and let him unwind with a bit of telly, Paul dropped onto the sofa and picked up the remote. Surely *Hell's Kitchen* was on somewhere...

"My son," Sharada began.

He groaned.

"Why do you always assume you won't like what I have to say?"

"History. Evidence. Deduction." He passed a hand over his face. "Can't you see I'm cream-crackered?"

"I'll put cream in your cracker. With all I do for you, you should thank me from the bottom of your heart. You should—"

"Thanks, Mum. Thanks for everything. Comprehensively. From my birth up to this moment."

"You should thank me with sincerity. Today, I compiled a list of developmental pediatric specialists. You and Emmeline must pick one and make an appointment. Heaven only knows how long it will take to get in. Early diagnosis, Deepal. Early intervention."

"Autism intervention starts around age two."

"You don't know it's autism. It might be delay. That's the word now. *Delay*. Not the other word."

Paul groaned again.

"I know why you resist," Sharada went on, undeterred. "You're afraid that if you get her checked, the problem will become real."

"We just got her eyes checked."

"You need to check her brain. Neural connections are most plastic between birth and three years."

"She's seven months." Paul shot his mother a pleading look. Tomorrow, he had to re-interview Marilyn and, if possible, get Lady Caryn on the record. He didn't need to be up all night, simmering in his own juices.

"Deepal. How many months might it take for the specialist to see Evvy?"

She had a point. Still, the idea of taking such an irrevocable step made his stomach drop.

"Maybe she's just a quiet baby. Maybe we've given her all the wrong toys. She likes to play with shiny things. She's always reaching for Em's necklace. Even when Em puts it in a pocket or under her shirt, Evvy tries to pull it out."

"I worry about her appetite, too," Sharada went on. "She won't eat her veg."

"Oh, come on. Did I eat mine?"

"You ate everything. Veg. Grass. Paste."

"She stole a bit of banana out of my cereal this morning. So, she likes fruit."

His mum took off her reading specs. "What?"

"I was eating muesli with cut banana on top. She was doing her thing, turning her face away from what Em was trying to feed her. Then, she reached over and plucked out one of my banana pieces. I reckon they looked like the best thing on offer."

Paul was surprised that Sharada even considered the banana story. He'd brought it up from sheer desperation.

"I wish Evvy would say something," she said at last. "*Ma* or *Ba*."

"Or *Sha?*"

She smiled tiredly. "Especially *Sha.*"

Chapter Eighteen

St. Ethelburga's was a lovely stone building with leaded-glass windows and a wooden door any eighteenth-century parish church would be proud to claim. All around it, glass and steel buildings soared, enhancing the center's rustic front and big, Roman-numeral clock. Kate went to the door and pulled the iron ring, but it was locked. A discreet sign pointed her through an alley with massive, cylindrical steel columns on one side and a crumbling brick wall on the other.

It was half-eleven, and the event inside was already underway. Kate thought the venue looked like a place for wedding dinners and upmarket baby showers. However, its public calendar listed only community-focused events: scholarship banquets, Save the Children fundraisers, and homeless advocate training. The Honorable Griselda Bothurst sat on the Royal Purfleet Cancer Charity board, which met for a mimosa brunch once a year. Judging by the concrete barriers and uniformed security guards, the charity safeguarded its members and their privacy.

"No press," a guard called to Kate conversationally. "No admittance without a ticket."

"MPS," she returned in the same breezy tone. "Scotland Yard. DI Hetheridge."

The guard looked her up and down. Her attire—red sheath, red heels, and little sparkly clutch—apparently didn't scream copper to him, which pleased her. She unsnapped the clutch and showed him her warrant card.

"Yes, ma'am. This way."

It was one of those stand-and-nibble affairs, with little round tables for members to rest their champagne flutes. Almost everyone carried a small glass plate bearing what Kate suspected were outstanding bites: prosciutto-wrapped melon, caviar and blini, *canelé*. The men were partaking heartily. The women sipped their mimosas, plates untouched.

Kate accepted a mimosa, had a sip, and let her gaze rove around the room. The PM for the Cities of London and Westminster was hobnobbing with the Lord Mayor of London himself, who'd forgone his chain of office for the occasion. Nearby was the retired BBC presenter who'd left under a cloud of scandal but come roaring back on ITV. He seemed to be chatting up a society maven Kate knew from somewhere but couldn't place. The power and influence contained in this single room was breathtaking.

And there's Neera Nausherwani, Kate thought, picking out a vision in wine-colored silk. She'd familiarized herself with Archie Hicks-Bowen's face, just in case he made an appearance, but didn't see him. She *did* see Lord Patrick Bruce, looking like a man who'd never heard of a £1 shop, much less got rich off it, talking to a young, green-haired woman who stood out among a crowd whose median age was at least fifty.

That's Damselfish's lead singer, Kate realized. *Elodie Queen. If she's here without her security detail, I'm grassing on her to Tony. Rent-a-cops out front or not, she needs top-shelf protection.*

No sooner did the thought cross her mind than she noticed a tall, bulky man in a dark suit lingering obtrusively a few feet away. He had no glass plate or champagne flute, but he did have an earpiece and a suitably grim expression.

Almost the same grim look was worn by a petite, slender old lady in a black organza gown with ruffled trim. Despite her slow, painful gait, she made the rounds in high heels, exchanging greetings with the great and good. Kate was suddenly reminded of the hostile cat who once lived next door.

What did Tony say? she thought. *"Bony, brittle, and unbowed."*

Handing off her empty flute glass to a server, Kate moved to intercept her prey.

"Excuse me, Lady Bothurst," she said, firmly enough to make the headmistress go rigid. "DI Kate Hetheridge, Scotland Yard. I need to speak with you, please."

Lady Bothurst fixed her with a gimlet eye. "This intrusion is unsupportable."

"This intrusion is necessary. How do you do?" Kate stuck out her hand. When the old lady didn't take it, she added, "I'm Tony Hetheridge's wife. I understand you share many of the same charities."

With evident reluctance, Lady Bothurst touched her hand. There was no shake or air kisses to follow, but Kate wasn't left hanging.

"Right. Now, let's step away from the crowd, shall we? I'm sure we can find some private nook to sit and talk."

"If I haven't made it abundantly clear, I have nothing to say to you."

"Lady Bothurst, one of your instructors, Cathleen Maitland-Palmer, was murdered. I happen to know you'd lost confidence in her over the last year or so. If you don't give me the truth, I'll have to get it from someone else. Probably someone who doesn't have Annabelle Carter's best interests in mind."

Lady Bothurst glared at her, trembling, though with emotion or a touch of palsy, Kate couldn't tell.

"Very well," she said at last. "Follow me."

They made slow progress through the guests, leaving a trail of curious expressions in their wake. Lord Patrick Bruce looked concerned; Elodie Queen watched them go with a curious half-smile. Neera Nausherwani pulled out a mobile and swept off, presumably to make a private call. One or two guests asked Lady Bothurst if she needed help, as if Kate were abducting her at gunpoint.

"Carry on," the old lady ordered them, unimpressed by the show of concern. "I have matters in hand."

As if to prove it, she led Kate past two comfortable-looking but less-than-private seating areas, tottered up to an office belonging to the Director of Public Events, and rapped on the door. When the woman answered, Lady Bothurst civilly but firmly told her to give them the room. To Kate's surprise, the cowed woman scooped up her things and departed, leaving them to talk privately.

"Because I respect your time, I'll get right to it," Kate said when the door was closed. "Please describe your professional relationship with Mrs. Maitland-Palmer."

"I hired her. In the beginning, she was an exemplary instructor. She believed wholeheartedly in Annabelle

Carter's mission. Her personal life was a fine example. I promoted her to deputy headmistress."

"And you gave her the London blue ring as a token of your esteem?"

"Don't be naïve," Lady Bothurst snapped. "Over time, as society changed for the worse, some of my instructors astonished me by suggesting we adulterate the curriculum. Outrageous. Cathleen and Ginny—Virginia Braide, the cookery teacher—were the only two who understood that Annabelle Carter must hold the line. So, I bestowed those rings on them as a warning to the other instructors. Every time they saw that ring on Cathleen or Ginny's finger, they'd remember that they weren't good enough to receive one."

"I've interviewed Mrs. Dankworth," Kate said. "It's hard to imagine her telling you to change with the times."

"Eleanor Dankworth is an able administrator. She has a degree in accounting. I appreciate her contribution and show appreciation by paying her salary. But she comes from nowhere, is married to no one, and marking her out for distinction would have been inappropriate. Ginny Braide may be rather homely, but she comes from good stock. Her great-uncle was PM."

"Getting back to Mrs. Maitland-Palmer. Mrs. Dankworth made it sound like she embarrassed herself by marrying a butler."

"Nonsense. Joseph Palmer was an exceptional butler. How he put up with Cathleen for all those years, I can't say. Probably for Marilyn's sake."

"So, what precisely soured your relationship with Mrs. Maitland-Palmer?"

"After Joseph divorced her, Cathleen was desperate to remarry. She was determined to elevate herself in the process—a ridiculous notion. Men of distinction were amused by her, but that was all. The rumors of her promiscuity even reached our students. I asked her to leave forthwith. But a friend convinced me to rescind the demand."

"Which friend?"

"Marilyn."

"I've interviewed her, too," Kate said. "Don't mistake this for criticism, but the way she talks and dresses seems incompatible with what you stand for."

"My dear DI Hetheridge, you have no idea what I stand for. Marilyn is a lovely woman. She's faced considerable difficulties without complaining. And she's always been a friend to Annabelle Carter."

"What sort of difficulties?" Kate asked.

"In the global financial crisis, she lost everything she'd put by for retirement. This time last year, she was almost bankrupt. She had to leave her townhouse and lodge above her computer repair shop, a humiliation I can scarcely imagine."

"She seems to be doing better these days," Kate said, remembering what Paul had said about Marilyn's real estate bid.

"Naturally. She's been trading in financial markets since age twenty. If not for the big crash, she'd be a multi-millionaire."

"You called her a friend to Annabelle Carter. In the course of our investigation, we discovered that after Marilyn learned of Cathleen's death, she immediately rang a government official called Neera Nausherwani. I saw her just now, exiting the building with her mobile in hand."

"Neera is also a faithful friend of the school."

"Even though she doesn't want anyone to know she attended?"

"Politics is a bloodsport. If she gives her enemies an opening, she'll be destroyed."

Kate had the inexplicable suspicion that something important had gone unsaid. There was an elephant in the room, an invisible one, and she could feel its breath on the back of her neck. Taking a wild stab, she asked,

"Lady Bothurst, do you know what Knight Club is?"

"Naturally."

"What do you understand it to be?"

"A secret society within Annabelle Carter. An open secret, I should say. Over time, it's become one of our greatest assets. An informal way to expose our brightest students to business opportunities without injuring our reputation or forcing us to compete directly with two and four-year institutions. In Knight Club, the right sort of girl can get a crash course in money management without wasting her best years taking a finance degree. And I'm told the club's network extends far beyond finance these days."

Kate said, "Last night, I watched that video from the *Secret Life of Lexie Lex*. In it, she referred to Knight Club as KC and Marilyn as M. Effectively, she's providing free advertising for what you just called a great asset. So—maybe you should drop the lawsuit?"

"What lawsuit?" Lady Bothurst seemed bemused. "Who told you that?"

"I'd have to consult my notes," Kate lied. Marilyn Maitland-Palmer was the person who'd claimed Annabelle Carter was suing Lexie Lex for breach of NDA. Even if the headmistress looked on Knight Club as a good thing, Kate found it hard to believe this achingly correct woman could stomach the video, which showed the school in a highly negative light.

Unless she despised Cathleen so much, Kate thought, *she couldn't resist leaving the video up for all to see.*

"Surely, I've answered all of your questions." The old lady stood up. "I expect you to see yourself out of this private party now that—"

"Sorry," Kate cut across her. "One last thing. In the investigation, we turned up something else: Cathleen was no longer being paid for teaching. Why?"

"I told you she was promiscuous. The first time her behavior embarrassed me, I sacked her, then took her back against my better judgment. The second time, I held firm."

"But why let her keep teaching for free?"

"Annabelle Carter teachers are not unceremoniously given the keys to the street. That would reflect poorly upon me as headmistress. Our instructors retire to marry, or they leave to spend more time with their families. *Always.*"

"Couldn't she have pretended to be doing one of those things?"

"She refused. We found ourselves at an impasse. She demanded severance. I said there'd be none until she returned the ring. In light of her behavior, allowing her to continue wearing it was an insult to the school."

Severance, Kate thought, glad Paul wasn't there. He would've found the obvious joke impossible to resist.

"Lady Bothurst, do you know how Cathleen died?"

"Not precisely. Only that it happened at home."

"Have you been told any other details?"

The old lady looked her steadily in the eye for a beat before saying, "No."

"I hope you'll forgive me for asking this, but I'm afraid I must. Did you, or someone close to you, arrange to have Mrs. Maitland-Palmer's ring cut off?"

"Don't be absurd."

The calm reply sealed Kate's belief that Lady Bothurst, like Neera, Elodie, Lady Caryn, and heaven knew who else, knew all of the murder's salient details.

"Could someone," she persisted, "some intensely loyal person, have done it in the belief it would please you?"

"No."

"Would you care to speculate on why Cathleen was murdered?"

"I suppose someone couldn't bear to have her in the world a moment longer."

"And the ring? What do you think happened to it?"

"I imagine it was swapped for drugs. Death and dismemberment are nothing new to London. I'd expect someone in your line of work to know that."

"Thank you, Lady Bothurst." Kate put out her hand, but with no audience to shame her into good manners this time, the old lady happily left her hanging. Seeming pleased with herself, she tottered away without even a sniff.

"Er...all finished?" The Director for Public Events peeked into her office, looking hopefully at Kate.

"Yes. Thanks, love," Kate said, putting her bag on her shoulder. "Bit of unsolicited advice. Next time someone tries something like that, lock your door and refuse to come out. Bluebloods wouldn't get away with half of what they do if we didn't let them."

As she rejoined the crowd, now on the dance floor swaying to slow music, it occurred to Kate that she might press Lord Poundland into committing to an interview. If she didn't, a perfect opportunity would go up in smoke.

Searching the dancers, most of whom were older couples, she picked out the tall form of Patrick Bruce, leaning over a much shorter partner. As they revolved, she recognized the green-haired figure as Elodie Queen. The proportions were silly, almost like a Daddy-Daughter dance, but the expression on Lord Dellkirk's face was far from paternal. Judging from Elodie's flirtatious smile, she welcomed the attention.

The Lord Mayor departed, taking the grim-looking guard with him. That meant Elodie hadn't brought along her own security detail.

I'll have to tell Tony. Not just about the lack of security, but Lord Dellkirk, too, Kate thought. *Probably has no bearing on his case, but you never know.*

Chapter Nineteen

Paul had offered to meet Marilyn at Cyber Monkeez, but she declined, saying she didn't want her customers distracted. Instead, they met at a Brixton coffee shop called Holy Grounds, where he had a flat white and she ordered a diet fizzy drink.

"These follow-up interviews are quite common," he told her, beginning on a friendly note. "Often, on the first day of an investigation, certain avenues are missed or misunderstood." Opening his notebook to a fresh page, he added, "For example, Cyber Monkeez. When you named it as your place of employment, I didn't realize you owned it."

Marilyn shrugged. She looked marginally more put-together today in a *Doctor Who* T-shirt and black jeans. Her hair was styled neatly, and she wore lipstick. However, the frames of her huge black specs still dominated her face, making every expression seem harsher than it probably was.

"Yeah, I was probably a bit rattled, if I'm being honest," she said, poking a straw in her drink. "I tried to come over all tough as nails. Then, I went home and boo-hooed like a bloody fool. Mum never loved me. But I loved her. And I hated her." She sighed. "Now that she's gone, it hit me: I can stop trying to make her care about me. First, I was giddy. Then I was gutted."

"I understand. But I was surprised to discover that you've never been married, since you specifically mentioned your ex to DI Hetheridge and me."

"Oh, that. Just as well you brought it up, as I need to say sorry. Calling you a Paki was just wrong," Marilyn said. "Not my best day, but it's no excuse. The minute it came out of my mouth, I wanted it back. So, I pulled out the lie I've been telling for twenty years—my ex, the mysterious man of color. The man no one ever met because it was a short marriage, and we kept it on the QT so as not to scandalize my older family members."

"Why have you been lying about an ex-husband for twenty years?"

"To spare my mum's feelings. And Lady Bothurst's. And so on and so forth. Suspecting I date women is one thing. Knowing it, and being forced to admit they know it, is more than they can handle."

"Oh." Paul had anticipated many possible excuses for the lie, but not that one. "Well, I'm afraid there's yet another inconsistency. A more serious one. On the night of your mother's death, you said you were at home, researching affordable flats. But not long ago—"

"—I put in a bid on a cracking new-build that reminded me of my old place. The place I had before the markets went boom," Marilyn interrupted. "It's true. I've been rebuilding my finances, trying to recreate the retirement fund I lost in the crash. I used to scoff at people who didn't have the stomach for high-risk, high-return investments." She shook her head. "I picked the absolute worst time to reach for the brass ring."

"But things are better now?"

"Yep."

"Then why did you say, 'affordable flats'?"

"Another die-hard habit of mine: never let on what I have, or what I know. Let 'em guess."

"Right. Just one last thing," Paul said casually, indulging his inner Columbo. "Why was your car parked near Cathleen's townhouse the night she died? And why did you lie about it?"

"Pull the other one."

"I'm quite serious. You drive a Ford C-MAX with a recognizable bumper sticker. One of your mum's neighbors was walking his dog between half-eleven and twelve that night. He saw your car parked two blocks from Mrs. Maitland-Palmer's home. Not your usual spot, but within easy walking distance."

"Good grief. One of those nosy parkers saw my car and did what? Rang Crimestoppers? Wankers, every last one of them."

"What were you doing there?"

"Not seeing Mum," Marilyn cried, sounding more like the angry woman he remembered from their first interview. "You know what happens to be in Shepherd's Bush besides No. 9 Bulwer Street? Anne Lister's. Heard of it?"

"No. Pub?"

"Private club. Ladies only. Get it? You have to belong to the sapphic sisterhood to enter."

"Oh. Well. That should be easy to verify," Paul said, amazed at how quickly she'd batted aside all his gotchas. "When I ring the manager to check, will your name be on the members list?"

"Of course. Now." Marilyn relaxed a little. "If you want a list of people who'll vouch for me, here are some. Lady

Bothurst has a soft spot. Mrs. Dankworth likes me better than she'll admit. And Caryn—sorry, Lady Caryn, now—used to idolize me. Maybe still does."

"If I run into one of them, I'll be sure to ask," he said, declining to add that he was meeting Lady Caryn at Annabelle Carter later that afternoon. First, however, he'd contact the management at Anne Lister's. Marilyn seemed on the level, but he'd dealt with plenty of smooth types who never broke a sweat. You couldn't always suss out someone by demeanor alone, even after years of practice.

"So, listen, Paul. Can I call you Paul?"

"Please." He finished his coffee, which had grown lukewarm during their talk. Noticing that Marilyn's fizzy drink had become nothing but ice, he added, "If you want another one, or maybe a pastry..."

"I'm fine. But if that's all, I need to get back to the shop. It can get a little wild in the monkey house without me there, cracking the whip."

"I'm afraid I have more questions. Why didn't you tell us about your mum's fiancé?"

"Because he wasn't real. She was tangling with some online scammer. I tried to tell her," Marilyn said, gathering steam. "It was your classic love 'em and bleed 'em scheme. She said I was jealous she'd found real love and wouldn't discuss it with me anymore."

"All the same, we need to rule him out definitively. What was his name?"

"I don't know. We just called him Sydney."

"Right. Next question. At the end of your interview with DI Hetheridge and me, you told us to take a good look around upstairs. What did you mean by that?"

"I meant the geriatric sex dungeon, obviously."

"How did you feel about your mum secretly filming sexual liaisons?"

Marilyn gaped at him. "She filmed herself with her boyfriends?"

"No. She filmed the ones who decided to go up with Daciana Botezatu instead of her."

"I don't believe it."

"You don't think your mum was capable of such a thing?" Paul asked.

"I don't think Dozy Bozo could pull off anything as intellectually taxing as a criminal act. She's a babe in the woods."

"She's the one who provided us with the home movies as evidence," Paul said, still not sure if he trusted Marilyn. She was saying all the right things in all the right ways, but with some quality he couldn't quite put his finger on. Almost—not quite, but almost—pleasure, as if the interview had become unexpectedly entertaining.

"We're going on the assumption that Mrs. Maitland-Palmer was blackmailing former boyfriends," he continued. "And that the tapes we were given might not be the entire collection. Any thoughts on that?"

Marilyn shook her head. "Blackmail. Wow. *Blackmail*. Hope Mum watched her step. If not..." She tailed off ominously.

"You think one of them might have taken revenge privately? As opposed to going to the police?"

She pursed her lips and said nothing.

"You singled out Patrick Bruce—Lord Dellkirk—in our first interview."

She groaned.

"Come on, Marilyn. Hints aren't enough for me to work with."

"Patrick Bruce is powerful. He could sue me into nonexistence without lifting a finger. Hell, truth be told, he could probably have me done away with if he really wanted to."

"Keep going." Paul's pen was poised to write.

"Ever wonder how Mum knew Patrick Bruce?"

"I assumed through Annabelle Carter."

"That, too, but the truth is, Mum was his Mrs. Robinson, if you know what I mean. When he was wet behind the ears and fresh out of uni, she took him in hand and made a man out of him." Marilyn sounded disgusted. "The kind of thing I'd rather not know, but Mum loved to brag."

"And the relationship continued?" Paul asked.

"On and off. Anyway, I mentioned she had a pacemaker, didn't I? When I explained why smoking was *verboten* in her house?"

He nodded, thrown by the verbal detour.

"Last year, Lord Dellkirk bought a medical supply company from one of his rivals. He liquidated it for the most part, but he kept the rare element magnet lab. Those magnets have uses beyond hospital MRIs. Military applications. Big government contracts."

Paul closed his notebook. He wasn't going to forget what she said next, and if it were as meaningful as he thought it might be, she'd be repeating it into a voice recorder at HQ.

"He had some kind of open house at the factory for his kind of people," Marilyn continued. "Masters of the universe people. He invited Mum, too. She was physically on the premises before she saw all the signs with the dire pacemaker warnings. So, she turned around, went home, and read him the riot act for not thinking to warn her. If she'd missed the signs, her pacemaker might have gone on the fritz."

"So, what are you telling me? That maybe your mum visited the factory later, despite the danger?" Paul asked. He knew perfectly well that she meant something else, but she needed to state it clearly, without prompting.

"She wouldn't have done that. It had to be an accidental exposure. I don't know how it could've happened... Maybe if he came to her place with one of those special magnets in his pocket or briefcase? Or a dusting of shop particulate on his hands? I don't know. But Mum died peacefully, so somebody ought to check her pacemaker." Suddenly angry, she added, "I haven't seen anything about him being questioned by police. You haven't even asked if he took Mum home that night, have you?"

"Voluntary interviews can take time to arrange."

"Especially when the interviewee can buy and sell Scotland Yard. I should've known," Marilyn sighed. "I really should've known."

***

"DC Baker's already looking into places that sell high-powered magnets," said Kate, who'd answered Paul's call on the first ring. She was at Wellegrave House, changing into her work clothes; Paul was sitting in one of Brixton's micro parks, eating his lunch. "I'll tell her to concentrate on Patrick Bruce's company. What's it called?"

"Massive Attraction."

"Sounds like a nightclub. I'm on it."

"Excited?"

"Can't help it. A magnet as a murder weapon. That's a new one for me."

"Marilyn never used the word murder. She was careful to theorize that if one of Lord Dellkirk's magnets killed CMP, it was probably accidental."

"Whatever. I don't know what to make of her after all the porky pies she reeled off in her first interview," Kate said. "I'm glad she came clean to you, assuming she really did come clean to you, but all those lies put her on the naughty step. And she'll stay on that step until she gives us something useful. Now—ask me what I learned from Lady Bothurst."

"Please tell me she's guilty as sin. It would be the pinnacle of my career—make that my life—to toss someone like her in the nick."

"Sorry to disappoint. She's inscrutable and still a bit of a question mark. I don't think it's impossible that she hired someone to kill Cathleen and get that ring back. She definitely thought Cathleen's public behavior tarnished the school."

"What if one of her teachers did it for her without being asked, to curry favor?"

"Could be. Ask me what else I accomplished at St. Ethelburga's."

"Persuaded them to change the name?"

"I leaned on Lord Dellkirk for an interview, and we fixed a date. Noon tomorrow at Cottlestone Manor, just you and me. He got shirty about what he called 'entourages.' Seemed to think we'd bring along a crowd of junior officers and uniformed coppers with a reporter or two hidden in the mix."

"Paranoid type?"

"Just angry, I reckon. Probably thought getting the earldom would be an end to all his problems."

"I assume you saved the question of blackmail for the one-on-one?"

"Yeah. By the way, I'd call Lord Dellkirk a man of wide-ranging tastes when it comes to the ladies. On the one hand, Cathleen Maitland-Palmer, reminding him of his uni days, and on the other, Elodie Queen, reminding him of—well, his uni days, but in a different way."

"That's the Damselfish singer, right? Tony's case?"

Kate made an affirmative noise.

"So we're back to coincidences."

Another affirmative noise.

"What did the chief say when you told him?"

Kate imitated her husband's interrogative rumble.

"You do that better than I ever could," Paul chuckled. "We're the perfect team. No words, only grunts."

Kate made an affirmative noise and rang off.

* * *

At Lady Caryn Hattersley's request, Paul met her at Annabelle Carter around four o'clock, when classes were over and the students were off on a cultural enrichment tour of the Victoria and Albert Museum.

"It's a last-minute change, and they weren't best pleased," she said, meeting him at the conservatory door. "It was supposed to be a day trip to Cottlestone Manor for the debutante ball dry run. But Lord Dellkirk sent us his regrets. Now, we're left scrambling for a venue with a grand staircase. We might have to forgo the whole thing."

Paul nodded along with this opening volley of information, struggling to contextualize it. He was accustomed to interviews where getting a simple answer was like pulling teeth. But Lady Caryn seemed genuinely pleased to see him and willing, at least at first blush, to talk about anything.

"Sorry if I come off a bit thick," he said. "My mum writes historical romance novels, so what little I know is from her books. But didn't the presentation of debutantes end in the Fifties?"

"Queen Elizabeth II ended the royal presentation in 1958," Lady Caryn agreed, leading him into the school proper. "But there are still private balls. The big one is Queen Charlotte's Ball, which is limited to one hundred and fifty girls. It's not an open invitation. Every girl has to apply for the privilege of attending. Those who don't make the cut will try a second-tier debutante ball like *Le Bal des Roses* in Paris. That's also for daughters of the very rich or very famous, but not as exclusive.

"Our pupils must set their sights a bit lower," she continued, starting down dim, steep stairs. "This year, Lady Bothurst arranged for our graduating debs to dance with their chevaliers"—she giggled—"yes, I know it's terribly silly, but the dance was meant to be at Cottlestone Manor. Then, Lord Poundland—oops, Lord Dellkirk—decided he needed to spend that particular weekend lowering prices, or some such. Do I sound bitter?"

They had arrived in a short corridor that led to two rooms. One, with deep porcelain sinks and steel hose sprayers, was a scullery not unlike the one at Wellegrave House. The other was a big white kitchen, garish under fluorescent lights. A wooden table laden with baked goods awaited them, as did a large, red-faced woman in stained chef's whites.

"Mrs. Virginia Braide is our cookery teacher and the rock that holds this place together," Lady Caryn announced. "Ginny, this is DI Bhar. DI Bhar, this is Ginny Braide."

"Hello," Ginny said without expression. Her small eyes were wary.

"Don't bowl us over with enthusiasm," Lady Caryn said. To Paul, she added, "When I was a student, my favorite class was cookery because Mrs. Braide didn't play mind games or try and tear us down."

"I think you'll find I've torn down many an egotistical girl in my time," Ginny sniffed. "I certainly had plenty to say about this benighted buffet." She indicated the plates and baskets loaded with fresh-baked treats, which all looked and smelled perfect to Paul.

"You have high standards," he told her, hoping a wistful note in his voice might prompt an invitation to tuck in.

"Of course. This is Annabelle Carter. Which I'm sure you'll remember," she added, touching Lady Caryn's arm. "Well. Must dash. Don't worry about shutting off the lights when you're done talking to the detective."

"What about all this food?"

"Leave it. I told the new janitor he can pack up as much as he likes. I have a feeling there are underfed little ones at home who won't mind soggy *pâte à choux* or underfilled éclairs. Good night," Ginny said, not looking behind her, and left.

"Oh, well. So much for my cunning plan to make Ginny talk to you," Lady Caryn said.

"You think she might have information pertinent to the case?"

Lady Caryn shrugged. Even in her silk wrap dress, court shoes, and hat, an ensemble more appropriate for a ribbon cutting than a workday, her easy informality put him entirely at ease.

"Ginny probably knows more about everything that goes on here than anyone, including Dankworth. Sorry—Mrs. Dankworth. At school, the nicest thing we called her was plain old Dankworth."

"And you think some incident at Annabelle Carter will help solve Mrs. Maitland-Palmer's murder?"

Playfully, she shook a finger at him. "Maneuvering me, are you? I didn't plan on doing a swan dive right into the deep end, but yes, there might be some facts you need to know."

"Let's sit." Paul pulled out a chair for her. "Mind if I drive?"

"Of course not. This is exciting. I've never been interrogated before."

"Consider it a friendly conversation. I'd like to begin with something a former student, Elodie Queen, said to one of my colleagues. Ms. Queen freely revealed confidential information about Mrs. Maitland-Palmer's death. These are details known only to the police and deliberately withheld from the press. Ms. Queen said she got them from you."

"Do you mean the missing finger?" Lady Caryn seemed delighted. "Yes, sorry. Guilty as charged. I probably told everyone at school and at least half the women I know from Knight Club. That's—"

"I'm familiar."

"Really?"

"Afraid so. Lexie Hicks-Bowen practically spilled the beans on YouTube. And it's always been an open secret with the faculty, hasn't it?"

Lady Caryn nodded. "Yes. We can't mention it on our website or in parent interviews because the students are sharing their own personal connections at their own risk. If Annabelle Carter acknowledges it, we take on the liability.

But the friendships I made in KC were the best part of being here."

"Are you acquainted with Marilyn Maitland-Palmer?"

"Of course."

"Do you look up to her?"

"Totally. She's a genius. But I'm only the second of us," she said proudly, "to marry a knight. Everyone else came out with terribly practical skills or introductions to people who could help them start a career. I came out knowing five very eligible bachelors, and one of them proposed. It's probably because Cathleen taught us how to bat our eyelashes." She demonstrated.

Paul laughed. "I appreciate your honesty. Now I have to ask—who shared those privileged details with you?"

"One of the KC mentors. She'd kill me if I named her. She's a public figure, and in her line, being an alumna would count as a strike against her."

Paul went cold. He could almost hear Kate crowing, "Told you so!"

"I really must ask you to tell me, Lady Hattersley."

"Neera Nausherwani. She's in government. DEFRA."

Paul was sitting too close to Lady Caryn to scrawl KILL ME in his notebook, so he settled for asking, "Why would Ms. Nausherwani want to spread those details around?"

"I have a theory. But you're better off asking her yourself."

"Oh, I will," Paul assured her. "But please, go on."

"Ever listen to podcasts?"

"When I can find the time."

"Well, you know how everyone's into true crime podcasts and Netflix specials and so on? I think Neera was crowdsourcing the killer's identity," Lady Caryn said, warming to her topic. "She didn't say it outright. But come on—the ring was missing. Lady Bothurst wanted it off her finger. Dankworth wanted it off her finger. Even Ginny probably felt soiled by association. The fact it's gone can't be a meaningless detail."

"Theft isn't a good enough motive?" he asked.

"It's a motive. But too easy."

"Tell me about your relationship with Cathleen."

Lady Caryn's eyes widened. "Oh-ho! It's like that, is it?" She sounded thrilled. "I'm a bit of a true crime junkie myself, if I'm being honest. Never thought I'd been considered a murder suspect."

"We're simply conducting routine interviews of everyone who—"

"No, no, don't ruin it, let me have my moment. Right. My relationship with Cathleen was exactly like Lexie's. She was cruel and rude and did her best to make us feel like troglodytes."

"And that continued when you returned to school as a teacher?"

"I was hired to take her place," Lady Caryn said. "She was already working on a volunteer basis, everyone knew that. She was meant to make a graceful exit, but she just kept making excuses. One day, in the faculty lounge, she called me a jumped-up student. So, I poured a cup of tea in her lap."

"Hot tea?"

"Not hot enough. It would've turned into a free-for-all—a twenty-something versus a seventy-something—except Dankworth and Ginny pulled us apart. And I would be banged up for GBH on a pensioner instead of sitting here with you."

"You're laughing about it now," Paul observed in his

most nonjudgmental tone. "At the time, did you really want to do grievous bodily harm?"

"I've wanted to for years. But I wouldn't. We still haven't heard exactly how she died. Was she beaten to death? Boiled in Darjeeling?"

"It's confidential."

"Right." Her eyes sparkled mischievously. "I know I should be all somber and respectful, but this is the clearest case of someone getting what they deserve that I've ever seen. That doesn't mean the people who did it aren't scumbags, of course."

"People?"

Lady Caryn put her head to one side. "I could speculate, if you're interested…"

He waited, trying to decide if she was simply indulging herself, enjoying a detective inspector's full attention, or sitting on information vital to the case.

"The thing you must understand about Cathleen was her vanity," Lady Caryn said. "We're all our own biggest fans, in one way or another, but Cathleen was always gagging for flattery. However much she got, it was never enough. And when someone hit the right button, her IQ dropped fifty points. Like with her so-called fiancé."

"Speaking of him, we're still trying to run down his name. We'll get it, of course, either through Zoom or by searching Cathleen's laptop. But in the meantime, do you know it?"

"Robert something."

"Raynard? Reynolds?"

"Raymond, I thought. We just called him Sydney. It wouldn't surprise me if you find no British expats in Australia living under that name."

"You think she was being catfished?"

"Had to be. I overheard a couple of their Zoom calls. No man on earth talks to a woman that way. I would've known instantly that he was a fraud. But she lapped it up and came back for more."

"How did he talk to her?"

"Like this. 'I'm counting the hours until I hold you in my arms. I tell my friends, wait till you see her. The clearest blue eyes. Bright golden hair. They'll all be so jealous that you're mine.'" Lady Caryn shook her head. "If a bloke texted me that rot, I'd think he was taking the mickey. If a bloke said it, I'd *know* he was taking the mickey. Or trying to shake me down. Which is what Sydney was doing to Cathleen."

"You heard him ask her for money?"

"Of course. 'Just another five thousand, darling, and the house will be ours, free and clear.' Or, 'The ATO will put me in prison for tax evasion if I don't pay up soon.'"

Those lines do sound ripped straight out of the international fraudster's playbook, Paul thought.

"Maybe he wasn't even a real, live scammer," Lady Caryn continued. "Maybe he was a deepfake. Great bod. Movie-star good looks. A total silver fox, always sitting on his back porch with the red desert for a backdrop. Way too good to be true."

"Are you suggesting the man behind the deepfake would've killed her?" Paul asked. "His golden goose?"

"Oh, no, that's not where I was going. I only wanted to explain how Cathleen's vanity was her Achilles heel. Anyone who flattered her was in. Even the old janitor, Rasvan Botezatu, led her around by the nose. And a man like that doesn't cozy up to you for no reason."

Recalling the photograph of Botezatu in blue overalls,

standing unsmiling several yards away from the faculty, Paul asked, "A man like what?"

"A foreign grifter who landed in London." Lady Caryn waved a hand dismissively. "Greasy. Oily. Always watching and always saying 'Trust me.' When his slag daughter needed a job, he got Cathleen to take her on as a cleaner."

"You've met Daciana Botezatu?"

"No."

"Then why do you call her a slag?"

"Because she's his daughter. Probably just an Eastern European tart who came here to reinvent herself. And Cathleen gave her a key. What better way to let dear old dad come in and kill her?"

Chapter Twenty

"We need to interview Daddy Botezatu," Kate said.

She and Paul were driving to Cottlestone Manor, located in Hampshire, and she'd borrowed Tony's Mercedes EQC 400 for the excursion. Though she had the right to requisition a car from Scotland Yard's vehicle pool, available to any detective traveling more than ten miles from the new HQ, she picked the Mercedes. Not only could it travel up to two hundred miles on a single charge, but it was outrageously comfortable. Harvey still loved their vintage Bentley, and Tony sometimes missed his Lexus. But to Kate, nothing could touch a late-model SUV when it came to sheer luxury.

"We probably need to speak with Daciana again, too. A uniformed officer is checking to make sure she doesn't leg it, right?"

"Yeah. She's been at her father's place since last Friday," Paul said. "But Lady Caryn didn't make a great case for the Botezatus murdering CMP. Just that they're from Romania and they're icky."

"Henry says squicky. But theft still seems good to me,"

Kate said. "I rechecked the SOCOs' crime scene inventory before we left. They didn't locate any additional sex tapes. Either Daciana turned them all over, which I have trouble believing, or we have to keep looking."

"You don't think a film or films were taken from her bookcase?"

"No. The person who rifled the office pulled the letters out of their envelopes. They were after something small and flat. Even a jump drive would be obvious, stuffed inside an envelope. CMP was no master criminal. She probably hid anything important in a bank deposit box. Speaking of that…"

"The warrant came through first thing this morning," Paul said. "I sent Sean to talk with the bank manager. No joy. Turns out CMP *was* renting a safe deposit box, but it was empty. According to their records, her final visit was a month ago. If any masters were kept inside, they were taken out then."

"Right. So, let's proceed on the assumption she *did* have special editions in that safe deposit box, and she *did* retrieve them for a purpose. What is it?"

"To blackmail the whole randy lot again."

"Yeah. Lady Bothurst said CMP hadn't been paid for teaching in about six months. She would've been desperate for money if she wasn't frugal with the cash the first time around."

"And, like Marilyn, Lady Caryn thought CMP was being catfished by Sydney the Aussie hunk."

"This is her theory?"

"Based on eavesdropping. She listened in on CMP and Sydney getting lovey-dovey. Overheard him telling sob stories about being on the hook to inland revenue. He'd be jailed if he didn't pay up, so he needed another loan."

"Right. So. CMP has been sacked from the job she held her whole life. She's destroyed her reputation with women because of her behavior, and with men because of blackmail," Kate said.

"She's ready to give up on England," Paul said. "Emigrate to Australia and live in a house overlooking the sea. But loverboy has siphoned off most if not all of her ready cash."

"She pulls out the special film of her biggest fish, Patrick Bruce, and decides to hit him again. She attends a party at Cottlestone Manor—"

"—and turns up dead a few hours later. It works," Paul said. "But what about the ring? Why would Lord Dellkirk want it?"

"I don't know. Theft of the ring only makes sense in the case of Lady Bothurst." Another dangling thread occurred to Kate. "Did the manager of Anne Lister's back up Marilyn's alibi?"

"Yes. I have a signed statement that MMP was in the club from about eight o'clock to closing time, which is two A.M. And by two A.M., Cathleen was already dead, per Dr. Stepp's report."

"Maybe MMP slipped out for a quick murder."

"The front door staff records all entrances and exits."

"Maybe her friends at Anne Lister's will say whatever she wants."

"Even to the police?" Paul chuckled. "Fine, she stays on the list."

"And so does Neera," Kate said sweetly.

"Come on. What's her motive?"

"I don't know, but even if her interference isn't illegal, I'd call it unethical. Why was Neera at Annabelle Carter when we turned up?"

"She left as soon as we arrived."

"Maybe she's the one who searched CMP's office. And only stuck around long enough to make sure the janitor took the blame."

"I admit she's been weird. I admit she's been indiscreet. But do you really like her as the killer?"

Kate pretended to be engrossed in checking their GPS route.

"Stop that. It's a straight shot for the next fifty miles," Paul said. "Seriously, Kate. If Neera did it, how did she get into CMP's house? Assuming she knew about the pacemaker, and assuming she knew a rare earth magnet might destroy it, how did she get her hands on one? And why did a magnet strike her as a better murder weapon than—I don't know, one of those vases Marilyn tipped her cigarette ash into?"

"To make it look like a natural death."

"Then why chop off the finger?"

"You've got me there," she admitted. "But as far as how Neera or anyone else got into CMP's house, don't you think Daciana would sell a copy of her key for the right price?"

"From what Sean said about her home movies, there isn't a lot she wouldn't do for the right price," Paul admitted. "He also said he wished there was such a thing as arse recognition software. It would've saved him from some awful sights."

"Sure, I'll bet it was a big sacrifice for him, going through fifty shades of Daciana." Kate meant to speak lightly, but the words came out sounding like a dig.

It was none of her business, of course, and not particularly fair, but the idea of Sean Kincaid enjoying Daciana's nudity made her want to punch something. Amelia Gulls hadn't been dead six months. Kate knew this because Nicky had been born soon after. It was a sad asterisk to her son's age; using it, Kate could always calculate how long Amelia had been gone.

His life has to go on, she thought. *And I need to sort out my own grief, not find fault with how he does or doesn't express his.*

To get them back on topic, she said, "I haven't read his report yet. What about someone called Hicks-Bowen? Or Hattersley? Or Nausherwani," she added, remembering that the DEFRA secretary was married.

"No. All the men are successful, most of them are married, and they range from sixty to eighty," Paul said. "But no familiar names. Including Lady Caryn's husband, Lexie Lex's dad, or Neera's husband."

"Too bad. Still, with any luck, we'll meet one or two of these successful, married, seasoned gentlemen this afternoon," she said, gauging his reaction with a sidelong look.

He sat up straighter. "What did you cook up?"

"I told you I got Lord Dellkirk to agree to the interview, but I didn't say how. It took some negotiating," Kate said. "He asked me if we meant to subject every single one of his party guests to an interrogation or just him. I said we'd probably speak to them all, since they were the last to see her alive.

"He didn't like that answer. He was gearing up to tell me off, but that's when Elodie Queen gave me an assist. She said, 'Somebody out there must know something about who killed Miranda, but they haven't come forward. Anyone who might know who killed Cathleen needs to say so, now.'"

"And that moved the needle?"

"In a big way. He really couldn't say no after that. So, he said, fine, but interview me at Cottlestone Manor where I can keep the press away. And he told me he'd ask back all his party guests so we could process them in one fell swoop."

"This could turn into a free-for-all. I love it," Paul said gleefully. "Let the blabbering begin."

"I know, right? Lord Poundland thinks it's checkmate. He was pleased to inform me that two of his guests are distinguished barristers and will act as counsel for the group."

"They can counsel away. My money's on us.

* * *

Cottlestone Manor was a grand old heap. It ticked all the boxes: Grade II listed, built of seventeenth-century stone, and thirty acres of parkland that commanded breathtaking views of the English countryside. According to the website, which offered Cottlestone Manor as an event venue with rates upon request, it had six bedrooms, a swimming pool, and a garden designed by Capability Brown. The estate also had three outbuildings: a barn, a cottage, and a coach house, all renovated with *en suite* bedrooms and satellite telly. The variety of interiors to choose from and its slightly forbidding look—it had once been a medieval nunnery—had won the house appearances in such cinema gems as *Zombies Eat the Rich 2*. Simultaneously sumptuous and severe, it looked like a place where the delicious rich would dwell, and peckish zombies would inevitably turn up.

Kate parked out front. As she paused to reapply lipstick, Paul, checking his hair in the sideview mirror, said, "Don't look now, but a disapproving man in a black suit is coming this way. I'm guessing he's the executive butler."

"Coming to warn us to be properly respectful."

"And to say that being received into the manor is a privilege."

"Lather, rinse, repeat." Kate snapped her compact shut.

The executive butler, Mr. McCall, was indeed coming to say all that, and also to inform them they couldn't park out front. Hollywood location scouts were coming; a large SUV by the stone fountain would spoil the period effect. He directed Kate to a car lot behind the renovated barn that was clearly for the help. One of the parked cars, an all-black, completely plain SUV, made Kate think of MPS undercover vehicles. Maybe the Hollywood people had sent a small security detail ahead?

To hammer home their inferior status, McCall led them in through "the trade entrance," or loading dock. A lorry driver was there, unloading crates of fresh seafood and boxes of bubbly.

"That's a lot of champagne," Paul observed.

"The Hollywood people expect it. And it's not champagne," the butler sniffed. "It's California sparkling wine. Lord Dellkirk prefers Laurent-Perrier *Blanc de Blancs Brut Nature* when he drinks champagne. Which doesn't arrive in packages of twelve."

"Of course. What would I know? I buy dodgy booze from places where everything's a pound."

McCall didn't even flinch. He led them briskly through the kitchen, past the scullery, up a flight of uncarpeted stairs, and down a long hallway. At last, they arrived in what looked like a formal reception room with dark-papered walls and a mix of Regency and Victorian furniture.

"Wait here for his lordship."

"Thanks ever so. In the meantime," Paul said, dropping into a chintz-covered sofa unasked, "we're inviting ourselves to sit." When the butler scowled, he added, "I was stabbed in the shoulder whilst on duty, protecting citizens like you from crazed killers and whatnot. I won't stand about indefinitely."

Kate, grateful for his cheekiness, also sat. Her knees and hips thanked her.

"I owe you one," she told Paul when the man was gone. "That was a long walk. Isn't it nuts how much Tony hates showing weakness in front of me? I'm still not a hundred percent. I do rehab once a week."

"It's a man thing."

"You've never been shy about bleating in pain."

"I'm in touch with my feelings." He shifted on the sofa's lumpy cushions. "This must be stuffed with horsehair. I detect a barnyard aroma."

They went on like that, critiquing the ugly antiques with which Patrick Bruce had surrounded himself, until the earl turned up an interminable forty-eight minutes later.

"In the interest of preserving my time, which I find valuable even if others do not," he announced, striding into the room mid-diatribe, "I've invited certain other parties to share in this interview. I'll introduce them before we begin. But first, your credentials. Now."

Kate dutifully brought out her warrant card as if she hadn't met him yesterday. Paul patted himself down. He dragged out the search for over a minute, even peeking inside his socks, before producing it from his inner coat pocket.

"I don't know why I always look there last."

Bruce made a show of scrutinizing each card. "Right," he said at last, handing them back. "Here's how this will go. My guests from last Thursday night's dinner party await you in the dining room. They're willing to answer your questions as a courtesy to me and to the Metropolitan

Police Service, which I think you'll find I've always supported.

"In exchange for our voluntary cooperation, I expect you to be respectful. To be brief. And to remember where you are, and to whom you speak, or you'll be told to piss off, sharpish. Is that understood?"

Behold the captain of industry, ordering us about like junior VPs, Kate thought. *Is he always like this, or do we make him nervous?*

"Understood, milord," she said smoothly. "Please accept my condolences."

"For what?"

"For the loss of your friend, Mrs. Maitland-Palmer."

"Oh." He cleared his throat. "Thank you. Come through."

Bruce led them into the manor's formal dining room. Bright afternoon sunlight streamed in from six windows overlooking the lawn and, more distantly, a wooded park. The ceiling soared; the wall hangings looked like medieval heraldry, though they might have been modern reproductions. All in all, it would have been a captivating room if not for the seven people ranged around the table. They regarded Kate and Paul with various expressions, few of them friendly.

"Clockwise from the left." Bruce started with the least hostile-looking couple. "Lord Lachey," he said, indicating a forty-something man with blond hair and a pretty face. "Beside him, Lady Lachey." The wife, blonder and prettier, smiled at Kate and Paul. She seemed pleased to assist the police with their inquiries.

"Ms. Vera Jane Mission." Bruce indicated an attractive woman in her late thirties. Kate recognized her as a failed Tory MP candidate for one London borough or other.

Olive-skinned, with flawless hair and makeup, she was both businesslike and beautiful. Although Kate had never thrown a formal dinner party at Wellegrave House—and hoped to evade the responsibility indefinitely, if she could manage it—she knew the host traditionally strove for an even number of guests, half male, half female. That meant Vera Jane was some man's counterpart.

She must be Lord Dellkirk's current squeeze, Kate thought. *But if she was his date for Thursday night, who was CMP paired up with?*

"Beside Ms. Mission," Bruce said, "the Viscount Lachey, OBE."

"Hello," said the stooped little old man cheerfully. "Is that Baron Wellegrave's wife?"

"It is, my lord." Kate smiled. "How do you do?"

"How do you do?" Pushing back his chair, he rose to Lord Lachey's clear disapproval—they seemed to be father and son—and shambled over, a trifle unsteadily, to shake her hand.

"You're quite a pretty one, aren't you?" The viscount beamed up at her.

"So my husband says, my lord."

"Never mind all that," said Viscount Lachey. "Only the Johnny-come-latelies want all that." With a pointed glance at his host, he added, "Forget to 'my lord' one of these newly created blokes, and they'll clap you in irons."

Lord Lachey stood up. "Father, let me help you back to your chair."

Paying no attention, the viscount turned to Paul. "And who's this intrepid young man?"

"DI Bhar, my lord," Paul said, throwing in a faint but perceptible bow that Kate knew wasn't meant sarcastically. That made it quite a compliment.

"Terrible thing about Cathleen. Shocking," the viscount said. "You'll get to the bottom of it, won't you?" In a lower voice, he added, "They were all jealous of her at that school, you know. Look for the most jealous bird in the bunch. That'll be your culprit."

Lord Lachey took hold of his father, firmly steering the old man back to his chair. "We mustn't exert ourselves. The doctor said take it easy for a few days, remember?"

"Who's this we? And who died and made you governor? I suppose if I disobey, you'll give me six whacks across the seat of my trousers," the viscount said, staring mutinously into the distance.

As if the interruption hadn't happened, Bruce resumed his introductions by indicating a compact, bearded man at the end of the long oval table. "Sir Kenneth Hattersley. Beside him, Lady Hattersley."

"Caryn," she added in the same chirpy voice Kate remembered from their first meeting. "Not the most jealous bird in the bunch."

"I didn't mean you," Viscount Lachey assured her.

"Beside Lady Hattersley, Conor Wilkinson." Bruce indicated a young man with multiple tattoos and piercings who looked barely twenty. "Beside him, Lottie Watson."

"AKA Elodie Queen." The young woman with green hair and pouty lips studied Kate. "I didn't put it together yesterday, but are you Tony's wife?"

"I am. How are you, Ms. Queen?"

"Desperate not to get grassed on again," she said pointedly. "*Someone* saw me yesterday at St. Ethelburga's without bodyguards. They told Tony, who rang me at half-seven to read me the riot act. Do you know what it's like having a peer tell you off at half-seven in the morning?"

"Actually, I do."

"Well, today, I brought my new security guys. See?" She pointed to the dark-suited man with the earpiece who stood motionless in the corner, radiating readiness like an especially vigilant potted plant. "One in here, one out front, and one in the back garden."

And Elodie makes nine, Kate thought. *The missing person is Cathleen, so the gang's all here.*

Despite an empty slot near the head of the table, there were no additional chairs. Bruce apparently expected them to stand throughout the group interview.

"Just a sec," Paul said, ducking into the adjoining parlor. There was a sound of heavy furniture being moved. He reappeared dragging two expensive-looking Queen Anne chairs across the floor, placing them with a satisfied thump. Kate avoided looking at him, aware that if she caught his eye, one of them would start laughing, and the whole enterprise would swirl down the drain.

"I do have a question before we begin," she said, sitting. "Conor Wilkinson, is that right? Are you the son of Will Wilkinson?"

"Yes. Um, yes, my lady." He had a deep voice, a neck covered with interlocking designs, and an incongruously wet-behind-the-ears air.

"DI Hetheridge is fine." She was tempted to ask Lord Dellkirk point-blank how he knew the Wilkinson family, but couldn't think of a way to justify it concerning the Cathleen Maitland-Palmer case. All she could do was keep her ears open for any tidbits Tony might find helpful.

"Thank you, Lord Dellkirk, for allowing us into your home," Kate said. "First, I'd like you all to know that the Metropolitan Police Service appreciates your time and will do everything in our power not to waste it. To maximize efficiency, this interview will be recorded. Any statement you make will be on the record and subject to fact-checking. Please be aware that we reserve the right to call any of you for a follow-up interview if we have further questions."

Producing his voice-activated recorder, Paul identified himself and Kate, the place, the time, and had everyone give their names, including Elodie's security guard.

"This is a voluntary interview. But the law requires me to read you this caution before we begin," he said. "'You do not have to say anything. But it may harm your defense if you do not mention when questioned something which you later rely on in court. Anything you do say may be given in evidence.' Right. Begin interview." He placed the recorder in the middle of the table and returned to his chair.

"Okay. Let's get to it," Kate said cheerfully. "Was anyone here being blackmailed by Mrs. Maitland-Palmer on threat of releasing a sex tape?"

Chapter Twenty-One

Reactions rocketed around the table. Bruce snapped, "What? How dare you?" Lord Lachey puffed up. Lady Lachey pressed her hand to her throat, clutching her metaphorical pearls. Elodie Queen and Conor Wilkinson grinned at each other in delight. They were like kids whose first Christmas lunch at the adults' table came with turkey, a sip of wine, and a bare-knuckle grownup row.

Kate thought Vera Jane Mission looked like an utterly unshocked woman doing her best to seem poleaxed. Lady Caryn gave a sort of hiccupping giggle that turned into a cough. Besides her, Sir Kenneth was reddening from the neck up.

"Patrick, this is a travesty." He glared at Kate. "You're a disgrace to Scotland Yard."

"Oh, come now." Viscount Lachey's eyes twinkled. If sheer pleasure could restore vitality, he would've grown younger by the minute. "Lady Hetheridge is only doing her job."

"You're not offended to be lumped in with that sordid accusation?"

"Of course not. I'm one of the men Cathleen tried to touch for money using, well, rather unorthodox methods," the viscount said calmly. "But that was months ago. Water under the bridge."

"Father, be quiet. I insist," said Lord Lachey.

"Excuse me, my lord, but that's out of order," Paul said. "Everyone is encouraged to answer truthfully. Viscount, anything you can tell us would be of assistance."

"You don't have to share highly personal details," Kate added. "Just the approximate date it happened, the sum she wanted, and how it was resolved."

"DI Hetheridge." Bruce stood up. "Sir Kenneth is quite right. This is a travesty, and I won't permit it."

"Lord Dellkirk." Kate's poise was hard-earned but genuine. Once upon a time, sprinting up the high street after a bag-snatcher had been the best part of her job. These days, confronting a jumped-up retailer like Patrick Bruce was the high-stakes equivalent: a kick, not a chore.

"If you consider this a travesty, let me remind you, a group interview was your doing, not ours. We agreed to bend the rules for you and your guests because, frankly, you seemed determined to put off your interview indefinitely, and we were willing to compromise. If Mrs. Maitland-Palmer's killer is to be brought to justice, Scotland Yard needs all of you to cooperate."

"I want the two of you gone before—" Bruce began.

"If you now regret your own scheme," Kate cut across him smoothly, "we're happy to revert to the traditional route. I can have a couple of Met people movers here within two hours. You're all welcome to pile in and take a day trip to the new HQ. It has lovely private interview rooms."

"Dispenser coffee. Pig snacks," Paul put in.

"She can't force us to go anywhere," Sir Kenneth told Bruce.

"That's right, she can't." Lord Lachey smoothed back his blond hair. "I trained as a barrister. University College, London. These voluntary police interviews are just that, voluntary. We need only stand up and walk away." Rising, he gestured toward his wife, who hopped to her feet obediently. He gestured to the viscount. "Father."

"Brian."

"We're leaving."

"No."

Feeling certain she read the viscount's attitude correctly, Kate told his son, "You and most of the others, including Lord Dellkirk, are certainly free to leave. But as this is a murder inquiry, and Viscount Lachey is now a material witness, I'm afraid things have changed. You and your family need to talk to us. If you don't, Scotland Yard will be forced to listen to anyone with something to say. Cleaners, maids, ex-employees..."

"That's a threat," Bruce said.

"Damn right it is." Lord Lachey glared down the table at Kate. "How dare you threaten my father? A vulnerable witness by anyone's standards, infirm and clearly in the grip of dementia—"

"Dementia," the viscount cried. "Brian Haworth McCullough Lachey. I knew sending you to UCL was a waste of time and money. Be quiet before I tell these people what kind of marks you received. And why you never sat for your bar exam."

Lord Lachey and his wife sank back into their chairs. So did Patrick Bruce, whose experience with compliant boardrooms had never prepared him for this sort of free-for-all.

"I happen to be an actual barrister," the viscount told

Kate. "A Gray's Inn man. I practiced for thirty-five years, and I'll gladly accommodate Scotland Yard. Make it easy on yourself." He thrust out his wrists. "Arrest me for murder and haul me back to London. I could use a day out."

"Now, this is getting out of control," Lady Caryn said, looking around with a nervous smile. "As the only representative of Annabelle Carter present, Viscount Lachey, I'm asking you to please imagine the headlines. If you're questioned on this topic, it's sure to get out. News that one of our teachers was blackmailing anyone, much less a peer, is a scandal that will kill the school once and for all." Her gaze flicked to Sir Kenneth as if checking his reaction. "I really think it's better if we all get up and leave, like my husband said."

"I understand your position, my dear." Viscount Lachey eyed Sir Kenneth. "Fortunately for me, I'm not obliged to walk on eggshells to keep anyone from erupting.

"Now, Lady Hetheridge, where were we?" he asked crisply. "Oh, yes. Blackmail. You must understand the situation from Cathleen's point of view. She'd never put by a penny in the years after her divorce. Keeping up appearances took everything she had. She would have been all right if she'd retired from Annabelle Carter twenty years ago and taken a flat outside the city. But she wanted to remarry, and that meant seeing and being seen."

"Excuse me, sir, but how do you know all this?" Paul asked.

"I can speak authoritatively about Cathleen because we had a love affair long ago," the viscount said. "We parted friends, and I saw her often, including at parties at her townhouse. At one such event, I confess that I became rather festive." He chuckled. "Too much Christmas punch.

Cathleen wanted one for old times' sake, but that book was closed. Instead, I toddled upstairs with her maid."

"Father," Lord Lachey groaned.

"Just because you don't know how to live, don't fault me for it. It was only a bit of fun. Six months later, when I'd quite forgotten the whole thing, Cathleen popped round to show me the video and shake me down for twenty thousand pounds." He laughed. "As if a man at my time of life would pay to suppress anything of the sort. I should have offered her money to put it about as proof of life. Viscount Lachey isn't quite dead yet, thank you very much."

"So, you chose not to report the crime?" Paul asked.

"Naturally. I scolded her a bit, then forgave her. And I told her, 'If you insist on seeking hush money, choose men with plenty of cash and something to lose. Not reckless old goats like me.'" The viscount sighed. "Ah, poor Cathleen. I've been told the killer lopped off her finger. For some reason, I keep coming back to that. An awful thing. Barbaric."

"It was the finger she wore her London blue ring on," Kate said. "Can you think of anyone who might have wanted it that badly?"

"No."

"I can," Vera Jane Mission said.

"Shut it," Sir Kenneth hissed.

"*Oi!* Chivalry really is dead, innit?" Elodie said.

Sir Kenneth gave her the same suppressive look he'd just given the politician. Elodie stuck out her tongue at him. "If Vera Jane wants to speak, let her."

"I'd prefer you didn't," Bruce told her.

Lord Lachey cleared his throat. "I am perfectly qualified to act as your brief in this matter. You're under no obligation to answer, Vera Jane."

"Technically, my son is correct," said Viscount Lachey. "Broken clock and all that. But I encourage you to speak out, dear. I know you had no use for Cathleen. You thought she was ridiculous. And I know you don't want to rock the boat with our host. But in a murder case, your paramount obligation is to give evidence."

"Perhaps you should look into Mrs. Dankworth, the deputy headmistress at Annabelle Carter," Vera Jane said. "Whenever she was included in a function, usually for Griselda's sake, she could barely manage to be civil to Cathleen. She was mad with envy. Or maybe the word is jealousy—jealousy over that ring. Mrs. Dankworth holds the school together. If she left, it would fall to pieces. But Griselda never rewarded her."

"I refuse to believe Cathleen was killed over a trinket," Bruce said angrily. "It was probably taken as a trophy. Serial killers do that."

"The manner of Mrs. Maitland-Palmer's death doesn't suggest a serial killer," Paul said. "She might have died without even knowing she was under attack. Her heart stopped when her pacemaker exploded. And it exploded because someone brought a powerful rare earth magnet within six inches of her chest."

Kate watched Bruce's face change. One moment, he was incensed by the foolish nattering of police. The next, he was shocked—genuinely shocked, unless she missed her guess.

"What did you say?" he asked.

"A rare earth magnet," Kate said, holding his gaze. "We understand she had a near-miss regarding her pacemaker outside one of your facilities, Lord Dellkirk. You invited her to Massive Attraction for—"

"I didn't know," he snapped. "How could I? She never

told me about her heart. She wanted me to think of her as young, strong..." Bruce tailed off, looking miserable. And regretful, since he'd engineered a situation where his society friends were present to witness this line of questioning.

Too clever by half, Lord Poundland, she thought. *Just like when you bought yourself an earldom and thought nobody would notice.*

"We've been told you had a long personal relationship with the deceased, Lord Dellkirk," Paul said. "That you've been linked since your uni days. Is that true?"

"Yes."

"Were you aware that she sometimes filmed men during sex with her cleaner?"

"Of course not."

"Did you ever have a liaison with that cleaner? Daciana Botezatu?"

"Absolutely not."

"To restate the question and answer for the record, did Mrs. Maitland-Palmer try to blackmail you with a sex tape or by threatening you in some other way?"

"No."

Kate turned to the viscount's son. "What about you, Lord Lachey?"

He shook his head.

"Or you, Sir Kenneth?"

Lady Caryn's knight didn't appreciate women speaking out of turn. He glared at Kate as if imagining he was disassembling her, limb by limb.

"Please answer for the recording, Sir Kenneth."

"No," he growled.

She pretended not to notice. "Right. Moving on. We've been told that Mrs. Maitland-Palmer didn't drive—"

"You skipped Conor," Elodie said.

The young man looked like he might melt into a puddle of tattoos.

"I mean, you are a guy, and Cathleen knew you," Elodie said mischievously. "You don't get skipped just because you're presumed a virgin."

As the young man colored, Kate asked with complete solemnity, "Did you receive a blackmail threat from Mrs. Maitland-Palmer?"

"No, ma'am."

"If you don't mind my asking, how did you know the deceased?"

"I was a chevalier."

Beside her, Paul coughed. It sounded suspiciously like a laugh.

As if she owed him a timely rescue, Elodie said, "His mum, Rebekah, knows someone at the school. Lady Bothurst, I think. She talked Conor into attending a debutante ball. The girls always need dance partners."

"I see. Thank you. Getting back to Mrs. Maitland-Palmer, who did not drive, how did she get to Thursday night's dinner party?" Kate asked.

"I gave her a lift," Bruce said. "I was on my way home from the city."

"Did you take her back to Bulwer Street after the party?" Paul asked.

"A round trip at that time of night? Ridiculous. Someone else must have given her a ride."

"Not me," Elodie said. "I offered. She said she wanted a man on her arm."

"I intended to offer," Viscount Lachey said. "But somehow, the night got away from me, and by the time I remembered, she was gone."

"I took her home," Conor said. "Let her off at her door.

She invited me to come up, but..." He looked embarrassed. "I had, er, things to do."

Kate said, "This is important, Conor. Think back. Did Cathleen say anything to you during the ride that stands out now?"

"Like what?"

"Like she was afraid of someone? Or that someone was waiting for her at home?"

The young man blew out his breath, considering. "She acted a little weird, I thought. Said someone scammed her out of a lot of money, and she didn't know what to do. Maybe she was hinting for a loan. I got uncomfortable. I said, look, my life's messed up, too. The other night, I went to a club, and—"

BOOM

One of the tall windows exploded. Glass showered on the tabletop and the floor. Amid screams and cries, Elodie Queen's security guard barreled across the room, seizing his charge and whirling so his back was to the open window.

BOOM

"Hit the deck!" Kate grabbed the viscount by his lapels, pushing him under the table. She didn't know if the security guard had taken the second shot in the back or not. Beside her, Sir Kenneth sat frozen in terror. Paul yanked the chair out from under him. The knight landed on the floor next to Lady Caryn, whose hands were clapped over her ears.

BOOM

Kate had done many active shooter drills over the course of her career; her response was muscle memory rather than instinct. First, she'd taken shelter. Second, she'd checked Paul's status. Third, she checked the status of everyone else hiding beneath the solid oak table.

"Be quiet," she ordered the jumble of faces, hands, and knees. Heart hammering, she took them all in.

Green hair: Elodie. Beefy arms: security guy, who didn't seem to be shot. Clutching one another: Lord and Lady Lachey. Near-fetal position: Lady Caryn. Still rigid with fear: Sir Kenneth. Equally blank with terror: Patrick Bruce. Finally, Viscount Lachey, who wore the canny look of a man who'd faced down real danger before.

"I was in the war," he whispered.

Conor, she thought. *Where's Conor?*

The viscount, apparently thinking the same thing, silently pointed. The guests' mad scramble under the table had knocked over most of the chairs, but one was still upright. A pair of legs in ripped jeans indicated that its occupant was still seated.

"Active shooter," Paul was muttering into his mobile. "Ten, strike that, eleven people sheltering in place. One injured or dead. Number of assailants unknown. Additional casualties unknown."

As Paul instructed the 999 operator, Kate mentally blocked out his voice, the sound of Lady Lachey's hitching breaths, and her own thunderous pulse. The pause in gunfire could mean many things. Maybe Elodie's other two security guards had found the shooter and neutralized him. Maybe he was reloading. Maybe he'd legged it. Or maybe, just maybe, he was advancing toward the house, intent on climbing through the broken window and finishing the job at close range.

For what seemed like eons, she waited, straining for the sound of footsteps crunching on broken glass. She didn't need Paul to tell her it would take at least fifteen minutes for the nearest village police to organize and arrive at the manor.

Fifteen minutes, she thought. *Fifteen lifetimes.*

When she could wait no longer, she began easing out of her jacket. These complicated movements in such a tight space alarmed everyone but Paul, who understood what she meant to do. It was a calculated risk—if Conor was still alive, they had to get to him and render aid until paramedics arrived.

"Ma'am, I don't advise—" began the security guard,

Silencing him with a look, Kate crawled out from under the table. Trying not to imagine the loud crack that would end her life, she scuttled on hands and knees toward the windows. Once there, she put her back against the wall. Then, rising as much as she could without exposing herself to the shooter, she checked on Conor.

His chin had fallen against his chest. There was a lot of blood, most of it splashed on the wall behind him.

Poor kid, Kate thought. *At least it was quick. Probably never knew what hit him.*

Forcing herself to count to sixty, she stayed like that, back pressed to the wall and jacket in hand. The count ended without another shot and without anyone climbing through the broken window.

Deep breath, she thought. *Go.*

Wildly, she waved her jacket in front of the window. If the shooter had a decent scope, he'd be able to tell it was just a garment, not a potential victim. But he'd probably be so hopped up on adrenaline that his finger would squeeze the trigger before his brain said no.

Nothing happened. Kate counted to sixty a second time. On fifty-eight, the rapid thump of boots echoed down the corridor.

"Elodie Queen," a man shouted. "It's Jimmy from ASC.

Are you injured? Kurt, my earpiece is out. Are you still with her?"

"Yep, she's A-OK," the security guard beneath the table called back.

"Who are you?" Jimmy from ASC asked Kate.

"DI Hetheridge."

"Are you injured?"

"No. Did you neutralize the shooter?"

"Negative, he beat feet. Mind you, we ran toward the shots," Jimmy added, as if Kate had accused him of cowardice. "When the shooter saw he'd been made, he dropped the weapon and legged it."

Kate, suddenly cognizant of her cramping legs, stood up shakily. Her tights were torn, her knees were scratched from broken glass, and she was trembling all over. Numbly, and with real difficulty, she pulled on her jacket. She would've buttoned it, but her fingers were on the fritz.

Paul was the first out from under the table. Helping the viscount up, he led the old man—arguably the calmest person in the room—to a chair. Kurt the security guard checked the lay of the land for himself, then told Elodie she should remain on the floor a little longer. Ignoring that, Elodie jumped up, saw Conor, and screamed.

This touched off fresh panic among those still under the table. Paul took charge of them, leading each out of hiding and into the parlor. Kate went to Elodie, who was still screaming. Before she could intervene, Jimmy administered an open-palmed slap. Shocked, Elodie gulped air instead of screaming again.

"Oi!" Kate yelled. "How 'bout I come over there and slap you back?"

"She's hysterical. That's what you do when someone's hysterical."

"What d'you do when security his so bleeding incompetent, they set hup their client hin front of windows! Fink habout that," she roared, shaking her fist. "That kid his dead because you people never checked the woods, did you? Did you?"

"You—you lot didn't either," he stammered.

He's right, damn him, Kate thought, the accusation piercing her rage. *We were here to talk about CMP. But we knew Elodie was at risk. And we assumed these muscle-bound doughnuts were doing their best to protect her.*

Elodie began to cry, first silently, then with rising anguish.

"You blokes go out front," Kate said tiredly. "Meet the local coppers. Tell 'em what you know."

"We can't leave Ms. Queen's side," Jimmy said.

"You're sacked," Elodie whispered between sobs. The security trio left without trying to change her mind.

Kate wished Amelia Gulls were there. She'd had a genius for putting people at ease. She'd know what to say.

No. Amelia wouldn't speak, Kate realized. *There are no words.*

She put her arms around Elodie, who whispered, "It was because of me."

Kate didn't answer, just held her tight. It was probably true: a young man was dead because an amateur killer took aim at Damselfish's lead singer and missed.

Chapter Twenty-Two

Thumping his way around the desk, Tony sat down heavily in his office chair. "Sorry I disappeared for so long," he said to his laptop. "Had to get Nicky off to sleep. There was some controversy as to the respective merits of the stuffed lion versus the stuffed zebra."

"And you checked on Kate?" Elodie asked over their video connection.

"Yes. I assure you, she's fine. Having a talk with our other son about his pocket money."

"So, almost getting killed is all in a day's work for you two?"

"No. But we're trained for the job, and we chose it." Smiling, Tony added, "I see you called in reinforcements for the evening."

"Yeah. This is Bartholomew Bear." Elodie made her old-fashioned brown stuffie wave at him. "He's giving me moral support."

"Of course he is." Elodie had always seemed like a child to Tony, but even more so after the shooting at Cottlestone Manor. He didn't begrudge her the teddy bear and the red McGregor tartan pajamas. This was turning into the sort of discussion that warranted extra comforting.

"Now, regarding your safety. I hope you don't mind that I took the liberty of sending you men from Schloss LTD."

She shook her head.

"Their bodyguards are among the very best. I asked them to go over your flat with a fine-toothed comb. It seems they've already found something."

"What? How do you know?"

"They texted me."

She glared at someone off-screen. "Adam! What the hell?"

"You were in the shower, Ms. Queen. Then you were on a call." A man's big, square face bobbed into view, asking Tony, "Okay to proceed, boss?"

"I'm the boss," Elodie snapped as Tony said, "Do it."

Adam opened his fist to reveal a palm-sized rectangle with braided red and black wires. At the end of those wires: a white, button-like device. "It's a GSM transmitter."

"A bug," Tony clarified.

"Where? Here?" Elodie said.

"In your bedroom," Adam said. "The body of the transmitter was hidden behind a ceiling panel. Only the microphone was exposed, and because it was white, it blended in."

"My bedroom?" Elodie repeated numbly. "How—how long has it been there?"

"There's no way to tell. It's a pretty simple covert listening device. The kind you buy online," Adam said. "When the device picks up sound, it alerts the spy. By remote, the spy can choose to ignore the sound, record it, or actively listen."

"Don't panic," Tony said. "What's done is done. At least now you know your flat is clean."

"But who could've put it in my *bedroom*?" she cried.

"Do you have a cleaner?"

She nodded.

"One person, or a service that sends different people?"

"A service."

"Then that's the most likely explanation. One of them was approached by the killer and hired to install that whilst cleaning."

"Do you think there was a bug in Miranda's place, too? In Zoë's?"

"Quite possibly. I'm actually relieved such a device was discovered," Tony said. "Kate put me in the picture regarding the group interview at Cottlestone Manor. It was arranged with only a day's notice. We wondered how the killer knew he needed to travel two hours, scout the location, find a spot to fire from, etc. Even so, the manor's interior is rather large. Would you mind letting Adam examine your bag?"

Wide-eyed, Elodie got up, picked up her handbag, and dumped it on her bed. Tony watched as Adam sorted through the usual feminine detritus before going over the bag itself.

"Here," he said. "Same white button microphone. The rest of the unit is stuck between the cloth liner and the bag material."

"Is the bug active now?" Tony asked.

Adam passed over the microphone with a handheld device roughly shaped like a selfie stick. "No."

"How can you be sure?" Elodie asked.

"This is a nonlinear junction detector," Adam said. "The RF—well, trust me, Ms. Queen. I'm sure."

"Wrap up the bug in something to muffle it. A throw from the sofa will do," Tony said.

"No, give it to me," Elodie cried. "I want to stomp it!"

"Adam, take custody of it," Tony said sharply. "We might make use of it later. The killer certainly made use of it today."

Elodie, perhaps unconsciously, clutched Bartholomew closer. "How?"

"He listened to everything you said and probably a good deal of what was said to you. He would've learned the meeting would be held in the dining room. Once he saw the windows, he probably started scouting a location to set up his gun rest. I imagine all this transpired while Lord Dellkirk was still greeting his guests."

Elodie covered her face with her hands. Her black nail lacquer was peeling; every fingernail was bitten down to the quick.

"Elodie," Tony said firmly. "*Elodie*."

She took her hands away and looked at him. Although she was still fighting tears, she seemed to be winning the battle.

"Kate told me the last question she posed to the group. It was about which guest drove Mrs. Maitland-Palmer home on the night of her death. I understand Conor Wilkinson identified himself. Do you recall what he was saying before he was shot?"

"Just that he drove her home."

"Nothing else? Think carefully." Tony already knew what Kate remembered; he wanted to see if Elodie recalled the same, or possibly more.

After consideration, Elodie said, "Seems like the question was, did Cathleen tell Conor anything important, like was she afraid for her life? Conor said she was upset over how weird her life was. He said his life was messed up, too, and I cringed for him." Elodie's voice broke. "I knew he was about to start talking about his dad's death, and nobody in that crowd cared about his feelings."

"It sounds like you had more than a nodding acquaintance with Conor."

"I met him through Damselfish. Early on, Will included Rebekah—his ex—in all the parties. Conor kept turning up, too, because he wanted to break into the music industry. Wanted to rap, like his stupid dad. But Conor was a good egg," Elodie said. "I even gave him industry advice, just generally. I said, it's no good cutting a basement demo when you've never even stepped on stage. The only way to make money anymore is in live performances. I said he needed to go to hip-hop clubs with open mic nights and start rapping for audiences. Even if they boo him at first."

"What did he mean, his life was messed up?"

"I don't think he ever dealt with losing Will. After the explosion, his sister and brother were gutted, but Conor felt nothing. He said it was because they were never close, but I reckon he was in shock. He didn't seem affected until recently. Delayed grief."

"Right. Now, I'm not sure if this is germane, but I'm afraid I must ask—do you have some sort of relationship with Lord Dellkirk?"

Elodie looked pained. Sighing, she put the bear aside as if protecting the stuffie's tender ears from what would come next.

"You know how my career started. Patrick is friends with Mal, and of course, Mal's an industry legend. Patrick introduced us, and we fell for each other. Then, Mal created Damselfish and tapped Will as our producer. The rest happened through talent and hard work. That's what I tell myself, anyway.

"After Zoë got stabbed and Miranda died, I realized Damselfish was finished. Even if the killer is caught—even if Zoë and I hire a replacement for Miranda—the magic is gone. Reinvention is the only way forward. And here's the thing about Patrick: he has industry connections besides Mal. Plus, he likes me. And I like him." She pursed her lips. "It will never be more than that. But I can see us dating for a while. And maybe he can help me and Zoë get back on top."

Tony pondered that.

"You think I'm a monster."

"Don't be ridiculous. Patrick Bruce isn't a wide-eyed innocent, and neither are you. If the terms of your relationship are mutually satisfactory, it's none of my business." He lapsed into silence again. New possibilities were occurring rapidly. They didn't quite make sense, at least not yet, but couldn't be eliminated.

"Is it possible," he said slowly, "that the person who wants to annihilate Damselfish isn't interested in you *per se*? That his true motive is to wipe out Will Wilkinson entirely? Him, his family, and Damselfish, which Will claimed was his creation?"

Elodie stared at him. "You think the gunman didn't miss me? That he deliberately shot Conor?"

"I don't know. I'll entertain the possibility until I prove it or rule it out. Kate said there were two more gunshots after the one that hit Conor. Maybe the shooter missed you. Maybe you were his second priority."

She took that in. "There's a problem with your theory. Rebekah's never been in hiding. She's lived like normal, out in the open, this whole time. And so did Conor. There must've been millions of opportunities to kill him. Without driving all the way to Cottlestone Manor, either."

"As I suspected. What about that list I asked you and Zoë to make?" Tony asked, switching gears. "Surely you can give me some names to look into. Not only stalkers. Someone you beat out for an award, or felt forgotten as Damselfish rose to success?"

"You think I haven't been racking my brains? I've gone over everyone I ever beefed with, starting in middle school. I mean, Caryn Hattersley and I are frenemies more than friends, but she'd never hurt me. She still calls or emails me once a week."

"And the origin of the conflict was...?"

"She always wanted to be a pop singer. She even got me to introduce her to Mal," Elodie said. "He wasn't impressed by her voice. Let her down easy, I thought, but she was never the same with me after that. She couldn't be the killer, though. She was right there in the room with us today, freaking out."

"Based on the previous attacks, if she is the killer, she would have hired someone to do her dirty work. And what better way to look innocent than to be physically present during an active shooter situation?"

"So, you think it's her?"

"No. It's only another possibility I can't ignore."

Elodie covered a yawn. "Wow. It's almost midnight."

"Indeed. High time you were in bed."

"As if I can sleep after what happened."

"Then stay up all night if you wish. Just don't pop down to the corner for pot noodles."

"Tony. Do you really think Scotland Yard will catch who's doing this?"

"They'll do their damndest. And so will I. I promise."

* * *

Knowing Kate had probably turned in, and unwilling to risk disturbing her by bringing his laptop to bed, Tony remained in his office for a little while, logging into various databases accessible through his PI credentials.

Lady Caryn Hattersley was clean. She'd never had so much as a parking ticket or done anything good enough or bad enough to make the society columns. She and her husband, Sir Kenneth, lived in a small but spendy mock Tudor only a mile from Annabelle Carter.

Sir Kenneth had been in minor trouble during his uni years. Two cautions for drink-driving, the second resulting in a massive fine and suspension of his driving privileges for three years. Now, he worked for his father's corporation, holding the title of Vice President for Intraoffice Communications.

What did Elodie call his type? A failson? Tony thought. *Vice President for Intraoffice Communications is a failson title if I ever heard one. Sounds like he spends all day forwarding emails.*

Without evidence linking them to a crime or personal histories that warranted more digging, Tony could only go with his gut. And his gut told him that Lady Caryn and Sir Kenneth lacked the drive to carry out a string of murders. Even if they outsourced the actual killings, one or both of them would soon get bored, probably before the job was finished.

Throughout his research session, the baby monitor on his desk hadn't broadcast any cries from Nicky. Still, it was half-midnight; time to shamble upstairs to look in on his wife and his youngest.

As it turned out, Kate wasn't asleep but sitting up in

bed reading. As for Nicky, Tony found the baby sleeping on his back with glorious abandon. The position was sometimes called the "Fencer's pose": one arm up, one akimbo.

"How is he?" Kate asked.

"Saying *en garde* in his dreams."

"That's your boy."

"How are you?" he asked pointedly, undressing.

"Fine. Wide awake, but fine."

"Have you put in a call to Alix?" he asked, meaning her therapist.

"No. It's not PTSD. Seems like that's all about home," she said, putting her ereader aside. "Today was scary, in the moment. Then it was done, and I shook it off. But here in our bedroom, if I think I hear an intruder downstairs, I'm a bundle of nerves for hours on end."

"Makes sense. Home is where we're meant to be safe. Mind you," he continued, putting on the pajamas he didn't much care for, but midnight feedings made necessary, "we *are* safe. Wellegrave House has multiple barriers to home invasion. You should be satisfied with them, as you chose them."

"I still want a safe room."

Tony pretended not to hear. He didn't care about the expense or about sacrificing a disused pantry for the purpose. He cared about helping Kate deal with her PTSD. In his view, a safe room wasn't the answer.

"How did your pocket money talk with Henry go?"

"I sat him down and told him about it," Kate said. "I expected him to do the Snoopy dance all over the house. £500 every month—honestly, I thought he'd jump on his computer and start shopping. He didn't. He was bowled over. Then, he confessed to me about unlocking his mobile.

He thought we should know because we'd want to rescind his pocket money increase."

"How did you handle it?"

"I told him we already knew. That the nanny software has shown us every single thing he's done with the phone since he unlocked it." She chuckled. "He was a little embarrassed."

"At some point, we'll have to give him his privacy." Tony propped his crutch beside the bed and climbed in. "But not yet. There are too many predators out there, and they get cleverer all the time. So—with his confession out of the way, did he go into shopping mode?"

"No." Kate sounded pleased and incredulous. "He said £500 a month was a big opportunity. And he'd need to talk to you about how to handle it."

Tony absorbed that. "We have a remarkable son."

"I know." Kate kissed him. "Believe me, I know.

Chapter Twenty-Three

"Why aren't you gone already? Did crime stop? Have we achieved a perfect society?"

Wandering into the kitchen, Paul scrubbed at his eyes, veering toward the smell of fresh coffee. The night before, he'd decided not to tell Emmeline about the shooting at Cottlestone Manor, at least not yet. She had enough to worry about at home. Besides, he processed these things better by not talking about them.

"Not that I blame you for having a lie-in." She was at the kitchen table feeding their daughter, or trying to. Evvy sat like a surly monarch in her high throne, casting a dubious eye on the spoon Emmeline offered.

"You surprised me last night," she added, giving him a sidelong grin.

"Couldn't resist you, babe. Even with spit-up on your trackies." He kissed the top of her head. "But we opened a new case yesterday, and I need to crack on. I'll be off as soon as I sit down and have some muesli."

"Must be nice."

"What? Muesli?"

"Sitting down to eat."

Coffee mug in hand, Paul turned and really looked at his wife. Her blonde hair needed a wash. She still wore those stained trackies from the day before. Had she eaten anything, even a bit of toast?

"Yes, well, do you know what I think would be nice?" He put down the mug. "If you'd stop hogging all the action and let me feed Evvy for once."

"Pull the other one."

"I mean it. Take a hot bath. I've got this."

"But it will make you even later. Can you really do that?"

"I'm in charge, babe. I can do anything."

"Sold!" Emmeline hurried off. Her giddiness at the prospect of a half-hour all to herself made Paul proud to have offered, and embarrassed that he hadn't offered sooner.

Now, their surly monarch had a new chamberlain. Paul sat down before her, smiled, and received the same jaundiced look.

"Ev-vvy," he crooned, picking up the little plastic spoon and reloading it with carrot puree. "It's Dad-ddy. I have some scrummy veg for you."

Evvy pursed her lips and turned her head.

"All right, fine. What about beef? Beef?"

That got her attention. He fed her a couple of spoonfuls, which she ate with gusto, then went back to the carrots.

"Come on, sweetheart. We English are beefeaters, but you can't live on beef alone. Veg is good for you."

Evvy made a supremely frustrated noise. It sounded almost like, "No."

Paul tried again. "Come on, Evvy. Veg is good for you. Eat some veg."

"No. No veg."

Paul stared. Was he imagining things? The words were recognizable but not perfectly articulated. Was his brain changing gibberish into speech?

"Eat some veg, Evvy."

Her chubby fist pounded the tray. "No veg, Daddy!"

"Right. Right. No veg." Hardly knowing what he was doing, he reloaded the beef medley. "Beef?"

She made a grab at the spoon.

"Beef?"

"Beep."

"Beef?"

"Beee-f!" More pounding. "Beef, Daddy!"

He fed her one spoonful, then another, then another. As he did so, his daughter's beautiful face swam in and out of focus, but he dashed away the tears unconsciously. When she'd had her fill, he picked her up and carried her to the bathroom, barging into Emmeline's steamy, lavender-scented escape.

"Oh, for God's sake," she barked at him. "It's been ten minutes!"

"She spoke."

"What?"

"She *spoke*." Carrying her to the lip of the tub, Paul said, "Evvy. Daddy's going to feed you veg."

"No veg, Daddy." Evvy, sensing her parents' pleasure, covered her face for a moment. Then, she shrieked happily, "No veg!"

Slopping bathwater out of the tub, Emmeline jumped on the mat so hurriedly that she almost fell. Automatically wrapping a towel around herself, she pleaded, "Say it again, darling."

Evvy, staring like a magpie at the gold locket at Emmeline's throat, tried to seize it.

"No, sweetheart."

"Hang on," Paul said. "I want to try something." He flipped the locket so that it hung down Emmeline's back. Evvy, not missing a beat, strained to reach behind her mum.

"She knows where it is. Is that...normal?" Paul asked in a hushed voice.

"I don't know," Emmeline whispered back.

Evvy was watching them curiously. "No veg, Daddy," Paul said like a stagehand supplying a line.

"No veg, Daddy." Her enunciation was startlingly crisp. A little back-and-forth had already given her the knack.

Emmeline squealed. Her towel, which she'd barely used, was mostly dry; the mat under her feet was wringing wet.

"Who's that?" Paul pointed at Emmeline.

Evvy again strained toward the hidden locket.

"Here. Here it is." Undoing the clasp with shaking fingers, Emmeline handed it over. Evvy clutched it, victorious at last.

"Evvy. That gorgeous lady who's quite like a mermaid. Tell me who she is. *Daddy*." He patted his chest. "*Evvy*." He patted hers. "And this is..." He patted Emmeline. "Who's this?"

Evvy, deep in her examination of the locket, had to be prodded to look up. Paul went through the "Me Tarzan, you Jane" routine again.

"This lady, Evvy. Who's this lady?"

"Babe."

"Mummy," he corrected.

"Babe! Babe!"

"You do call me that a lot," Emmeline said hoarsely.

"I do." Paul smiled at his wife. Weeping and beaming, she was beyond perfect, just like their little girl.

***

I hate it when Mum cries, Paul thought. *But at least they were happy tears.*

The moment she heard, Sharada had rushed over to confirm the miracle for herself. Then, she'd started ringing everyone she knew, with the exception of Paul's father, who'd made it clear he didn't care about his old family, and Buck Wainwright, who'd flown back to Texas three sheets to the wind.

"Seven months old and speaking in sentences," Sharada had said over and over. "Not one word. Listen to me. I'm telling you, *sentences*..."

Only after he, Emmeline, and Sharada talked themselves blue in the face about the implications had Paul remembered he was meant to meet Tony at half-nine. By the time he reached Wellegrave House, it was pushing noon, and he was so disoriented, he couldn't recall a single detail from the tube. Before he set out, Evvy had learned a new word, locket, which she pronounced "ock-it." For all he knew, she'd master the tongue placement necessary to pronounce the letter *l* before he returned that night.

Tony said mildly, "I did say I'm happy to work alone."

"What?" Paul sat up straight. "Off with the fairies again. Sorry. I'm working, I promise."

They were on their laptops in Tony's office. While Paul was at home, delighting in Evvy's surprise milestones, Tony had reexamined all the data on Zoë Schultz's knife attack and Miranda Griffin's murder. Now, he'd gone back to the bus explosion that kicked it all off, which made Paul uneasy. He'd been in charge of the Wilkinson case. If he'd missed something the first time around, he wanted to be the one to find it. But that meant concentrating on what was in front of him.

"I was thinking," Tony said, still in that mild tone, "I could reach out to Oliver and Priya if you wish. They might be happy to talk with you."

Paul came back to earth with a guilty start. "What? Who?"

"Oliver and Priya Vine-Jones. From the Galen case?"

"The what? Oh, yeah, sorry." He lightly slapped his cheek. "Rise and shine, Paulie. You're still in touch with them? Scratch that, idiot question. How are they?" Though he couldn't guess how former suspects from a solved murder case factored into anything, he was eager to seem awake and rational.

"As their eldest, Nathan, is an exceptional young man born with many gifts, I merely thought..." Tony tailed off politely.

"Oh. Yeah! That would be brill. Thanks, Chief." Paul chuckled uneasily. "Before, I was scared witless that Evvy was way behind on her milestones. Now, there's a whole new map of responsibilities. And pitfalls." He groaned. "Listen to me bleating again. I don't suppose you'd like to whinge for once?"

"I wish I'd never had the bloody knee surgery. I resent being in pain, and I resent creeping about like an antediluvian tortoise."

"My God! This is a breakthrough. Lord Anthony Hetheridge and his flexible upper lip."

Tony chuckled. "Lady Margaret forbade me from whinging. And I can't very well go moaning to Kate. She's endured so much more and come through strong."

"Maybe. But take it from me. Sometimes, a good whinge makes the impossible possible."

London Blue

"I'll take that under advisement." Tony pushed himself to his feet, located his crutch, and came around to Paul's side of the desk. "What precisely *are* you doing, anyway? Online solitaire? Ah. Something even less helpful. The bus explosion footage."

"Not just that." Paul toggled to another window. "This video is from one of the arena's backstage CCTV cameras. See the time stamp? Eight minutes before things go boom."

"Is that Wilkinson?"

"Yeah."

"Is he dancing?"

"Maybe."

"To employ one of Elodie's phrases," Tony said, "the man looks like a ginormous git."

"If we had audio or could zoom in somehow, I could say for sure," Paul said. "But I don't think he's just dancing. I think he's practicing his rap routine."

Wilkinson, a clean-cut, middle-aged man with hair gelled straight up, wore a dark suit, thousand-pound sneakers, and shades. During three painful minutes of footage, he paced back and forth, swaying from side to side and swinging his arms like a gorilla driven out of the troop for being a prat. He scowled, grinned, and threw in threatening hand gestures as his lips moved.

"Was he apprehensive for some reason, do you think?" Tony asked. "Or just entertaining himself?"

Paul considered. "Maybe he was rehearsing for—"

"Wait. Sorry. This is ringing a bell." Returning to his side of the desk, Tony clicked keys, then spun his laptop around, showing Paul an article from the web archive of an industry magazine called *Song Spinner*.

"From the second paragraph," Tony said.

Paul read aloud, "'Wilkinson, who often displays the

demeanor of a much younger man, isn't cagey about his hopes for mid-life fame.

"'I went to uni, had my internships, and made a name for myself as a producer. But I'm more than a producer. I write. I rap. I express myself in music. I *am* music.'

"'If this sounds grandiose, perhaps it is,'" Paul read. "'As Wilkinson passionately enumerates his talents, he paces like a b-boy poised for a dance-off. His hands gesticulate constantly: the pointing finger, the closed fist, the karate chop. Five minutes in his presence is exhausting.'" Paul chuckled. "Yikes. If someone wrote that in a profile about me, I'd crawl in a hole and never come out."

"Yes, well, it's brutal, but it isn't helpful," Tony said. "How does this backstage footage end? I don't suppose a sinister-looking culprit arrives to lure Wilkinson to his death?"

"No. He gets a text or a phone call, I reckon. Pulls out his mobile, looks at it, and off he goes. He disappears from the backstage CCTV camera and reappears on an exterior camera that shows him entering the bus. One minute later—boom."

"Ah, well. There's never a culprit on CCTV when you need one."

Tony resumed clicking at his keyboard. Paul, still struggling to be productive, checked his MPS email to see if DC Kincaid or DC Baker had sent him any updates.

"Paul."

Startled by Tony's tone, Paul looked up guiltily. Had he been off with the fairies yet again?

"Look at this."

On Tony's screen was another mute, grainy, black-and-white CCTV feed. The action was paused.

"This is from a Barclays security camera across the

street from where Miranda Griffin was attacked," Tony said. "It was filed away as useless because the man's face isn't visible. But it did capture what the assailant was doing before Miranda's car stopped at the light."

At the beginning of the video, a man sprinted into view. Tall and bald, Paul judged him to be middle-aged and exceptionally fit. The passersby flowed around him as he leaned against a lamppost to catch his breath.

"Traffic was quite slow," Tony said, clicking pause. "According to the witnesses, it was the sort of afternoon where a brisk pedestrian can move faster than the cars, at least for a block or two. I believe our killer sprinted to this corner because he missed Miranda at an earlier light. He would have needed specific conditions to approach her car and get her to lower the window." He clicked play.

"He's caught his breath. Looking antsy," Paul observed.

"Pacing. And perhaps—rapping?"

Paul stared at the screen. The man was essentially featureless; the video would be ruled inadmissible in the courtroom because there was no means of identification. But the killer's swaying walk, apelike swinging arms, and hand gestures were unmistakable.

"Holy shit," Paul breathed. "Wilkinson is alive."

Chapter Twenty-Four

"Hiya, guv. You at HQ yet?" asked DC Kincaid.

"I'm on the Embankment. In the doughnut queue." Kate tapped her foot impatiently. It was a quarter till nine, the sky was overcast, and the smell of fried dough was making her stomach rumble. "The world and his wife is in front of me, getting sugared up. And I expected an update from you by three P.M. yesterday."

"Weren't you being shot at just then?"

"Nope, I was being debriefed. Talking about earning a bag of doughnuts. Seriously, though—why didn't you email me a progress report at the very least?"

"I was trying to dig up something better than goose eggs. And I think I did. But first, the CMP blackmail list. My interviews with the men didn't go the way we hoped."

"What, they all said they were happy to pay up?" Kate asked, thinking of the inimitable Viscount Lachey.

"Close. They all insisted we'd been fooled by deepfakes or body doubles," Kincaid said. "Not one said an unkind word about CMP. They all pretended to be sad about her death."

"So, they figure playing dumb is the best defense. And maybe it is. Any one of them could have killed her."

"With a magnet?"

Realizing that people in the queue were becoming interested in her side of the conversation, Kate gave up on the doughnuts. She found a more private place directly overlooking the Thames and said, "That's a good point, Sean. I need to have another go at Lord Dellkirk."

"Maybe not. I finally got through to the right person at Massive Attraction. They have an online store for retail purchases. When customers purchase an industrial magnet above a certain level, their names and addresses are kept for ten years. That's because powerful ones have been used in corporate sabotage, wiping hard drives, and so on. Someone we know bought a rare earth magnet last month. Want to guess who?"

"Lady Griselda Bothurst," Kate said, mostly joking.

"Daciana Botezatu."

"Oh! Of course she did. That's great work, Sean. Bring her in. If Rasvan looks at you the wrong way, bring him in, too. Maybe this case really is as simple as an employee who decided to do in her boss."

"You got it, guv. What time do you want to do the interview?"

She started to answer, "ASAP," and stopped herself. Sean had dug out the name; the best reward for an up-and-coming detective was greater responsibility.

"I have an appointment with Virginia Braide at Annabelle Carter. Just want to be sure she isn't sitting on vital information. It's probably a moot point, given your news, but I'll see it through. In the meantime, you handle the interview. Bring along DC Baker. Of course, she's no—" Kate cut herself off before she could finish.

"No Amelia," he said. "No. But she's good. I like her."

"Oh, Sean. Foot in mouth. Sorry."

"Don't be. Sometimes I wish people wouldn't avoid mentioning her."

"I'll try to remember that. Go arrest Daciana. And be sure to keep me posted, even if it all comes up goose eggs." Before she could change her mind and seize control of what promised to be a juicy interview, Kate rang off. This time, Sean would get the confession, and she'd get a pointless follow-up with a cookery teacher.

I hope today's lesson is doughnuts, Kate thought, heading for the tube station.

* * *

"Disaster," pronounced Ginny Braide.

Standing beside what appeared to be a leaning tower of shiny rocks, her pupil looked appropriately chagrined.

"Your *pâte à choux* puffs are meant to be of uniform size. Your tiny ones contain little or no filling. The big ones are like boulders. They'd be a nightmare to eat. Before you piped your dough, did you draw your pastry template as instructed?"

"No, ma'am."

"You simply worked freehand and hoped for the best?"

"Yes, ma'am."

"Faiza, I despair of you. Take your seat."

As Braide cast her beady eye on the next *croquembouche*, Kate googled the French celebration dessert. They were a fixture at the galas she attended with Tony; Harvey had done one for their wedding. To Kate, they looked simple and not especially appetizing. But, judging from the rapturous reception Harvey's croquembouches always received, the dessert was a crowd-pleaser.

"Marielle, your croquembouche looks good. The caramel is a touch dark for my taste, but still acceptable." Withdrawing a tape measure from her apron pocket, Braide checked the dessert's height. "Twenty-two inches. Disappointing. I did say the proper height is twenty-four inches, minimum." Removing a cream puff, the cookery teacher took one bite and binned the rest.

"Marielle, what is the direct English translation of the word croquembouche?"

"Crunch in mouth."

"When did you fill those puffs?"

"Last night."

"Didn't I say you must not fill them until the moment before you assemble the tower? Your puffs are soggy. Take a seat."

It went on like that for some time. Kate checked her Met email, personal email, and text messages. Tony had sent her a video of Nicky snuggling his stuffed lion. She was smiling fondly at it when Ginny said, "I'm sorry class ran over, Lady Hetheridge. What would you like to speak with me about?"

"DI Hetheridge is fine." Kate put away her mobile. She'd been so caught up in watching her son that she'd failed to notice the class filing out. Now, the kitchen was empty apart from her, the cookery teacher, and some wonky pastry trees.

"I can't imagine what you want to ask me." Ginny's tone was miles from the brusque one she used with her students. A big woman, she hunched as Kate approached, hands awkwardly clasped before her.

"I haven't anything to offer," Ginny added. "If I'm being

honest, I'm still gutted over what happened yesterday. Poor Conor. He was a lovely chevalier. Lady Bothurst was deeply shocked."

"I'm sure she was. Mrs. Braide, you're not wearing your London blue ring."

"Not for class." Stripping off her food prep gloves, Ginny opened a drawer, plucked out the ring, and slipped it on. It twinkled on the third finger of her left hand, symbolizing the professional union.

"Did those rings create envy among the staff?"

"Oh, yes, terrible envy. Cathleen loved hers and lorded it over everybody. But I never wanted mine. If I could've returned it without giving offense, I would have."

"Lady Bothurst told me you and Mrs. Maitland-Palmer were singled out simply to put the rest of the teachers on notice."

"It was more than that." Ginny seemed surprised that the headmistress would make such a claim. "It was a reward for loyalty. I found myself in a tricky scrape and came out okay. Did right by the school, I mean. Same with Cathleen. We proved our allegiance, and Lady Bothurst recognized us for it."

"Tell me what happened." Whether it ultimately mattered to the case or not, Kate was intrigued.

"It was twenty-five years ago. Who cares anymore?" Ginny's small eyes darted to the wall clock.

"I'm not trying to make you anxious or put you on the spot," Kate said. "But someone cut off Mrs. Maitland-Palmer's finger to get that ring. Maybe it was pure theft. But for some reason, I don't believe that."

As if playing for time, Ginny removed her flour-dusted apron, hung it on a peg, dusted off her shapeless black maxi dress, and smoothed her hair. "You must understand, DI

Hetheridge. Lady Bothurst insists that all inquiries about the school's controversies are answered by her."

"You just told me Lady Bothurst lied about the reason you received the ring." Watching the cookery teacher twist her hands, Kate added, "Makes sense that you wear the ring on your wedding finger. Working for her is like being in a bad marriage, isn't it?"

Ginny's eyes widened. "You've no idea."

"You're afraid Mrs. Bothurst will sack you?"

"Oh, no. She couldn't find anyone else to do my job without paying them triple," Ginny said matter-of-factly, without a trace of ego. "The school's barely hanging on financially. Besides—no young teacher fresh out of the culinary institute could ever live up to Griselda's standards."

"Which gives you the whip hand over her."

"No. Now, especially with Cathleen gone, Griselda's my only friend. Without her, I'd never be invited anywhere."

"What kind of invitations are you angling for?" Kate tried not to laugh. "To manor houses where young men get shot dead and people sit around, obviously despising each other?"

"You shouldn't mock. You're Lady Hetheridge. You get invited everywhere."

Kate could have rebutted that sentiment with a frank description of her more onerous social obligations, but she didn't think it would solve Ginny's problem. The cookery teacher's real issue wasn't loneliness but fear. Fear of not pleasing the most powerful person in her life, Lady Griselda Bothurst. And fear of deliberate rule-breaking, when she spent her working life pummeling the young women who broke hers.

"I know you must think me a great, daft cow," Ginny said. "But I'm too old to change."

"How old are you?"

"Sixty."

Kate grinned. "I have a story for you about a man who turned sixty."

* * *

Ginny's new office was Cathleen Maitland-Palmer's old one. The wall décor and knickknacks were gone, but the furniture hadn't changed. The Mills and Boon paperbacks were packed in a cardboard box marked CHARITY. Life was going on without Cathleen; before long, every trace of her would disappear, except possibly for Lexie Lex's YouTube video. That amateur exposé might become her most enduring tribute.

"So romantic," Ginny said when Kate finished her story. "I gave up on finding a husband ages ago. But a story like that makes me wonder."

"Mrs. Maitland-Palmer found love online, or so I was told," Kate said, nudging the woman to talk about the case.

"Yes. That's one of the things Griselda told me to keep schtum about. How Cathleen was convinced she'd been scammed and was suddenly desperate for money."

"She confided in you?"

"Yes. Sydney—his real name was Robert Raynard—turned cruel when she said she couldn't wire him any more cash. He called her an old cow and said he'd already traded her in for a younger model. Then he changed his number. She tried to get him back by mobile, text, everything. He was gone. Disappeared in a puff of smoke." After a pause,

Ginny added, "I did try to tell her. I grew up on tales of Raynard the Fox."

"Remind me." Kate didn't recognize the name.

"He's a trickster from European folk tales. If he seemed to be kind to you, he was actually picking your pocket."

"Had Cathleen heard of that character?"

"Of course. I'm sure it was in a book of fairy tales she or her daughter grew up on. Anyway," Ginny continued, "there was something Sydney said before he signed off for good. He told Cathleen his new woman was Romanian. It was filthy, and I'd rather not repeat it. But the gist was, Romanian women are better in bed."

"Did that make her suspicious of her cleaner, Daciana?" Kate asked.

"Oh, yes. I thought she'd sack the little minx. But she wanted answers, and more than anything, she wanted her money back," Ginny said. "So, she stole the cleaner's passport and refused to give it back unless she confessed."

"Why did Lady Bothurst want you to keep that from me?"

"Because stealing a passport to keep an employee from leaving work is a crime. And Cathleen stashed the passport in this office."

"In the bookcase," Kate said. "Hidden in her old letters."

Ginny nodded. "The day after Cathleen died, someone rifled the place and took the passport. Mrs. Dankworth thought it must have been the janitor. And maybe it was. He was the type to do anything for a tenner."

"All this would've been quite useful information last week, but as it happens, Daciana's being arrested right now. Have you been sitting on anything else? Why did Lady Bothurst lie to me about the rings?"

"Probably to keep from embarrassing former students. Girls who grew up well and support the school better than most." Ginny twisted her London blue ring. "Did you know Marilyn Maitland-Palmer was a student here?"

Kate nodded.

"There's a woman in government now who was a student at the same time. Neera Nausherwani. Have you heard of her?"

"Oh, yeah."

"Well, I caught Marilyn and Neera breaking the rules. At first, I wanted to pretend I didn't know. But loyalty—or fear, if I'm being honest—won out, and I told Griselda. She was furious. She ordered Cathleen, who was deputy headmistress at the time, to fix the situation or get out. And Cathleen proved her loyalty by fixing it. Afterwards, it came to light that all the other teachers knew what was going on but said nothing. That's why Griselda presented the two of us with rings and no one else."

"All right. That's interesting, I suppose. But I already knew about Marilyn and Knight Club. And I figured the entire faculty knew as well."

"Knight Club?" Ginny looked blank.

"Marilyn founded Knight Club. Neera was in it, too. That's what you're talking about, isn't it?"

"No. I'm talking about Marilyn and Neera having sex every chance they got. I'm afraid we weren't very understanding. Griselda called it deviance," Ginny said. "Even twenty-five years ago, that felt a bit harsh. But back then, no lesbian behavior at Annabelle Carter was an unwritten rule. And it's been an explicit rule ever since."

"Neera Nausherwani had a fling with Marilyn Maitland-Palmer?" Kate asked, gobsmacked.

"More than a fling. They were wild about each other. Young love."

Kate took a moment to absorb that. "Ginny. Is it possible they're back together now?"

"Oh, I think they grew out of it. Moved on. As I said, it was stamped out pretty definitively. Cathleen was furious. She made Marilyn see a psychiatrist. And Neera's family was ready to sue the school. They said our environment corrupted their daughter. But in the end, it was all smoothed over, and neither of them seems to remember it now. Marilyn married a Jamaican handyman, didn't she? And Neera did very well. Caught herself the CEO of Talk-Talk, you know. It's been an enduring marriage. They have four boys, all handsome young athletes."

"Marilyn and Neera are still friendly at the very least," Kate said. "Neera is DEFRA Secretary. She has nothing to do with the Metropolitan Police Service. But she knew about Cathleen's death before the authorities did, because Marilyn rang her before 999."

"Hmm. Probably just loyalty to the school. But who knows? My mum used to say first loves never die."

"Right. Thank you, Ginny." As Kate rose to go, the other woman removed her London blue ring. "Going back to the kitchen?"

"No, I'm going home, unless Cohen's Fine Jewelry is still open. The owner has remarked on my ring many times. I feel sure he'll make me an offer."

"That should make for an interesting conversation with Lady Bothurst." Kate was astonished. There was no way her story about Tony's changes since his sixtieth birthday had freed Ginny from decades of fearful loyalty. This mutiny must have been simmering in the pot for a long time.

"I'm sure it will. But Annabelle Carter has been dead

for a long time. I'm tired of painting rouge on the corpse. Besides." Ginny smiled at Kate, a gleam in her eyes. "If Griselda wants, she's welcome to replace me. *If* she can find another cookery teacher who'll do this thankless job for less than triple my salary."

* * *

"Hiya, guv." DC Kincaid answered his mobile in a wary tone, as if Kate were the last person he wanted to talk to.

"Seannie, my lad, how goes the interview?"

"It doesn't. I'm in Hackney, talking to the Botezatus' neighbors. Their flat is still furnished, but no one's there."

"I suppose Daciana's not answering her mobile, either?"

"No. But she was seen in the building yesterday. So was Rasvan. It's not impossible they'll come home."

"And it's not impossible they've done a runner," Kate said. "You know the drill. Have a couple of uniformed officers wait at the flat in case they return. Meanwhile, you and DC Baker contact HMPO and Border Security Command. If the Botezatus try to travel on their real passports, picking them up should be easy."

And if they got themselves top-drawer fraudulent passports, this could turn into a long chase, Kate thought. Any UK citizen who wanted a phony passport could get one if they had cash and working knowledge of the dark web.

Kincaid sighed. "I hope we don't have to turn this over to Europol."

"Think positive. Daciana wanted her real passport badly enough to steal it back. Maybe she and Daddy are traveling under their real names."

And maybe, Kate thought, *Daciana's purchase of the magnet isn't the smoking gun I thought it was.*

Chapter Twenty-Five

"I'll kill him," Elodie Queen shrieked. The virtual connection didn't dim the force of her fury and grief. "I should've known that egomaniacal bastard would never top himself! He'd burn down the whole world first!"

"That's our impression of Wilkinson's character, certainly," Tony said. Outside, the sun was going down; Paul had left for HQ hours ago. Their afternoon of quietly reviewing the details of a cold case had transformed into a manhunt for a double murderer.

"You're sure about this? You can prove it?" Elodie wore her usual Goth-rocker clothes. Her green hair was brighter, as if recently refreshed, and her eyeliner was as black as her lipstick. Still, she looked as much like a child to Tony as she had the night before, even without the pajamas and stuffed bear.

He said, "For now, it's only informed supposition. But the theory fits the facts so far. To pull off the bus explosion, Wilkinson needed a professional. As I mentioned before, one of his rapper clients stood trial for murder. That client might have provided him with the necessary connections.

"To ensure human remains were among the rubble, Wilkinson would've invited some as-yet-unidentified person, perhaps a fan, to wait on the tour bus. Possibly, he promised them a meet-and-greet. Or maybe he lured a homeless person onboard with the offer of a meal. Either way, someone else died in his place.

"A backstage camera filmed Wilkinson pacing and performing, if you can call it that," Tony said archly, "until the time drew near. Then, he boarded the bus, making certain to pass by a CCTV camera as he did. The bus was parked facing the camera, so its emergency exit window wasn't visible. No doubt Wilkinson asked the driver to park in the optimal spot. He planned his 'death' meticulously."

"I'm shocked he didn't use the bomb to wipe us out," Elodie said. "Zoë, Miranda, and I were *in the bus* during intermission. It would've been so easy."

"Yes, but what then? Wilkinson still would have been a middle-aged music executive, one public humiliation under his belt, in the middle of a messy divorce that was sure to cost half his assets. He might've hidden them as best he could, but even if he survived the forensic audits, Rebekah's lawyers would've pounced the first time he touched the money. He needed a new identity. So, he gradually transferred his assets to a new identity, then 'died' in order to claim them.

"Of course, this would've been right after Christmas," Tony said. "I don't yet have a theory as to why he waited over eight months to try and settle the score with Damselfish."

"I know why. We were on a world tour," Elodie said. "He had to wait for us to get back to London. I just can't believe he went after Zoë first. He loathed me. You'd think I would have been top of the list."

"I believe you were. That mugger you mentioned, the one your dog, Patience, bit? You said it happened before Zoë's stabbing, yes? That may have been Wilkinson's first attempt at murder. He may not even have brought a weapon. Egomaniacal men tend to assume that choking a woman to death will be easy. Even when she has a large, loyal Rottweiler beside her.

"Once he recovered sufficiently from the dog bite, he went after Zoë," Tony continued. "As with you, he knew exactly where and when to find her alone. Possibly because the bug was planted in your flat, or perhaps because he had the three of you under visual surveillance. For his second attempt, he disguised himself and brought a weapon. But committing murder with a knife designed for dicing veg didn't work.

"So, with Miranda, he took his time and executed the kind of carefully thought-out plan he devised for his sham death," Tony said. "He was swift. He was ruthless. And after he killed her, he locked her body in the car boot to make her murder seem professional rather than personal."

Elodie gave an incoherent cry of rage.

"Then, there's Conor. I confess, I'm glad it won't fall to me to tell Rebekah Wilkinson who is responsible for her son's death," Tony said. "Either Wilkinson pulled the trigger himself, or he hired a gunman. But based on his DIY behavior thus far, I assume he fired the fatal shot, probably whilst aiming at you."

"Please," Elodie said in a low voice. "*Please* tell me you'll catch him."

"DI Bhar's team is already searching. We know Wilkinson changed his appearance based on eyewitness testimony from Miranda's kidnapping. Shaved his head, grew a beard. A smart man who successfully faked his death would start a new life far away. That's the typical MO. But fakers have been known to revisit key places from their previous identity or refuse to leave home altogether. Given London's size, Wilkinson probably thought he didn't have to go. Let's hope he hasn't changed his mind just yet."

"Oh, God," Elodie said. "*Conor.*"

The small hairs on the back of Tony's neck rose. "Tell me."

"Remember when you asked why Conor thought his life was messed up? I said, delayed grief. That he must've never dealt with his feelings about his dad. I said that because he went from not caring at all to claiming he'd seen Will. Alive and in London."

"Where?"

Elodie continued as if he hadn't spoken. "Rebekah and I used to complain about Will to each other, and she still calls sometimes. The other day, she rang me up to say Conor should go to therapy. He'd been doing what I told him to do —going to hip-hop clubs with open mic nights. He was still working up to it, haunting a club called the Ministry of Rhythm. When it's open mic, anyone can have three minutes in front of the toughest crowd in London. Most performers, even the decent ones, are booed off the stage. The rappers who survive have a future. Conor was at the Ministry on Monday night and—"

"Three days ago?"

"Yeah. He saw a man get booed off the stage. The guy was doing a variation of 'Go Down Hoedown.' Conor said at first, he thought the dude had stolen his dad's song. Then, he realized it *was* his dad. He told Rebekah that Will looked different—bald, a beard, a stone heavier—and when he tried to confront Will outside the club, he legged it."

"Rebekah assumed Conor was having a breakdown?"

"Yeah. And so did I. He told me about it yesterday, before the interview started." Elodie blinked back tears. "He was desperate to make me believe him, but I didn't."

"You couldn't have known," Tony said. "It seems likely that Will was eavesdropping via the bug in your handbag. When Kate asked Conor to describe Mrs. Maitland-Palmer's state of mind on the night of her death, and Conor referred to his own life being, as he put it, 'messed up'..." Tony tailed off, thinking it over. "Yes. Those words probably spurred Wilkinson to shoot his own son dead, rather than let him describe the sighting in the police's hearing."

"You think he did it on purpose?"

"Why not? A man willing to desert his children and leave them penniless, relatively speaking, can do a great deal worse under pressure. But whether all three shots were intended for you or only the second and third shot, the result is the same. He murdered his son."

"I want him caught," Elodie said fiercely. "I want him punished."

"Hold on to that feeling. You're the key to making it happen."

* * *

Around ten P.M., Tony was standing beside Nicky's cot, watching the boy sleep, when Kate entered the room.

"Where's your crutch?"

He smiled at her. "Today, Paul invited me to whinge freely about my knee. I did—and now it seems I can stand unaided. Perhaps there's some value to strategic venting, now and again. Alas, walking still presents a challenge."

"Onward and upward, zaddy."

Chuckling, he settled into bed and pointedly performed a bed slide. "Ninety degrees flexion."

"And barely a grimace. Still wish you hadn't done it?" she asked, sliding in beside him.

"I never said that. Not to you."

"You didn't have to. *Zaddy*," she repeated. "Do you even know what that means?"

"Naturally. I believe I own the copyright."

Kate snuggled up to him. "Maybe you learned 'zaddy' from your sexy young client."

"No, but I'll be sure to tell Dame Ingrid you find her young and sexy."

"So bizarre. A case where the victim turns out to be alive and rapping. *Poorly*. Wish I was on it with you."

"Really?"

"I miss working together. You're solving cases from home, Paul's swanned off to manage his manhunt, and I'm babysitting DCs."

"I don't believe for a minute that you'd willingly go backward. You like being in charge. And you've earned it."

"Being the guv is nice. Tomorrow, I plan to hit Marilyn Maitland-Palmer again. The more I think about it, the more I feel like she's behind her mum's death. Anyway..." She traced a design on his chest. "Now that you can stand without a crutch, it doesn't mean you should start trying to walk without it. Just because you'll be sixty-two and think you have something to prove."

"You haven't mentioned my birthday in, what? A week? Admirable self-restraint."

"Harvey told me you put the kibosh on a special menu. Because that's an unbearable thing for a man's family to do: serve a meal in his honor."

"I'm pleased you agree."

"And since the occasion is less than two weeks away, I might as well tell you there *will* be a special dinner on your birthday." Kate spoke fast, as if he might jump up and run away. "The details are confidential, but I can promise you this. The venue is private. The view is impressive. One table only. There will be no streamers, noisemakers, or singing of any kind. And you don't have to wear evening dress, but I wish you would because you're utterly scrummy in it." She paused, clearly waiting for an objection, then added, "Don't you dare threaten not to go."

"I'll go," he said, relishing her surprise. "And I know the venue will be posh, since you went to the trouble of opening a secret checking account to put down the deposit."

"You drove me to it. You might've canceled the check if I'd used the joint account. So, you've been surveilling me, have you? Charting my movements?"

"Not at all. I trust you completely, apart from ignoring my wishes about birthdays. Only the bank manager gave me a bell. He thought I'd want to know that my wife opened a solo account. And had paid a rather large amount to something called GDS Catering."

"The bank manager? What business of it is his?"

"He considered it a courtesy. I've banked with them for years."

"Right. Tomorrow, I'll march in there, warrant card in hand, and give him a crash course in banking confidentiality laws."

"In this instance, they don't apply," he said, hiding his pleasure. No woman in the world was as desirable as Kate Wakefield Hetheridge when she was riled up.

"Fine. Then I'll bang him up for ruining my surprise. Did you look into GDS Catering? Admit it. I know you did."

"Only enough to learn they provide event management to several venues belonging to the National Trust. So, wherever you take me, I know it won't be KFC."

"I suppose you got other alerts, too?"

"No. I told the manager not to trouble me again." Tony was poised to shift their discussion into the physical realm, but Kate's secure MPS trilled. She had three ringtones: colleagues, the Met switchboard, and everybody else. This was the "everybody else" tone, which was highly unusual for a Thursday at half-ten. Groaning, she picked up.

"DI Hetheridge, it better be good." A pause. "Ms. Nausherwani. How can I help?"

Chapter Twenty-Six

"I'm sorry to call you at this hour, but it can't be helped." Neera spoke briskly, like a woman accustomed to being obeyed. "I rang Paul Bhar first, and he told me he'd been reassigned. I'm not happy to find myself abandoned, but I'll deal with that later. In the meantime, he named you as my point of contact."

"Yes."

"Get on with it, then. Give me a progress report on the investigation."

Kate bit back a laugh. "Sorry, not possible. Anything else before I hang up?"

There was a beat that Kate interpreted as incredulous silence. Then: "You should know I spoke to Lady Bothurst this evening. She'd just sacked the cookery teacher, Ginny Braide, for speaking at length to you earlier. Apparently, you received certain privileged details. I want to know what she said."

"I'm sure you do. But ringing me at home isn't the way to go about it. Furthermore," Kate said, gathering steam, "you have no business interrogating an MPS officer on any topic. I find your behavior inappropriate and potentially unethical. When Scotland Yard calls a press conference to update the public on the Maitland-Palmer case, you'll be briefed along with everyone else. Not before."

"Who do you think you are?" Neera asked coldly. "If you don't start doing your job, I'll see you're replaced. Why are Rasvan Botezatu and his daughter still at large? He was tried for murder twice in Romania. Acquitted, yes, but you know what the courts are like. Those two should've been your prime suspects from the start."

"When Scotland Yard wants your input—"

"Listen to me," Neera cried. "I'm serious. The Botezatus are dangerous, and I'm afraid for Marilyn's life."

"Marilyn Maitland-Palmer?"

"Yes. I tried to call her earlier, but she didn't pick up. I went to her place in Brixton. I found the door unlocked and her things strewn about like a tornado. She's gone, DI Hetheridge! I think the Botezatus have her."

"When did you discover the flat had been tossed?"

"Half an hour ago. Less."

"Call 999."

"I'm calling you. First, they killed the mother. Now they have the daughter. If you don't do something, I'll have your job, I swear I will!"

Kate wanted very much to tell Neera to go work on her fundraising, or whatever it was that politicians did, but the situation warranted follow-up. Especially in light of her rising suspicions about Marilyn.

"Address? Right. I'm putting it into my GPS. Okay. It looks like I can get there in forty minutes. An hour at most. In the meantime, ring 999."

"*You* ring them. I can't. I—I'm busy."

Out of bed and striding to the walk-in closet, Kate stopped dead. "Where are you, Ms. Nausherwani?"

"How is that relevant?"

"Are you home?"

"Yes."

"You went to Marilyn's place, discovered what you consider evidence of a crime, left the scene without calling the authorities, and only rang me once you were home again?"

"Yes. I couldn't stay there and wait on the police. Not that it's any of your business," Neera said stiffly, "but my family needs me. Now, then. When you have news about Marilyn, ring me on this line. *Only* this line."

"Of course. You wouldn't want me to mention her to your hubby." Checking her mobile screen, she added. "You're calling from a 076 number. Burner phone?"

"Whatever suspicions Ginny Braide put in your head, she had no right to judge me. And neither do you. I may still have your job, *Ms.* Hetheridge, so tread lightly. Good night." She disconnected.

"Whelp. Off to Brixton I go," Kate told Tony.

"You could send Sean."

"I need to reinterview Marilyn myself. If someone's kidnapped her, I'll lead the search."

"Why was the politician shouting? Is she having it off with the daughter on the side?"

"Yes. The only question in my mind," Kate said, stepping into the trousers she'd so recently vacated, "is whether or not Neera was involved with Cathleen's murder, or if Marilyn did it alone."

"No rest for the weary."

"Or the wicked." Kate reached for her blouse.

Nicholas made a fussy sound from his cot. It swiftly transitioned into a wail.

"He can't be hungry yet. Teething, I shouldn't wonder." Tony reached for his crutch. "As you said—no rest for the wicked."

* * *

On Kate's first attempt to find Marilyn Maitland-Palmer's shop, Cyber Monkeez, she turned down the wrong side street. In the headlights of Tony's SUV, vibrant portraits stood out on dirty brick walls. A polar bear in outer space. A velociraptor in Victorian clothes. A dreamy sylph with constellations for hair. There was plenty of graffiti, too: band names, obscenities, anarchy symbols. Looping around the block, Kate found the correct street. There was Cyber Monkeez, sandwiched between a punk salon and a charity shop.

She parked behind a panda car—or what she still thought of as a panda car, even though the colors had changed to blue and yellow—and was greeted by DC Kincaid, who looked as sleepy as she felt.

"Wotcha, Sean."

"Hiya, guv. Marilyn lives in the flat above the shop. Two uniforms are up there going over the scene."

"A kidnapping and robbery, d'you think? Or just a burglary?"

"There's no visible blood. Door was kicked in, from the looks of it. Kitchen canisters dumped out. Freezer emptied. Every drawer and cupboard tossed."

"Right. Better take a look."

Rolldown security gates protected Cyber Monkeez's shopfront. In the back, a rusty external staircase led up to

London Blue

Marilyn's flat. Its door was more than kicked in—it was kicked off its hinges.

Not much of a feat, Kate thought, *when the door is cheap plywood with a standard knob and no bolt lock.*

"I don't believe this," she told Kincaid. "It's the Tower Jewel House out front but come-in-and-kill-me back here?"

"Looks like there used to be a security door." Kincaid's torch picked out empty holes and scrapes around the cracked frame. After shining the torch at the ground, he added, "Not only off, but gone. That's one determined intruder."

"No. A security door can't be removed from the outside," Kate stated with confidence. "Not unless a moron installed it. MMP struck me as many things, but stupid wasn't one of them."

Inside the flat, Kate greeted a pair of young, fresh-faced coppers who seemed thrilled to work beside a Scotland Yard detective. As she followed them from space to space, checking for any detail they might have missed, Kincaid answered his mobile's buzz.

"Yeah. No. Uh-huh. I doubt it. Yeah. I'm sorry. I'll ring you tomorrow afternoon. Of course. Uh-huh."

"Interrupted your evening, too, eh?" Kate said. "I had something much nicer lined up myself." She meant to sound matey but didn't quite succeed. It was ludicrous. How did she know Sean's call came from a woman? Why did she assume he'd already moved on from Amelia? And when did her DC's love life become any of her business?

"Nothing major." Kincaid smiled sheepishly. "My friend Octavia's a bit of a night owl. Sometimes we meet up for a midnight hot cocoa."

"Oh." Kate strove for a polite tone. "Lovely. Right. Let's crack on."

Why, Kate thought, *do I ever open my stupid mouth?*

The interior search turned up nothing. Sean directed the uniformed officers outside, asking them to check nearby rubbish bins. Sometimes, important clues, like discarded murder weapons, bloody clothes, and even corpses, were stuffed in a bin awaiting discovery.

"Listen, guv," he said when they were alone. "Can I be honest for a sec?"

"I'm sorry, Sean. I don't know what I was thinking. You don't owe me an explanation."

"Maybe I do. You were Amelia's friend. But you're also my guv, so I can't really talk to you about losing her," he said awkwardly. "But Octavia's different. Her mum was murdered, and she knew her dad did it. She had to live with knowing the truth, but not being able to prove it, for years and years. The rage made her do crazy things. I think..." He sighed. "I think the rage I feel over Amelia would make me do crazy things, too, if I couldn't talk with someone who understands."

"I fouled up, Sean, full stop. When I ran into you and Octavia at Peregrine's, I jumped to conclusions. I thought Amelia was history and you'd found someone new."

"I'll never forget Amelia. As for Tave and me, I never meant for it to happen. She's not even my type, and God knows I'm not hers. Half her mates won't talk to her now that she's seeing a copper. But..." He tailed off, shrugging. "There it is. I don't know what else to say."

As Kate searched for a way to conclude the exchange besides doing a runner, one of the uniformed officers outside shouted,

"Oi! I said you can't go up there. Stop!"

Neera, Kate thought, relieved by the idea of a face-to-face throwdown. *If she thinks she can push me around in person, she has another thing coming.*

Hurrying to the busted doorframe, Kincaid arrived in time to block the interloper. The short, dark-skinned man he grappled with was like a wild animal. "Hetheridge," he cried, trying to make eye contact. "I need DI Hetheridge."

"I'm DI Hetheridge. Sean, it's all right. Let him go for now." As the man in a dark coat, trackies, and a knit beanie pulled himself together, she tried to square his image with the photo she'd seen at Annabelle Carter. It was him, she decided, several years older and out of his blue janitor overalls. "You're Rasvan Botezatu."

"Yes. You are Hetheridge? I—"

"I'm afraid you can't be here, Mr. Botezatu. It's a crime scene."

"There's a crime, all right." The little man seemed on the verge of hysteria. "My daughter, Daciana. She's missing. Go out for lunch yesterday. Never come back!"

Kate swapped glances with Kincaid. "Are you sure? She's a grown woman. Could she have—"

"I look all night. I don't sleep," he said in almost a howl. "She would never do this. Never, not even for one night. This is dangerous city. I must know where she is, always."

Kincaid looked openly skeptical. He'd probably read up on Rasvan's Romanian troubles and concluded the man was, if not a gangster, certainly gangster adjacent. But for Kate, Rasvan's dodgy reputation was the only reason to believe him. Street-level criminals were always at risk of being attacked by rivals. For a man like Rasvan, who'd twice faced the prospect of a life sentence in a Romanian prison, personal risk was part of the game. But if he loved Daciana as fiercely as he seemed to, she was his greatest vulnerability.

"DI Hetheridge, please. My daughter has been taken, I know it. Help me get her back. Please help me."

"How did you know where to find me?" Kate asked.

Botezatu looked at her blankly. "What?"

"How did you know I'd be in Marilyn Maitland-Palmer's flat at this time of night?"

"I didn't. I came here to beat the truth out of that woman." Despite his small stature, Rasvan's threat wasn't comical. Kate had no doubt Rasvan had administered beatings in the past and was willing to do it again if that's what it took to find Daciana.

"Bragging about intent to commit GBH, are you?" Kincaid asked, still skeptical.

"It's not a crime to destroy evil," Rasvan said with startling sincerity. "Listen to what I tell you. Many times I tell my daughter, shun such women. But Marilyn, she is worst. Pure evil."

Chapter Twenty-Seven

"I want the whole story. No omissions. Leave nothing out," Kate said. It was eleven A.M. the following day, a cold Friday that felt more like November than September. She was running on two hours' sleep and two Pret A Manger flat whites, and she sounded like it—impatient, with a side of menace.

"I think you already know most of it," Neera Nausherwani said, almost meekly.

They were sitting in Tony's SUV, parked on a street near Hyde Park that Kate had chosen at random. She had no interest in deliberately humiliating the politician by hauling her into Scotland Yard HQ for an interview. She only wanted the uncensored truth as fast as possible.

"Ginny Braide lost her job telling me how you and Marilyn first got together," Kate said. "The least you can do is pick up the story after the two of you were found out."

"It was awful," Neera said flatly. "My parents couldn't believe it. They grew up in a culture with no tolerance for— for that sort of thing. I had to beg and plead and promise them anything to keep them from sending me away to live with my auntie. I mean it. They almost disowned me."

"What about Marilyn?"

"It's not like Cathleen ever cared for her in the first place. She was disgusted. Forced Marilyn to go to a shrink and say she was cured."

"I thought you were at least eighteen years old when this happened."

"We were."

"So, neither of you were forced to do anything. You both could've packed up, left Annabelle Carter, and ridden off into the sunset together."

"Would you do such a thing? Turn your back on your parents? Leave them to despise you forever?"

Kate softened. "Maybe I'm not the best person to ask. And even if eighteen is legally grown up, most people are still pretty dependent at that age. But when the smoke cleared, it seems like you moved on. Got married to the TV exec?"

"Yes. We've been together twenty-two years. Our sons are beautiful. I have a good career. But I was still...." Neera looked away. "You wouldn't understand."

"I think I do. Did you two decide to be good little Annabelle Carter alumni so you could stay in touch?"

"Yes. Marilyn was doing well after graduation and could afford to donate generously. I was a rising star, if I say so myself, and did everything I could for the school, short of telling the world I'd gone there."

"From what I've gathered, you were a favorite with the faculty. Especially Lady Bothurst and Mrs. Dankworth. Even Cathleen seemed to have forgiven you."

"She did. She never blamed me. She thought Marilyn was the bad seed who seduced me." Neera shook her head.

"But even they came to terms eventually. When Marilyn was flush from her investments, she went on an island sabbatical for six months. Came back telling everyone she'd had a whirlwind marriage and a quickie divorce. That made things easier for her, and no one asked too many questions."

"Did you keep up the affair in secret all these years?"

"No. I didn't marry Quint just to cheat on him." Neera sounded slightly offended. "I did my best to make a go of the marriage, and Marilyn did her own thing. Moved to Brixton and pretended like she'd grown up there. Took a computer degree. Opened the shop. All the while, she was still playing the markets. She could've retired at thirty and lived comfortably for the rest of her life. But she was a risk junkie. Always going all-in on the penny stocks, trying to hit it big. When the global economy crashed, she lost everything."

"And ended up living in the flat above Cyber Monkeez," Kate said. "I know you probably don't see her as capable of committing a crime. But did she ever say or do anything that struck you as antisocial?"

"No. I don't know why you keep trying to paint her as a villain. I don't even know what we're doing here, digging up the dead past when she's *missing*, for God's sake."

"There's a method to my madness," Kate said, impatient again. "When did you and Marilyn start things up again?"

"Last spring."

"Was it serious?"

"Yes."

"Divorce-your-husband serious?"

"Yes. Someday," Neera said evasively. "In my career, image management is everything."

"Did the two of you make concrete plans?"

"Not yet," Neera said. "And not just because of me. Marilyn was rebuilding her nest egg from nothing."

"Right. Switching gears. Did Cathleen tell you about her new man? Robert Raynard, from Sydney, Australia?"

"A few times."

"What did Marilyn think about the affair?"

"What does it matter? Why do you keep trying to make me say something that will cast her in a negative light?"

"Just answer the damn question."

"She thought Cathleen was being catfished," Neera said. "That the man wasn't even real, just a deepfake. A Nigerian prince, maybe, sitting on the other side of the Zoom call, with computer software making him look and sound like Hugh Jackman. She laughed about it all the time."

"And that's the kind of thing Marilyn had the skill to pull off, yes?"

"What? No. I mean, yes, probably, but why would she do that?" Neera sounded genuinely appalled.

"I've been told that Cathleen was constantly wiring cash to this Robert Raynard person. And when she ran out, he turned cruel and ghosted her. Before he disappeared, he bragged about trading Cathleen in for a younger model," Kate said. "From what I gather, that was probably her greatest fear. The kind of button someone who knew her would push. Marilyn needed money to rebuild her nest egg. If she found out Cathleen made a mint blackmailing old flames, she might have cooked up a scheme to siphon off the cash."

"How could you even come up with such a cruel idea?"

"Experience. Switching gears again. When you rang me last night, you accused the Botezatus of hurting Marilyn. Have you ever met Daciana?"

"No."

"Did Marilyn ever mention her?"

"Yes. She didn't like her. Called her dozy."

"Is there any chance that was a smokescreen? That Marilyn was seeing Daciana as well as you?"

Neera gaped at her. "Of course not. There's really something wrong with you."

Kate silently promised herself another flat white when the interview ended.

"This is what we know," she said patiently. "Cathleen was blackmailing old flames who spurned her. Daciana took them upstairs, turned on the camera, and created home movies for Cathleen to use as bargaining chips. Last night, Rasvan Botezatu told me he recommended his daughter for the job. He hoped sleeping with men would make her give up women."

"That's disgusting."

"Yes, dads pimping daughters, who'd believe it," Kate said wryly. "This is what we theorize. Marilyn and Daciana got together, possibly before you came back into the picture. At some point, Daciana spilled the beans about the blackmail scheme. Marilyn saw an opportunity, and Robert Raynard was born."

"Next, you'll tell me Marilyn killed Cathleen. That's where you're going, isn't it? You'd rather pin it on her than the Botezatus."

Kate studied Neera impassively, trying to decide if the other woman was as clueless about her first love as she seemed.

"Let's do a thought experiment," she said at last. "Cathleen Maitland-Palmer was half of the Annabelle Carter duo that split up you and Marilyn. No doubt it was a traumatic experience. Yet that trauma was Cathleen's career high point. Lady Bothurst even gave her a London blue ring to commemorate it."

"Ginny has a ring, and no one's taken hers."

"Yes, but Ginny wasn't Marilyn's mother. Cathleen threw her daughter to the wolves. Now, fast-forward twenty-five years. Marilyn takes several thousand pounds from Cathleen. Cathleen panics. She steals Daciana's passport because she suspects Daciana sold her out and wants a confession. Then she rings up Marilyn and says, sign over your bank account to me or I'll end your lady's career."

Neera gaped at her. "But Cathleen didn't know we were back together. She knew we were friendly...ran into us at dinner one night, but ..." She tailed off. "Oh, no."

"How do you think Marilyn would've reacted to a blackmail threat from Cathleen?" Kate asked.

Neera didn't answer.

"I think she saw two choices. Pay up to protect you and your career. Or get rid of Cathleen."

"You're wrong. Whoever killed her chopped off a finger. The sheer *brutality*," Neera said. "It was the Botezatus. It had to be."

"I'm not saying Daciana wasn't involved," Kate said. "We know she purchased the murder weapon, a magnet, even though she might not have realized what it was for. Last Thursday night, Marilyn drove to Bulwer Street. She parked near her club, Anne Lister's, so her friends inside would vouch for her. Then, she slipped away to No. 9, let herself in, and waited. When Cathleen returned from the party, Marilyn killed her. Before she left, she took the ring. Cathleen's trophy for betrayal became Marilyn's trophy for revenge.

"The next morning," Kate continued, "Daciana and Marilyn handled things like they'd practiced. They—"

Her MPS secure mobile buzzed.

"What? Right." She scanned the park, which was people-heavy for such a brisk day. "Good job."

Slipping the phone back into her pocket, she said, "Where was I? The next day. Marilyn delayed calling 999 to ring you, supposedly because she wanted to protect the school from scandal. What she really wanted was to keep you as her ace in the hole. She probably thought you had the power to slam on the brakes. And you'd use it if we got too close to the truth, since you refuse to think badly of her."

To Kate's surprise, Neera made no protest. She seemed too shocked to speak.

"I need a couple more things from you," Kate said harshly, trying to snap the other woman back to reality. "Marilyn told us she was looking for a new home. She said somewhere cheaper, but I reckon she preferred upmarket. Tell me what you know about that."

"She was moving houses to Shoreditch. Into a brand-new building," Neera said numbly.

"Last night, when you went to Cyber Monkeez and found the upstairs flat tossed, did you go straight home? Or stop by the new building to see if she was there?"

"I went home. The building's only half-finished. No one lives there yet."

"Give me the address." Kate entered it into her GPS app. "When did Marilyn tell you she was moving houses?"

"Yesterday afternoon. We met for lunch, and she took me round to see the building. The construction manager was on site. She's friendly with him. The lifts were running, so he let us take a look around. Didn't even make us bother with hardhats."

"If you saw Marilyn at lunch, why did you go to her flat later that night?"

"She asked me to. Texted."

"Let me see."

Kate examined the text, which read simply,

> I need you. Things are going pear-shaped.

"Right. Well. That concludes our interview, Ms. Nausherwani. I must caution you not to repeat anything we've discussed with anyone. Do not try to contact Marilyn. If she contacts you, which I think highly unlikely, ring me directly." She handed over her card. "Not 999. Not DI Bhar. Me."

"Why do you say, 'highly unlikely?' Do you think she's dead? Did the Botezatus kill her?"

Kate resisted the temptation to grab Neera by the shoulders and scream, "Wake up!"

"No. I don't think she's dead. I think she's done with you. Yesterday afternoon, she showed you someplace where she might hide. Demonstrated that she had access to the building. Later that night, she lured you to her flat so you'd see the mess she staged and hit the panic button. Now," Kate said rather heartlessly, "you've told me about her new digs, which is the last thing she required of you. Go back to your life, Ms. Nausherwani. Whatever happens next, Marilyn's history."

"I don't believe you. I don't believe any of this," Neera cried. "How do you know she masterminded all this? How can you be sure she's not dead, just like her mum?"

Kate blew out a sigh. "Because the plainclothes officer I stationed in the park just called to say Marilyn's watching us from about fifty yards away. Next to the park bench. She must've followed you from the office—no," she snapped, catching the other woman's hand before she could signal. "She's walking away. I told you, she's done with you."

"If you're convinced she's guilty, why doesn't your officer arrest her?"

"Because I'm not ready."

"But why?"

"Why, indeed," Kate muttered. Maybe someday, somebody would pour a bucket of cold water over Neera's head, but Kate was done trying. "I have lots to do. Where can I drop you?"

Chapter Twenty-Eight

The young woman with green hair exited her building through a back door that opened onto a small courtyard. The area was popular with Marcham Court's resident gardeners, who harvested vegetables from their five-by-five raised beds and planted delicate vines along the wooden fence. A door in that fence led to the alley between Marcham Court and Ultra-Modern Fitness, the only health club in the area with an indoor swimming pool.

It was twilight in London, and the streetlamps, shop signs, billboards, and headlights combined to nullify the darkness into mere gloom. Stars winked faintly overhead, ignored by the city folk below.

The green-haired woman wasn't alone. She was flanked by a tall, heavily built man on her left and a leashed Rottweiler on her right. The man stepped in front of her, opened the alley door, and looked around as she and the dog passed through. The dog was straining at its lead, impatient to see someone or something.

From his rooftop perch on Marcham Court's next-door neighbor, Paul could have observed all that with the naked eye. His weather app had prepared him for a clear night with good visibility. That hadn't stopped him from requisitioning one of SCO19's coolest items ever: gen-three night vision binoculars with a white phosphor screen. The binocs were black, bulky, slightly impractical for the job at hand, and the most marvelous toy he'd had in eons. He almost wished Will Wilkinson had ignored the bait offered via his covert listening devices, just so he could hang on to the binocs for a little longer.

But Wilkinson had taken the bait, at least up to this point. Like the green-haired woman, he was under close surveillance. By shifting his binoculars, Paul quickly picked out Wilkinson in Ultra-Modern Fitness's car park, lurking behind a skip overflowing with rubbish.

Maybe he chose that because he feels like rubbish, thought Paul, who doubted it. He recognized Wilkinson as the type whose confidence in his own rightness was rock-solid. If his rap stylings weren't appreciated, that was the industry's fault, and Damselfish's fault, not his fault. If his son had to die to keep Wilkinson's "death" and rebirth a secret, well, sometimes sacrifices were necessary. If Elodie Queen were fool enough to go to the gym after dark, even in the company of a bodyguard, she'd brought her murder on herself. Wilkinson didn't fear being caught by the idiot police, who were totally baffled. He was laser-focused on eradicating everyone who'd ever let him down.

Wilkinson's willingness to believe his bugs were still undiscovered—that both of Elodie's security companies had failed to discover them, and conversations he overheard with them were utterly candid—was about to be his undoing. If not for the bugs, this manhunt might have gone on for weeks. In a sprawling metropolis, all the CCTV cameras and cashpoints in the world couldn't pinpoint a specific white man with a beard and a bald head; his kind were legion. As technically sophisticated and well-managed as Paul's team was, Wilkinson's alias was still unknown. It would take ages to discover his mailing address, new bank, and new hangouts, now that he knew to keep away from rap clubs for a while. But Paul's script, spoken by Elodie in range of the bugs, had lured out an overconfident killer bent on committing murder number four.

In the alley, the young woman, dog, and bodyguard walked slowly toward the crosswalk. Patience was still yanking hard on the lead, intent on surging ahead, and the bodyguard's head was on the swivel.

Behind the skip, Wilkinson removed the bolt-action hunting rifle from his yoga mat carrier. It was an all-weather gun, common throughout farm country. Although intended for deer stalking, pest control, and target shooting, it could as easily target humans if enhanced by a good scope.

Thank heaven for the hubris of amateurs, Paul thought. *A professional would never attempt this on the ground. He'd be on a rooftop, like me, or sighting his vic through an open window. I reckon after escaping Cottlestone Manor despite those ASC morons, he thinks he's untouchable.*

The unmistakable voice of Elodie Queen rang out: "Patience!"

The dog was off like a shot, dragging her loose lead behind her. The green-haired woman tried to go after the wayward Rottie, but the bodyguard caught her and wouldn't let go.

A dog on a mission, Patience galloped away. Paul held his breath, praying the dog wouldn't scent Wilkinson and go after him prematurely. To his relief, she veered in the opposite direction, disappearing around a corner.

In the street, the green-haired woman said something too low to hear.

"Fine," replied the bodyguard in a carrying voice. "I'll see if I can get her back." Not only was he on script, but he also sounded genuinely annoyed.

Everyone wants to be the next Stallone or Schwarzenegger, Paul thought, watching the man jog off in pursuit of the Rottweiler.

Night vision binoculars in his left hand, Paul reached for the bullhorn with his right. As Wilkinson stepped away from the skip, rifle in hand, he brought the bullhorn to his lips. And as Wilkinson took aim at the woman standing alone in the street, Paul's amplified command rang out:

"Will Wilkinson! Drop it! You're under arrest."

Wilkinson jerked. Looking around wildly, he made a complete turn before checking the roofs. Again, Paul blessed the hubris of amateurs. Most professionals would cast down their weapons when they heard a police command. An instant later, they'd be legging it—not in a panic, but according to a predetermined escape plan. A very resolute killer might have still taken the shot—the green-haired woman was well within range—and *then* cast down his rifle to flee. Wilkinson, apparently without an escape plan or the sheer determination to kill his quarry no matter what, fired wildly at the rooftop.

Paul hugged shingles. The lip of the roof, three feet tall and made of reinforced concrete, proved a good shield. Wilkinson got off two more wild shots before a woman cried, "Game's up. You're nicked!"

Leaving his night vision binocs and bullhorn behind, Paul pounded down the building's metal fire escape and sprinted toward the action.

The obvious pleasure the bewigged policewoman took

in her role reminded Paul of Kate. She would never play street-level decoy again; such a thing wasn't commensurate with her rank. Besides, playing decoy was a job for eager new recruits with high energy and two good knees.

Wilkinson, who seemed shellshocked by his reversal of fortune, was in cuffs. The now-wigless policewoman was bagging his long gun for evidence as her colleague read Wilkinson his rights.

"Well, aren't you decked out for the occasion." Paul looked the man up and down. The would-be rapper wore multi-pocket tactical trousers, combat boots, a utility belt, and a bulletproof vest under his t-shirt. He looked like an eight-year-old boy's idea of a tough guy. Even the back of his hoodie featured that ultra-violent comic book character, the Punisher.

"Even with SCO19 as backup, you were never in danger of being shot," Paul said conversationally. "To bring you down, all we needed was an eight-stone lady in a green wig."

"Nine stone," said the wigless policewoman. "Pure muscle."

"Nine stone. By the way," he continued in the same affable tone, "thanks for taking a shot at me. That's attempted murder of a police officer, mate. Add that to Miranda's murder and Conor's murder, and guess what? You're never getting out. But I just have to ask—what do you keep in that utility belt, Batman?"

"Will!" Elodie Queen arrived with Patience back on the lead. Her part in the ruse had been minimal but important. When Elodie, safely out of sight, called Patience's name from around the corner, the decoy officer had released the lead, allowing the dog to dash away. Then the bodyguard went after the dog, presenting Wilkinson with an irresistible target.

"You killed Miranda," Elodie shouted at him. "You killed Conor! You—you no-talent! You absolute joke!"

Patience put back her ears and growled menacingly. Paul decided it was time to intervene.

"Sorry, love, but I can't let you throttle him. Due process and all that."

"You're nothing without me," Wilkinson told Elodie. "You and Zoë are finished. Get yourself a job at McDonald's."

Afterward, Paul couldn't say precisely how it happened. Either Patience surged harder than her mistress could handle, or Elodie deliberately let go of the lead. Either way, Patience bounded at the handcuffed Wilkinson, knocking him to the ground. The officers managed to pull the Rottweiler off their suspect—but not before she administered one good, hard bite.

Chapter Twenty-Nine

I wonder what Paul's doing right now, Kate thought, approaching the half-finished building called Sanctuary on Tabernacle Street. Its neighbors seemed venerable and mysterious in the twilight; Sanctuary looked like a giant blue LEGO stood on end.

The blue site tarp, ugly but necessary, shielded the open west face from wind and weather. As Kate entered the lobby, she found the tarp kept it relatively warm, even without heat. As Neera had mentioned, the lifts were powered; their floor indicators glowed faintly in the blackness.

Flicking on her iPhone torch, Kate looked around. The uneven floor was grooved concrete, no doubt awaiting marble tiles to justify Sanctuary's exorbitant rent. In the center of the room, a four-by-four hole in the floor was taped off. A pipe stuck out of the dirt, indicating where a decorative column or infrared fireplace would soon be installed.

Kate ignored the lifts in favor of the stairs. Short by modern standards, Sanctuary had only three stories. The ground floor, or lobby level; the first floor, divided into four deluxe flats; and the second floor, split between two luxury units. In such a small, quiet building, the *ding* of the lift would sound like a fire alarm.

Marilyn Maitland-Palmer had leased flat 1B, but Kate didn't expect to find her holed up there. Its window was tarped, rendering the flat dark and smelling of industrial plastic. No, Marilyn had commandeered the second floor, which had better airflow and glazed east-facing windows to let in natural light. Moreover, heat rose; most of the building's warmth would be on the second floor.

Marilyn might be a risk junkie, but she surely never meant to cut things this close, Kate thought. *Maybe someone like Caryn Hattersley or Daciana Botezatu accidentally tipped her off. Or maybe she just did the math and gave Scotland Yard a little credit.*

On the stairwell, Kate paused on the first floor, listening. Easing open the door, she peered into the darkness, hearing and seeing nothing.

She found herself with her back to the wall because of the money, Kate thought, climbing again. *Tony's perp, Wilkinson, spent months divesting himself while he enriched a new identity. Marilyn didn't have time for that. She only had two choices: flee the UK and live dirt-poor, or flee the UK with cash in hand. And that meant making sure somebody else took the fall.*

On the second-floor landing, Kate saw a faint light under the door. She heard someone talking animatedly, but the words were indistinguishable.

Slowly, she opened the door onto a bare space that would probably become the lifts lobby. When finished, the flats would be separated by a corridor, but for the moment, they flowed together: no separating walls, no doors, only beams and columns. The tarped west side was dark, but the

London Blue

east side windows overlooked a fine view—the Honorable Artillery Company's green lawn—that faded as twilight turned to evening.

Following the sound of a woman's voice, Kate ventured into a wide space destined to become a living room. It was empty except for a camp chair, a battery-powered lantern, and an inflatable mattress.

In what would be the kitchen space, distinguished only by a half-constructed breakfast bar, a woman paced back and forth with her mobile, speaking in a thick German accent.

"That's good. *Ja*, I understand. I have papers. ID. Passport. *Nein*. I can't give you my car's number plate because I don't have it yet. The car will be rented. *Ren*-ted," she repeated louder. "You don't understand me? Never mind. Give me supervisor."

After a brief interval, the speaker said, "*Ja. Danke.* I don't have the number plate yet. Rent car in London. Ring you on the drive to Folkestone. Then—number plate, *ja*? *Perfekt*. Of course I have valid driving license. B entitlement..."

Folkestone, Kate thought. *She plans to escape Britain by Chunnel.*

Warrant card in hand, Kate strolled up to the breakfast bar, low heels clicking with every step. Marilyn whirled. Eyes widening, she stopped mid-sentence.

"Call you back," she muttered.

Kate smiled. "Hiya, Marilyn. Heading to France on a German passport?"

"*Ja*." She'd gone from cyber monkey to knockout. The big black specs were gone. Her makeup was bold; her hair, formerly short and brown, was now a shoulder-length bob in sizzling red.

"Nice wig."

"Extensions, actually."

"Are you leaving without Daciana?"

Marilyn didn't answer.

"You are, eh? That's not very nice. Rasvan says you were his daughter's fatal attraction. We know she conspired with you to murder your mother. Bought the magnet for you at the very least."

Marilyn still said nothing.

"Where is Daciana, anyway?" Kate sniffed the air. "Is that her I smell? Or did you forget to empty the bin?"

"You don't smell anything," Marilyn snapped. "She hasn't been dead long enough."

"I do smell her. But maybe my nose is more sensitive than yours after all these years on the job. Where's the body?" Kate glanced around, looking for a corpse in the lantern's dim light.

When Marilyn didn't answer, Kate asked, "Was it ever serious for you? Or was Daciana just a means to an end?"

"Everything is a means to an end."

"Including Neera?"

She seemed to have recovered from the shock of turning to find a DI standing behind her. Now her posture was tense, ready.

No weapon on her person, Kate thought. *Or she would've gone for it already.*

"Come on, Marilyn. I know you wanted the police to take the bait and search Sanctuary. I just turned up a few hours earlier than you planned. So tell me—what exactly did you do to Daciana?"

"Go through." Marilyn pointed in the direction of the flat's future master bedroom. "See for yourself."

Kate walked toward the windows. Deeper in the flat,

city lights revealed a silhouetted figure hanging from a beam.

Her eyes flicked back to Marilyn. In the seconds it had taken Kate to register Daciana's body, Marilyn had closed the distance. Now she was only a meter away. The woman was light on her feet.

Kate turned her back to the windows. There were only two exits, the lift and the stairs, both yards away.

"Let me guess. You lured her here. Probably told her to pack a bag for the trip to France. When she got here, you choked her out and strung her up. You wanted it to look like suicide. Like she couldn't live with the guilt of killing Cathleen."

"The guilt of killing Cathleen *and* me," Marilyn corrected, moving fractionally closer. "Sadly, my body will never be found. And by the time I'm declared dead, a new woman will be living the good life in parts unknown with what used to be my retirement fund."

"I don't know," Kate said skeptically. "The part about Daciana topping herself is classic, I guess. But why would she do it here, in what would have been her lover's future home?"

"Truthfully? Because it was fit for purpose. Private, with exposed beams. But I think it works. You said it yourself, I was her fatal attraction." Marilyn edged closer, hawk-like gaze trained on Kate. "I read up on you, DI Hetheridge. When you faced off with Sir Duncan, you got hurt. Needed a long leave of absence. Lost your edge."

Kate ignored that. "I'm not convinced about Daciana as the remorseful killer. It doesn't quite add up. Unless she was considerate enough to leave a confession?"

"Of course. You and your team were meant to find it

tomorrow morning. It could have been easy-peasy." Marilyn's lip curled. "But you had to go off the rails."

"Meaning what?"

"Meaning, you didn't behave like a rational person. I expected you to take Neera's info to your boss. Assemble a team. Follow procedures. By the time Sanctuary was surrounded and the police robot rolled in, I would've been long gone. You lot would've found Dacy, read her confession, and popped the bubbly. Instead—"

She feinted at Kate, who flinched reflexively. Marilyn laughed.

"I really can't believe you did this." Maintaining eye contact, Marilyn swayed from side to side as if about to spring. "The first time you landed in the papers was for being a dumb blonde. Trying to confront a killer solo. If a man hadn't rescued you, you'd be dead."

"I know about me," Kate said, keeping herself loose and unblinking. "But cutting off the finger wasn't rational, either. If you wanted the ring, you should've pulled it off."

"It wouldn't come off. She'd worn the bloody thing for twenty-five years."

"Then you should have left it. If you hadn't cut off that finger, you might have got away with murder."

"I don't care," Marilyn cried. "I wanted to wear the gaudy thing and laugh every time I looked at it. When it wouldn't come away, I chopped it off. Best moment of my life."

She feinted again. Kate didn't flinch.

"If you wanted it so bad, why aren't you wearing it?"

"Because Dacy had to look guilty. So, I sacrificed the ring. Placed it in her hand." She jerked her head toward the hanging silhouette. "Look."

Without waiting to see if Kate obeyed, Marilyn lunged.

Because she was heavier, the *smack* of impact drove Kate backward against a cold glass pane. Because she was taller, the attack left her throat exposed.

Kate gripped Marilyn under the chin, pushing sideways without mercy. Grunting in surprise and pain, Marilyn tried to yank free, but she couldn't. She tried to pry off Kate's grip with her fingers, but the vicious pressure on her neck made her hands weak. In desperation, Marilyn dropped to her knees, pulling Kate down with her.

They crashed into cold concrete. Freed by the impact, Marilyn scrabbled on hands and knees to the inflatable mattress. She flipped it over, revealing a 9mm Glock, the kind routinely smuggled into the UK and worth seven hundred Euros on the street.

Marilyn reached for the gun, then screamed when Kate yanked her back by the hair. Hands clutching frantically at the air, she strained toward the weapon. Holding her fast, Kate dug her hooked fingers into the other woman's nostrils. Marilyn tried to scream again, but only an animal gurgle came out.

Gritting her teeth, Kate got to her feet, dragging Marilyn up by the nose. When she withdrew her fingers and spun Marilyn around, the other woman cried out in relief. It didn't last. Kate's elbow came up in a smooth arc, slamming into her chin. The impact knocked Marilyn flat on her back.

"Right." After ten seconds to catch her breath and rub her aching elbow, Kate produced the handcuffs tucked in her waistband. Since her uniform days, she'd carried a backup there, cold against the small of her back. Even off duty, she rarely left home without that comforting steel.

Marilyn lay dazed, bleeding from the mouth. Kate looked down on her dispassionately. Probably, she'd bitten her tongue. The move was a throat strike—the least lethal one in Kate's arsenal. A vicious two-fingered thrust to the windpipe would've been easier but potentially fatal. Kate was in the business of making killers face the music, not providing them an easy out.

"Right," Kate repeated louder. "Roll on your side and put your hands behind your back. You're under arrest."

Marilyn moaned. Nudging her over with a foot, Kate seized one of Marilyn's wrists, twisting it till she screamed.

"I said, hands behind your back."

The other woman complied. Kate snapped on the cuffs and hauled her to her feet.

"I want you to see something." Kate shoved Marilyn toward a window. The lantern's weak glow created two reflections, faint and faceless, that didn't resemble Kate or Marilyn. Those figures might have been any two women, perhaps even Cathleen Maitland-Palmer and Daciana Botezatu, watching proceedings from some other plane.

"Look down," Kate said.

Three red dots floated in the center of Marilyn's chest, trembling slightly but almost in unison. This remarkable precision was emblematic of SCO19—three different police snipers, three different angles, but each laser dot trained on the target's center mass.

"Just so we're clear," Kate told Marilyn. "If at any moment I'd feared for my life, all I had to do was point at the ceiling. On that signal, you would've been shot dead. But I never feared for my life. You can't fight for toffee, and even if you got your hands on that gun, you couldn't kill me with it. You're too soft. You should've stuck with flower arranging and sewing knickers. Leave the rough stuff to us East End girls."

Chapter Thirty

In 1878, when Queen Victoria sat on the throne and Benjamin Disraeli was Prime Minister, the venerable City of London Corporation decided that something had to be done about Temple Bar. The bar, or gate, was the most important entrance from Westminster to the City, and its bottleneck of horse and cart traffic was infamous. Upon inspection, the Christopher Wren-designed monument was discovered to be falling apart. The stones were carefully pulled down, numbered, and stored away until 1880, when a baronet, Sir Henry Bruce Meux, and his wife, Valerie, bought and reassembled them in Hertfordshire as an ornament to Theobalds Park.

In 1976, Hugh Wontner, a former Lord Mayor of the City of London, decided to bring the monument home. He established the Temple Bar Trust, which purchased the stones for the princely sum of £1. In 2004, the trust rebuilt the arch in Paternoster Square. There, it enjoys a place of honor opposite St. Paul's Cathedral in the heart of London.

Kate, a typical Londoner born and bred, had barely noticed the arch or given it the slightest thought. But when in search of the perfect birthday party venue, one that even the most resistant husband couldn't reject, Temple Bar appeared on her radar.

The Wren Room's upper chamber, done in warm terracotta tones, was welcoming and sophisticated. Entering on the arm of that resistant husband—who had indeed worn evening dress and looked unbearably suave as a result—she was pleased to find the space configured precisely as requested: a long rectangular table with eight place settings, crisp white table linen, silver candelabras, and an autumn bouquet in yellow, orange, and red.

The place card for the empty seat at the head of the table read,

TONY

The place card to Tony's right read,

HENRY

There sat Henry Hetheridge in his new three-piece suit and tie, hair combed back, pink with pride.

The place card to Tony's left read,

PAUL

Paul Bhar was kitted out to the nines. He wore his best Tom Ford suit, an ultraviolet necktie, and jet-black locks straight from the salon. His cheeky grin reminded Kate of the week they'd met.

Tony clenched her arm. She'd expected a strong reaction when he discovered the party wasn't just for the two of them. Holding her breath, Kate risked a glance at her husband.

He wasn't looking at her. He was looking at the party's special guests.

An elderly Chinese gentleman with white hair smiled benignly. A woman of late middle age polished thick-lensed spectacles. A massive man with a beard like Falstaff sat with a book open before him. He might have been a grizzly bear that someone had wrestled into a suit and taught to read. Beside him, a slender, immaculately attired man of ninety-three sat up straight, birdlike eyes roving. At the foot of the table sat the grad student who served as dogsbody to this distinguished quartet, ready to project slides or facilitate the discussion as needed.

The five remaining place cards read:

DR. WU

DR. FOX

DR. GERSTEIN

DR. PAULSON

DOCTORAL CANDIDATE MR. LEEDS

"Good evening, everyone." Kate smiled at each guest in turn. "I'd like to introduce you to my husband, Tony Hetheridge. He very much wanted to attend your last military history conference, but the birth of our youngest son, Nicky, forced him to cancel. When he realized he'd missed your final public meeting, he was gutted. So, thank you all very much for coming. And for reuniting for a private conference to celebrate his birthday."

"A command performance," boomed Dr. Gerstein, who not only looked like Falstaff but sounded like him, too. "We're like the Beatles at the Royal Albert Hall."

"For once, Daniel, I agree with you." The bespectacled Dr. Fox winked at Kate. She'd been the last to say yes, agreeing only after a long personal conversation over Zoom. Her late, beloved husband had hated birthdays, too, and she understood how creative Kate had to get to celebrate properly.

Risking another look at Tony, Kate found him playing for time, fighting to keep his emotions at bay. In his gaze, she saw everything he would have said to her in that moment if he could've trusted himself to speak.

Leaning on his walking stick, Tony approached the table and addressed his guests.

"Thank you all for coming. I'm a policeman by trade. I never served in the armed forces, and when it comes to global military history, I'm best described as an enthusiastic dabbler. Having said that, I must tell you I've read most, if not all, of your books. I can't imagine a better conversation over dinner than the one I'll be privileged to share tonight."

Everyone clapped. Tony sat down. From an unobtrusive position, the Wren Room's head waiter glided forth, wine bottle in hand, and offered the label for his approval.

"One moment, please." Tony turned in his chair to look at her. "Kate, aren't you staying? Where's your seat?"

Smiling, she put her lips close to his ear and whispered, "This is father-son bonding. I threw in Paul because he's good for a laugh."

Straightening, she addressed the room. "Well. Must be

off. Enjoy your dinner, everyone. The room's booked for the night."

At half-nine, she returned to the Wren Room, where the guests were embroiled in a freewheeling debate about Scipio Africanus, the man who conquered Spain, then defeated Hannibal. Lurking just outside the door, Kate watched as Dr. Fox, who was knitting a sweater, occasionally glanced up to interject a point. Dr. Wu, whose arms were folded across his chest, looked quietly amused. Dr. Gerstein was arguing loudly against something Dr. Paulson had published. The ninety-three-year-old, completely unbothered, deflected each of his colleague's arguments like a mountaintop guru batting away flies. As for Tony, she couldn't remember the last time he'd looked so relaxed and happy.

Paul's having fun, too, Kate thought. *But poor Henry looks knackered.*

He loved nothing better than sitting at the adults' table and soaking in what was said. But the informal conference was likely to go on into the wee hours. Judging by the boy's drawn face and suppressed yawns, it was time to go home.

Abruptly, Tony turned in his chair. "I know that perfume. Kate. Come and join us."

"In a minute. Harvey's come to drive you home, Henry. Time to say goodnight."

Kate thought she detected genuine warmth as the historians told him farewell. He'd made a good impression on these eminent scholars. But of course, he had—he was Henry.

"Did you enjoy yourself?" Harvey asked the boy when Kate and Tony accompanied him into the lobby.

He nodded. "Did you bring it?"

"Yes." Harvey passed him a fancy wooden box tied with

a red ribbon, which Henry presented to Tony. "You can have *one* of these for your birthday. The rest are for your guests."

"Oh, my." Tony opened the box containing *Fuente Fuente OpusX Reserva d'Chateau* cigars. Selecting one, he passed it under his nose. "Magnificent. Thank you, Henry." He hugged the boy, tousling his hair. "You needn't worry about my lungs. One per year is enough for me."

When they returned to the dining room, Kate realized she'd forgotten to bring a cigar cutter. Tony brought out one from his jacket's inner pocket, along with a lighter.

"Damn it. You knew!"

"No, I didn't. I always carry a cutter on my birthday. From time to time, a very fine cigar falls from the sky, and I like to be ready."

Lighting it, Tony leaned back and puffed with the greatest pleasure. Kate, finding the sight irresistible, committed it to memory.

"You really did surprise me, Kate."

"I'm just getting started," she said, and winked.

THE END

To My Readers

First, I'd like to thank you all for your kind words, loyalty, and patience. Especially patience!

Second, allow me to thank you for buying this book or checking it out from the library. Events beyond our control are hitting authors, especially independent authors like me, hard. When you buy one of my books, or a library stocks one of my books, it makes it possible for me to continue writing for publication.

New readers always ask, "Will there be more Lord & Lady Hetheridge books?"

Yes, absolutely. I can't imagine myself without the Hetheridges. Even as I get ready to publish **London Blue**, a tiny glimmer of book nine, **Bolt from the Blue**, is forming in the back of my mind.

New readers also ask, "What else have you written?"

I'm thrilled to tell you about the **Dr. Benjamin Bones Mysteries**. Set in 1940s Cornwall, they follow the adventures of Ben Bones, a young doctor chosen by his government to serve a rural community during World War II. As the widower and native Londoner adjusts to life in

To My Readers

the tiny village of Birdswing, where the tiniest nugget of gossip can keep tongues wagging for weeks, he meets a fiery aristocrat named Lady Juliet. Together, they discover a taste for solving mysteries—and love along the way. Packed with great characters, a sweeping romance, and complex mysteries, the Dr. Benjamin Bones series is a perfect choice for anyone waiting (patiently, or impatiently) for another Hetheridge book.

I'm also starting a new adventure-mystery series called Skullduggery. Populated with Brits, Americans, cryptid monsters, phantasms, and an ancient society beneath the oceans, it's a story I've been working on for twenty-five years. I can't wait for you to read book one, **Hunting the Beast**, which will arrive in 2025.

I also write the ***Jem Jago Mysteries***, published by Bookouture. Set in the Isles of Scilly, an English archipelago off the coast of Cornwall, it concerns Jemima Jago—librarian, thirty-something singleton, and intrepid amateur sleuth. There are five books in all, and they contain some of my funniest scenes.

Finally, please visit my website for news, a look at **SPELLBOUND** Mystery Magazine, or to shop at the Emma Jameson Book Shop. You can also sign up for my newsletter there or by clicking this link. It's the very best way to learn about my new releases, giveaways, and author news.

Cheers!

EMMA JAMESON

2025

Also By Emma Jameson

Ice Blue (Lord & Lady Hetheridge Mysteries #1)

Blue Murder (Lord & Lady Hetheridge Mysteries #2)

Something Blue (Lord & Lady Hetheridge Mysteries #3)

Black & Blue (Lord & Lady Hetheridge Mysteries #4)

Blue Blooded (Lord & Lady Hetheridge Mysteries #5)

Blue Christmas (Lord & Lady Hetheridge Mysteries #6)

Untrue Blue (Lord & Lady Hetheridge Mysteries #7)

London Blue (Lord & Lady Hetheridge Mysteries #8)

Bones in the Blackout (Dr. Benjamin Bones Mysteries #1)

Bones at the Manor House (Dr. Benjamin Bones Mysteries #2)

Bones Takes a Holiday (Dr. Benjamin Bones Mysteries #3)

Bones Buried Deep (Dr. Benjamin Bones Mysteries #4)

Bones in the Blitz (Dr. Benjamin Bones Mysteries #5) — forthcoming

Hunting the Beast (Skullduggery Book One)—forthcoming

Published by Bookouture:

A Death at Seascape House (Jem Jago Mysteries #1)

A Death at Candlewick Castle (Jem Jago Mysteries #2)

A Death at Silversmith Bay (Jem Jago Mysteries #3)

A Death at Neptune Cove (Jem Jago Mysteries #4)

A Death at Bay View Hotel (Jem Jago Mysteries #5)

Made in the USA
Columbia, SC
24 March 2025